Deemed 'the father of the s  **Austin Freeman** had a long and distinguished career, not least as a writer of detective fiction. He was born in London, the son of a tailor who went on to train as a pharmacist. After graduating as a surgeon at the Middlesex Hospital Medical College, Freeman taught for a while and joined the colonial service, offering his skills as an assistant surgeon along the Gold Coast of Africa. He became embroiled in a diplomatic mission when a British expeditionary party was sent to investigate the activities of the French. Through his tact and formidable intelligence, a massacre was narrowly avoided. His future was assured in the colonial service. However, after becoming ill with blackwater fever, Freeman was sent back to England to recover and, finding his finances precarious, embarked on a career as acting physician in Holloway Prison. In desperation, he turned to writing and went on to dominate the world of British detective fiction, taking pride in testing different criminal techniques. So keen were his powers as a writer that part of one of his best novels was written in a bomb shelter.

BY THE SAME AUTHOR
ALL PUBLISHED BY HOUSE OF STRATUS

A CERTAIN DR THORNDYKE

THE D'ARBLAY MYSTERY

DR THORNDYKE INTERVENES

DR THORNDYKE'S CASEBOOK

THE EYE OF OSIRIS

FELO DE SE

FLIGHTY PHYLLIS

THE GOLDEN POOL: A STORY OF A FORGOTTEN MINE

THE GREAT PORTRAIT MYSTERY

HELEN VARDON'S CONFESSION

MR POLTON EXPLAINS

MR POTTERMACK'S OVERSIGHT

THE MYSTERY OF 31 NEW INN

THE MYSTERY OF ANGELINA FROOD

THE PENROSE MYSTERY

THE PUZZLE LOCK

THE RED THUMB MARK

THE SHADOW OF THE WOLF

A SILENT WITNESS

THE SINGING BONE

John Thorndyke's Cases

R Austin Freeman

HOUSE OF
STRATUS

This edition published in 2001 by House of Stratus, an imprint of
Stratus Books Ltd., 21 Beeching Park, Kelly Bray,
Cornwall, PL17 8QS, UK.
www.houseofstratus.com

Typeset, printed and bound by House of Stratus.

A catalogue record for this book is available from the British Library
and the Library of Congress.

ISBN 0-7551-0365-3

John Thorndyke's Cases
Related by Christopher Jervis, MD
and edited by R Austin Freeman

To my friend
Frank Standfield
In memory of many a pleasant evening
Spent with microscope and camera
This volume is dedicated

CONTENTS

ONE

The Man with the Nailed Shoes

There are, I suppose, few places even on the East Coast of England more lonely and remote than the village of Little Sundersley and the country that surrounds it. Far from any railway, and some miles distant from any considerable town, it remains an outpost of civilization, in which primitive manners and customs and old-world tradition linger on into an age that has elsewhere forgotten them. In the summer, it is true, a small contingent of visitors, adventurous in spirit, though mostly of sedate and solitary habits, make their appearance to swell its meagre population, and impart to the wide stretches of smooth sand that fringe its shores a fleeting air of life and sober gaiety; but in late September − the season of the year in which I made its acquaintance − its pasture-lands lie desolate, the rugged paths along the cliffs are seldom trodden by human foot, and the sands are a desert waste on which, for days together, no footprint appears save that left by some passing sea-bird.

I had been assured by my medical agent, Mr Turcival, that I should find the practice of which I was now taking charge "an exceedingly soft billet, and suitable for a studious man"; and certainly he had not misled me, for the patients were, in fact, so few that I was quite concerned for my principal, and rather dull for want of work. Hence, when my friend John Thorndyke, the well-known medico-legal expert, proposed to come down and stay with me for a weekend and perhaps a few days beyond, I hailed the proposal with delight, and welcomed him with open arms.

"You certainly don't seem to be overworked, Jervis," he remarked, as we turned out of the gate after tea, on the day of his arrival, for a stroll on the shore. "Is this a new practice, or an old one in a state of senile decay?"

"Why, the fact is," I answered, "there is virtually no practice. Cooper – my principal – has been here about six years, and as he has private means he has never made any serious effort to build one up; and the other man, Dr Burrows, being uncommonly keen, and the people very conservative, Cooper has never really got his foot in. However, it doesn't seem to trouble him."

"Well, if he is satisfied, I suppose you are," said Thorndyke, with a smile. "You are getting a seaside holiday, and being paid for it. But I didn't know you were as near to the sea as this."

We were entering, as he spoke, an artificial gap-way cut through the low cliff, forming a steep cart-track down to the shore. It was locally known as Sundersley Gap, and was used principally, when used at all, by the farmers' carts which came down to gather seaweed after a gale.

"What a magnificent stretch of sand!" continued Thorndyke, as we reached the bottom, and stood looking out seaward across the deserted beach. "There is something very majestic and solemn in a great expanse of sandy shore when the tide is out, and I know of nothing which is capable of conveying the impression of solitude so completely. The smooth, unbroken surface not only displays itself untenanted for the moment, but it offers convincing testimony that it has lain thus undisturbed through a considerable lapse of time. Here, for instance, we have clear evidence that for several days only two pairs of feet besides our own have trodden this gap."

"How do you arrive at the 'several days'?" I asked.

"In the simplest manner possible," he replied. "The moon is now in the third quarter, and the tides are consequently neap-tides.

2

You can see quite plainly the two lines of seaweed and jetsam which indicate the high-water marks of the spring-tides and the neap-tides respectively. The strip of comparatively dry sand between them, over which the water has not risen for several days, is, as you see, marked by only two sets of footprints, and those footprints will not be completely obliterated by the sea until the next spring-tide – nearly a week from today."

"Yes, I see now, and the thing appears obvious enough when one has heard the explanation. But it is really rather odd that no one should have passed through this gap for days, and then that four persons should have come here within quite a short interval of one another."

"What makes you think they have done so?" Thorndyke asked.

"Well," I replied, "both of these sets of footprints appear to be quite fresh, and to have been made about the same time."

"Not at the same time, Jervis," rejoined Thorndyke. "There is certainly an interval of several hours between them, though precisely how many hours we cannot judge, since there has been so little wind lately to disturb them; but the fisherman unquestionably passed here not more than three hours ago, and I should say probably within an hour; whereas the other man – who seems to have come up from a boat to fetch something of considerable weight – returned through the gap certainly not less, and probably more, than four hours ago."

I gazed at my friend in blank astonishment, for these events befell in the days before I had joined him as his assistant, and his special knowledge and powers of inference were not then fully appreciated by me.

"It is clear, Thorndyke," I said, "that footprints have a very different meaning to you from what they have for me. I don't see in the least how you have reached any of these conclusions."

"I suppose not," was the reply; "but, you see, special knowledge of this kind is the stock-in-trade of the medical jurist, and has to be acquired by special study, though the present example is one of the greatest simplicity. But let us consider it point by point; and first we will take this set of footprints which I have inferred to be a fisherman's. Note their enormous size. They should be the footprints of a giant. But the length of the stride shows that they were made by a rather short man. Then observe the massiveness of the soles, and the fact that there are no nails in them. Note also the peculiar clumsy tread – the deep toe and heel marks, as if the walker had wooden legs, or fixed ankles and knees. From that character we can safely infer high boots of thick, rigid leather, so that we can diagnose high boots, massive and stiff, with nailless soles, and many sizes too large for the wearer. But the only boot that answers this description is the fisherman's thigh-boot – made of enormous size to enable him to wear in the winter two or three pairs of thick knitted stockings, one over the other. Now look at the other footprints; there is a double track, you see, one set coming from the sea and one going towards it. As the man (who was bow-legged and turned his toes in) has trodden in his own footprints, it is obvious that he came from the sea, and returned to it. But observe the difference in the two sets of prints; the returning ones are much deeper than the others, and the stride much shorter. Evidently he was carrying something when he returned, and that something was very heavy. Moreover, we can see, by the greater depth of the toe impressions, that he was stooping forward as he walked, and so probably carried the weight on his back. Is that quite clear?"

"Perfectly," I replied. "But how do you arrive at the interval of time between the visits of the two men?"

"That also is quite simple. The tide is now about halfway out; it is thus about three hours since high water. Now, the fisherman walked just about the neap-tide, high-water mark, sometimes above it and sometimes below. But none of his footprints have been obliterated; therefore he passed after high water – that is, less than three hours ago; and since his footprints are all equally distinct, he could not have passed when the sand was very wet. Therefore he probably passed less than an hour ago. The other man's footprints, on the other hand, reach only to the neap-tide, high-water mark, where they end abruptly. The sea has washed over the remainder of the tracks and obliterated them. Therefore he passed not less than three hours and not more than four days ago – probably within twenty-four hours."

As Thorndyke concluded his demonstration the sound of voices was borne to us from above, mingled with the tramping of feet, and immediately afterwards a very singular party appeared at the head of the gap descending towards the shore. First came a short burly fisherman clad in oilskins and sou'-wester, clumping along awkwardly in his great sea-boots, then the local police-sergeant in company with my professional rival Dr Burrows, while the rear of the procession was brought up by two constables carrying a stretcher. As he reached the bottom of the gap the fisherman, who was evidently acting as guide, turned along the shore, retracing his own tracks, and the procession followed in his wake.

"A surgeon, a stretcher, two constables, and a police-sergeant," observed Thorndyke. "What does that suggest to your mind, Jervis?"

"A fall from the cliff," I replied, "or a body washed up on the shore."

"Probably," he rejoined; "but we may as well walk in that direction."

We turned to follow the retreating procession, and as we strode along the smooth surface left by the retiring tide Thorndyke resumed: "The subject of footprints has always interested me deeply for two reasons. First, the evidence furnished by footprints is constantly being brought forward, and is often of cardinal importance; and, secondly, the whole subject is capable of really systematic and scientific treatment. In the main the data are anatomical, but age, sex, occupation, health, and disease all give their various indications. Clearly, for instance, the footprints of an old man will differ from those of a young man of the same height, and I need not point out to you that those of a person suffering from locomotor ataxia or paralysis agitans would be quite unmistakable."

"Yes, I see that plainly enough," I said.

"Here, now," he continued, "is a case in point." He halted to point with his stick at a row of footprints that appeared suddenly above high-water mark, and having proceeded a short distance, crossed the line again, and vanished where the waves had washed over them. They were easily distinguished from any of the others by the clear impressions of circular rubber heels.

"Do you see anything remarkable about them?" he asked.

"I notice that they are considerably deeper than our own," I answered.

"Yes, and the boots are about the same size as ours, whereas the stride is considerably shorter – quite a short stride, in fact. Now there is a pretty constant ratio between the length of the foot and the length of the leg, between the length of leg and the height of the person, and between the stature and the length of stride. A long foot means a long leg, a tall man, and a long stride. But here we have a long foot and a short stride. What do you make of that?" He laid down his stick – a smooth partridge cane, one side of which was marked by small lines into inches and feet – beside the footprints to demonstrate the discrepancy.

"The depth of the footprints shows that he was a much heavier man than either of us," I suggested; "perhaps he was unusually fat."

"Yes," said Thorndyke, "that seems to be the explanation. The carrying of a dead weight shortens the stride, and fat is practically a dead weight. The conclusion is that he was about five feet ten inches high, and excessively fat." He picked up his cane, and we resumed our walk, keeping an eye on the procession ahead until it had disappeared round a curve in the coast-line, when we mended our pace somewhat. Presently we reached a small headland, and, turning the shoulder of cliff, came full upon the party which had preceded us. The men had halted in a narrow bay, and now stood looking down at a prostrate figure beside which the surgeon was kneeling.

"We were wrong, you see," observed Thorndyke. "He has not fallen over the cliff, nor has he been washed up by the sea. He is lying above high-water mark, and these footprints that we have been examining appear to be his."

As we approached, the sergeant turned and held up his hand.

"I'll ask you not to walk round the body just now, gentlemen," he said. "There seems to have been foul play here, and I want to be clear about the tracks before anyone crosses them."

Acknowledging this caution, we advanced to where the constables were standing, and looked down with some curiosity at the dead man. He was a tall, frail-looking man, thin to the point of emaciation, and appeared to be about thirty-five years of age. He lay in an easy posture, with half-closed eyes and a placid expression that contrasted strangely enough with the tragic circumstances of his death.

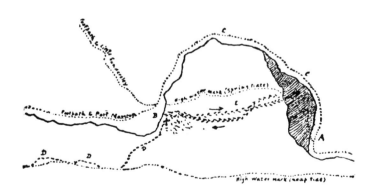

PLAN OF ST. BRIDGET'S BAY

†	Position of body	D D D	Tracks of Hearn's shoes
A	Top of Shepherd's Path	E	Tracks of the nailed shoes
B	Overhanging cliff	F	Shepherd's Path ascending
C	Footpath along edge of cliff		shelving cliff

"It is a clear case of murder," said Dr Burrows dusting the sand from his knees as he stood up.

"There is a deep knife-wound above the heart, which must have caused death almost instantaneously."

"How long should you say he has been dead, Doctor?" asked the sergeant.

"Twelve hours at least," was the reply. "He is quite cold and stiff."

"Twelve hours, eh?" repeated the officer. "That would bring it to about six o'clock this morning."

"I won't commit myself to a definite time," said Dr Burrows hastily. "I only say not *less* than twelve hours. It might have been considerably more."

"Ah!" said the sergeant. "Well, he made a pretty good fight for his life, to all appearances." He nodded at the sand, which for some feet around the body bore the deeply indented marks of feet, as though a furious struggle had taken place. "It's a mighty queer affair," pursued the sergeant, addressing Dr Burrows. "There seems to have been only one man in it − there is only one set of footprints besides those of the deceased − and we've got to find out who he is; and I reckon there won't be much trouble about that, seeing the kind of trade-marks he has left behind him."

"No," agreed the surgeon; "there ought not to be much trouble in identifying those boots. He would seem to be a labourer, judging by the hobnails."

"No, sir; not a labourer," dissented the sergeant. "The foot is too small, for one thing; and then the nails are not regular hobnails. They're a good deal smaller; and a labourer's boots would have the nails all round the edges, and there would be iron tips on the heels, and probably on the toes too. Now these have got no tips, and the nails are arranged in a pattern on the soles and heels. They are probably shooting-boots or sporting shoes of some kind." He strode to and fro with his notebook in his hand, writing down hasty memoranda, and stooping to scrutinize the impressions in the sand. The surgeon also busied himself in noting down the facts concerning which he would have to give evidence, while Thorndyke regarded in silence and with an air of intense preoccupation the footprints around the body which remained to testify to the circumstances of the crime.

"It is pretty clear, up to a certain point," the sergeant observed, as he concluded his investigations, "how the affair happened, and it is pretty clear, too, that the murder was premeditated. You see, Doctor, the deceased gentleman, Mr Hearn, was apparently walking home from Port Marston; we saw his footprints along the shore – those rubber heels make them easy to identify – and he didn't go down Sundersley Gap. He probably meant to climb up the cliff by that little track that you see there, which the people about here call the Shepherd's Path. Now the murderer must have known that he was coming, and waited upon the cliff to keep a lookout. When he saw Mr Hearn enter the bay, he came down the path and attacked him, and, after a tough struggle, succeeded in stabbing him. Then he turned and went back up the path. You can see the double track between the path and the place where the struggle took place, and the footprints going to the path are on top of those coming from it."

"If you follow the tracks," said Dr Burrows, "you ought to be able to see where the murderer went to."

"I'm afraid not," replied the sergeant. "There are no marks on the path itself – the rock is too hard, and so is the ground above, I fear. But I'll go over it carefully all the same."

The investigations being so far concluded, the body was lifted on to the stretcher, and the cortège, consisting of the bearers, the Doctor, and the fisherman, moved off towards the Gap, while the sergeant, having civilly wished us "Good evening," scrambled up the Shepherd's Path, and vanished above.

"A very smart officer that," said Thorndyke. "I should like to know what he wrote in his notebook."

"His account of the circumstances of the murder seemed a very reasonable one," I said.

"Very. He noted the plain and essential facts, and drew the natural conclusions from them. But there are some very singular features in this case; so singular that I am disposed to make a few notes for my own information."

He stooped over the place where the body had lain, and having narrowly examined the sand there and in the place where the dead man's feet had rested, drew out his notebook and made a memorandum. He next made a rapid sketch-plan of the bay, marking the position of the body and the various impressions in the sand, and then, following the double track leading from and to the Shepherd's Path, scrutinized the footprints with the deepest attention, making copious notes and sketches in his book.

"We may as well go up by the Shepherd's Path," said Thorndyke. "I think we are equal to the climb, and there may be visible traces of the murderer after all. The rock is only a sandstone, and not a very hard one either."

We approached the foot of the little rugged track which zigzagged up the face of the cliff, and, stooping down among the stiff, dry herbage, examined the surface. Here, at the bottom of the path, where the rock was softened by the weather, there were several distinct impressions on the crumbling surface of the murderer's nailed boots, though they were somewhat confused by the tracks of the sergeant, whose boots were heavily nailed. But as we ascended the marks became rather less distinct, and at quite a short distance from the foot of the cliff we lost them altogether, though we had no difficulty in following the more recent traces of the sergeant's passage up the path.

When we reached the top of the cliff we paused to scan the path that ran along its edge, but here, too, although the sergeant's heavy boots had left quite visible impressions on the ground, there were no signs of any other feet. At a little distance the sagacious officer himself was pursuing his investigations, walking backwards and forwards with his body bent double, and his eyes fixed on the ground.

"Not a trace of him anywhere," said he, straightening himself up as we approached. "I was afraid there wouldn't be after all this dry weather. I shall have to try a different tack. This is a small place, and if those boots belong to anyone living here they'll be sure to be known."

"The deceased gentleman – Mr Hearn, I think you called him," said Thorndyke as we turned towards the village – "is he a native of the locality?"

"Oh no, sir," replied the officer. "He is almost a stranger. He has only been here about three weeks; but, you know, in a little place like this a man soon gets to be known – and his business, too, for that matter," he added, with a smile.

"What was his business, then?" asked Thorndyke.

"Pleasure, I believe. He was down here for a holiday, though it's a good way past the season; but, then, he had a friend living here, and that makes a difference. Mr Draper up at the Poplars was an old friend of his, I understand. I am going to call on him now."

We walked on along the footpath that led towards the village, but had only proceeded two or three hundred yards when a loud hail drew our attention to a man running across a field towards us from the direction of the cliff.

"Why, here is Mr Draper himself," exclaimed the sergeant, stopping short and waving his hand. "I expect he has heard the news already."

Thorndyke and I also halted, and with some curiosity watched the approach of this new party to the tragedy. As the stranger drew near we saw that he was a tall, athletic-looking man of about forty, dressed in a Norfolk knickerbocker suit, and having the appearance of an ordinary country gentleman, excepting that he carried in his hand, in place of a walking-stick, the staff of a butterfly-net, the folding ring and bag of which partly projected from his pocket.

"Is it true, Sergeant?" he exclaimed as he came up to us, panting from his exertions. "About Mr Hearn, I mean. There is a rumour that he has been found dead on the beach."

"It's quite true, sir, I am sorry to say; and, what is worse, he has been murdered."

"My God! you don't say so!"

He turned towards us a face that must ordinarily have been jovial enough, but was now white and scared, and, after a brief pause, he exclaimed: "Murdered! Good God! Poor old Hearn! How did it happen, Sergeant? and when? and is there any clue to the murderer?"

"We can't say for certain when it happened," replied the sergeant; "and as to the question of clues, I was just coming up to call on you."

"On me!" exclaimed Draper, with a startled glance at the officer. "What for?"

"Well, we should like to know something about Mr Hearn — who he was, and whether he had any enemies, and so forth; anything, in fact, that would give us a hint where to look for the murderer. And you are the only person in the place who knew him at all intimately."

Mr Draper's pallid face turned a shade paler, and he glanced about him with an obviously embarrassed air.

"I'm afraid," he began in a hesitating manner, "I'm afraid I shan't be able to help you much. I didn't know much about his affairs. You see he was — well — only a casual acquaintance — "

"Well," interrupted the sergeant, "you can tell us who and what he was, and where he lived, and so forth. We'll find out the rest if you give us the start."

"I see," said Draper. "Yes, I expect you will." His eyes glanced restlessly to and fro, and he added presently: "You must come up tomorrow, and have a talk with me about him, and I'll see what I can remember."

"I'd rather come this evening," said the sergeant firmly.

"Not this evening," pleaded Draper. "I'm feeling rather — this affair, you know, has upset me. I couldn't give proper attention — "

His sentence petered out into a hesitating mumble, and the officer looked at him in evident surprise at his nervous, embarrassed manner. His own attitude, however, was perfectly firm, though polite.

"I don't like pressing you, sir," said he, "but time is precious – we'll have to go single file here; this pond is a public nuisance. They ought to bank it up at this end. After you, sir."

The pond to which the sergeant alluded had evidently extended at one time right across the path, but now, thanks to the dry weather, a narrow isthmus of half-dried mud traversed the morass, and along this Mr Draper proceeded to pick his way. The sergeant was about to follow, when suddenly he stopped short with his eyes riveted upon the muddy track. A single glance showed me the cause of his surprise, for on the stiff, putty-like surface, standing out with the sharp distinctness of a wax mould, were the fresh footprints of the man who had just passed, each footprint displaying on its sole the impression of stud-nails arranged in a diamond-shaped pattern, and on its heel a group of similar nails arranged in a cross.

The sergeant hesitated for only a moment, in which he turned a quick startled glance upon us; then he followed, walking gingerly along the edge of the path as if to avoid treading in his predecessor's footprints. Instinctively we did the same, following closely, and anxiously awaiting the next development of the tragedy. For a minute or two we all proceeded in silence, the sergeant being evidently at a loss how to act, and Mr Draper busy with his own thoughts. At length the former spoke.

"You think, Mr Draper, you would rather that I looked in on you tomorrow about this affair?"

"Much rather, if you wouldn't mind," was the eager reply.

"Then, in that case," said the sergeant, looking at his watch, "as I've got a good deal to see to this evening, I'll leave you here, and make my way to the station."

With a farewell flourish of his hand he climbed over a stile, and when, a few moments later, I caught a glimpse of him through an opening in the hedge, he was running across the meadow like a hare.

13

The departure of the police-officer was apparently a great relief to Mr Draper, who at once fell back and began to talk with us. "You are Dr Jervis, I think," said he. "I saw you coming out of Dr Cooper's house yesterday. We know everything that is happening in the village, you see." He laughed nervously, and added: "But I don't know your friend."

I introduced Thorndyke, at the mention of whose name our new acquaintance knitted his brows, and glanced inquisitively at my friend.

"Thorndyke," he repeated; "the name seems familiar to me. Are you in the Law, sir?"

Thorndyke admitted the impeachment, and our companion, having again bestowed on him a look full of curiosity, continued: "This horrible affair will interest you, no doubt, from a professional point of view. You were present when my poor friend's body was found, I think?"

"No," replied Thorndyke; "we came up afterwards, when they were removing it."

Our companion then proceeded to question us about the murder, but received from Thorndyke only the most general and ambiguous replies. Nor was there time to go into the matter at length, for the footpath presently emerged on to the road close to Mr Draper's house.

"You will excuse my not asking you in tonight," said he, "but you will understand that I am not in much form for visitors just now."

We assured him that we fully understood, and, having wished him "Good evening," pursued our way towards the village.

"The sergeant is off to get a warrant, I suppose," I observed.

"Yes; and mighty anxious lest his man should be off before he can execute it. But he is fishing in deeper waters than he thinks, Jervis. This is a very singular and complicated case; one of the strangest, in fact, that I have ever met. I shall follow its development with deep interest."

"The sergeant seems pretty cocksure, all the same," I said.

"He is not to blame for that," replied Thorndyke. "He is acting on the obvious appearances, which is the proper thing to do in the first place. Perhaps his notebook contains more than I think it does. But we shall see."

When we entered the village I stopped to settle some business with the chemist, who acted as Dr Cooper's dispenser, suggesting to Thorndyke that he should walk on to the house; but when I emerged from the shop some ten minutes later he was waiting outside, with a smallish brown-paper parcel under each arm. Of one of these parcels I insisted on relieving him, in spite of his protests, but when he at length handed it to me its weight completely took me by surprise.

"I should have let them send this home on a barrow," I remarked.

"So I should have done," he replied, "only I did not wish to draw attention to my purchase, or give my address."

Accepting this hint I refrained from making any inquiries as to the nature of the contents (although I must confess to considerable curiosity on the subject), and on arriving home I assisted him to deposit the two mysterious parcels in his room.

When I came downstairs a disagreeable surprise awaited me. Hitherto the long evenings had been spent by me in solitary and undisturbed enjoyment of Dr Cooper's excellent library, but tonight a perverse fate decreed that I must wander abroad, because, forsooth, a preposterous farmer, who resided in a hamlet five miles distant, had chosen the evening of my guest's arrival to dislocate his bucolic elbow. I half hoped that Thorndyke would offer to accompany me, but he made no such suggestion, and in fact seemed by no means afflicted at the prospect of my absence.

"I have plenty to occupy me while you are away," he said cheerfully; and with this assurance to comfort me I mounted my bicycle and rode off somewhat sulkily along the dark road.

My visit occupied in all a trifle under two hours, and when I reached home, ravenously hungry and heated by my ride, half-past nine had struck, and the village had begun to settle down for the night.

"Sergeant Payne is a-waiting in the surgery, sir," the housemaid announced as I entered the hall.

"Confound Sergeant Payne!" I exclaimed. "Is Dr Thorndyke with him?"

"No, sir," replied the grinning damsel. "Dr Thorndyke is hout."

"Hout!" I repeated (my surprise leading to unintentional mimicry).

"Yes, sir. He went hout soon after you, sir, on his bicycle. He had a basket strapped on to it – leastways a hamper – and he borrowed a basin and a kitchen-spoon from the cook."

I stared at the girl in astonishment. The ways of John Thorndyke were, indeed, beyond all understanding.

"Well, let me have some dinner or supper at once," I said, "and I will see what the sergeant wants."

The officer rose as I entered the surgery, and, laying his helmet on the table, approached me with an air of secrecy and importance.

"Well, sir," said he, "the fat's in the fire. I've arrested Mr Draper, and I've got him locked up in the court-house. But I wish it had been someone else."

"So does he, I expect," I remarked.

"You see, sir," continued the sergeant, "we all like Mr Draper. He's been among us a matter of seven years, and he's like one of ourselves. However, what I've come about is this; it seems the gentleman who was with you this evening is Dr Thorndyke, the great expert. Now Mr Draper seems to have heard about him, as most of us have, and he is very anxious for him to take up the defence. Do you think he would consent?"

"I expect so," I answered, remembering Thorndyke's keen interest in the case; "but I will ask him when he comes in."

"Thank you, sir," said the sergeant. "And perhaps you wouldn't mind stepping round to the court-house presently yourself. He looks uncommon queer, does Mr Draper, and no wonder, so I'd like you to take a look at him, and if you could bring Dr Thorndyke with you, he'd like it, and so should I, for, I assure you, sir, that although a conviction would mean a step up the ladder for me, I'd be glad enough to find that I'd made a mistake."

I was just showing my visitor out when a bicycle swept in through the open gate, and Thorndyke dismounted at the door, revealing a square hamper – evidently abstracted from the surgery – strapped on to a carrier at the back. I conveyed the sergeant's request to him at once, and asked if he was willing to take up the case.

"As to taking up the defence," he replied, "I will consider the matter; but in any case I will come up and see the prisoner."

With this the sergeant departed, and Thorndyke, having unstrapped the hamper with as much care as if it contained a collection of priceless porcelain, bore it tenderly up to his bedroom; whence he appeared, after a considerable interval, smilingly apologetic for the delay.

"I thought you were dressing for dinner," I grumbled as he took his seat at the table.

"No," he replied. "I have been considering this murder. Really it is a most singular case, and promises to be uncommonly complicated, too."

"Then I assume that you will undertake the defence?"

"I shall if Draper gives a reasonably straightforward account of himself."

It appeared that this condition was likely to be fulfilled, for when we arrived at the court-house (where the prisoner was accommodated in a spare office, under rather free-and-easy conditions considering the nature of the charge) we found Mr Draper in an eminently communicative frame of mind.

"I want you, Dr Thorndyke, to undertake my defence in this terrible affair, because I feel confident that you will be able to clear me. And I promise you that there shall be no reservation or concealment on my part of anything that you ought to know."

"Very well," said Thorndyke. "By the way, I see you have changed your shoes."

"Yes, the sergeant took possession of those I was wearing. He said something about comparing them with some footprints, but there can't be any footprints like those shoes here in Sundersley. The nails are fixed in the soles in quite a peculiar pattern. I had them made in Edinburgh."

"Have you more than one pair?"

"No. I have no other nailed boots."

"That is important," said Thorndyke. "And now I judge that you have something to tell us that bears on this crime. Am I right?"

"Yes. There is something that I am afraid it is necessary for you to know, although it is very painful to me to revive memories of my past that I had hoped were buried for ever. But perhaps, after all, it may not be necessary for these confidences to be revealed to anyone but yourself."

"I hope not," said Thorndyke; "and if it is not necessary you may rely upon me not to allow any of your secrets to leak out. But you are wise to tell me everything that may in any way bear upon the case."

At this juncture, seeing that confidential matters were about to be discussed, I rose and prepared to withdraw; but Draper waved me back into my chair.

"You need not go away, Dr Jervis," he said. "It is through you that I have the benefit of Dr Thorndyke's help, and I know that you doctors can be trusted to keep your own counsel and your clients' secrets. And now for these confessions of mine. In the first place, it is my painful duty to tell you that I am a discharged convict – an 'old lag', as the cant phrase has it."

He coloured a dusky red as he made this statement, and glanced furtively at Thorndyke to observe its effect. But he might as well have looked at a wooden figure-head or a stone mask as at my friend's immovable visage; and when his communication had been acknowledged by a slight nod, he proceeded: "The history of my wrong-doing is the history of hundreds of others. I was a clerk in a bank, and getting on as well as I could expect in that not very progressive avocation, when I had the misfortune to make four very undesirable acquaintances. They were all young men, though rather older than myself, and were close friends, forming a sort of little community or club. They were not what is usually described as 'fast'. They were quite sober and decently-behaved young fellows, but they were very decidedly addicted to gambling in a small way, and they soon infected me. Before long I was the keenest gambler of them all. Cards, billiards, pool, and various forms of betting began to be the chief pleasures of my life, and not only was the bulk of my scanty salary often consumed in the inevitable losses, but presently I found myself considerably in debt, without any visible means of discharging my liabilities. It is true that my four friends were my chief — in fact, almost my only — creditors, but still, the debts existed, and had to be paid.

"Now these four friends of mine — named respectively Leach, Pitford, Hearn, and Jezzard — were uncommonly clever men, though the full extent of their cleverness was not appreciated by me until too late. And I, too, was clever in my way, and a most undesirable way it was, for I possessed the fatal gift of imitating handwriting and signatures with the most remarkable accuracy. So perfect were my copies that the writers themselves were frequently unable to distinguish their own signatures from my imitations, and many a time was my skill invoked by some of my companions to play off practical jokes upon the others. But these jests were strictly confined to our own little set, for my four friends were most careful and anxious that my dangerous accomplishment should not become known to outsiders.

"And now follows the consequence which you have no doubt foreseen. My debts, though small, were accumulating, and I saw no prospect of being able to pay them. Then, one night, Jezzard made a proposition. We had been playing bridge at his rooms, and once more my ill luck had caused me to increase my debt. I scribbled out an IOU, and pushed it across the table to Jezzard, who picked it up with a very wry face, and pocketed it.

" 'Look here, Ted,' he said presently, 'this paper is all very well, but, you know, I can't pay my debts with it. My creditors demand hard cash.'

" 'I'm very sorry,' I replied, 'but I can't help it.'

" 'Yes, you can,' said he, 'and I'll tell you how.' He then propounded a scheme which I at first rejected with indignation, but which, when the others backed him up, I at last allowed myself to be talked into, and actually put into execution. I contrived, by taking advantage of the carelessness of some of my superiors at the bank, to get possession of some blank cheque forms, which I filled up with small amounts – not more than two or three pounds – and signed with careful imitations of the signatures of some of our clients. Jezzard got some stamps made for stamping on the account numbers, and when this had been done I handed over to him the whole collection of forged cheques in settlement of my debts to all of my four companions.

"The cheques were duly presented – by whom I do not know; and although, to my dismay, the modest sums for which I had drawn them had been skilfully altered into quite considerable amounts, they were all paid without demur excepting one. That one, which had been altered from three pounds to thirty-nine, was drawn upon an account which was already slightly overdrawn. The cashier became suspicious; the cheque was impounded, and the client communicated with. Then, of course, the mine exploded. Not only was this particular forgery detected, but inquiries were set afoot which soon brought to light the others. Presently circumstances, which I need not describe, threw some suspicion on me. I at once lost my nerve, and finally made a full confession.

"The inevitable prosecution followed. It was not conducted vindictively. Still, I had actually committed the forgeries, and though I endeavoured to cast a part of the blame on to the shoulders of my treacherous confederates, I did not succeed. Jezzard, it is true, was arrested, but was discharged for lack of evidence, and, consequently, the whole burden of the forgery fell upon me. The jury, of course, convicted me, and I was sentenced to seven years' penal servitude.

"During the time that I was in prison an uncle of mine died in Canada, and by the provisions of his will I inherited the whole of his very considerable property, so that when the time arrived for my release, I came out of prison, not only free, but comparatively rich. I at once dropped my own name, and, assuming that of Alfred Draper, began to look about for some quiet spot in which I might spend the rest of my days in peace, and with little chance of my identity being discovered. Such a place I found in Sundersley, and here I have lived for the last seven years, liked and respected, I think, by my neighbours, who have little suspected that they were harbouring in their midst a convicted felon.

"All this time I had neither seen nor heard anything of my four confederates, and I hoped and believed that they had passed completely out of my life. But they had not. Only a month ago I met them once more, to my sorrow, and from the day of that meeting all the peace and security of my quiet existence at Sundersley have vanished. Like evil spirits they have stolen into my life, changing my happiness into bitter misery, filling my days with dark forebodings and my nights with terror."

Here Mr Draper paused, and seemed to sink into a gloomy reverie.

"Under what circumstances did you meet these men?" Thorndyke asked.

"Ah!" exclaimed Draper, arousing with sudden excitement, "the circumstances were very singular and suspicious. I had gone over to Eastwich for the day to do some shopping. About eleven o'clock in the forenoon I was making some purchases in a shop when I noticed two men looking in the window, or rather pretending to do so, whilst they conversed earnestly. They were smartly dressed, in a horsy fashion, and looked like well-to-do farmers, as they might very naturally have been since it was market-day. But it seemed to me that their faces were familiar to me. I looked at them more attentively, and then it suddenly dawned upon me, most unpleasantly, that they resembled Leach and Jezzard. And yet they were not quite like. The resemblance was there, but the differences were greater than the lapse of time would account for. Moreover, the man who resembled Jezzard had a rather large mole on the left cheek just under the eye, while the other man had an eyeglass stuck in one eye, and wore a waxed moustache, whereas Leach had always been clean-shaven, and had never used an eyeglass.

"As I was speculating upon the resemblance they looked up, and caught my intent and inquisitive eye, whereupon they moved away from the window; and when, having completed my purchases, I came out into the street, they were nowhere to be seen.

"That evening, as I was walking by the river outside the town before returning to the station, I overtook a yacht which was being towed down-stream. Three men were walking ahead on the bank with a long towline, and one man stood in the cockpit steering. As I approached, and was reading the name *Otter* on the stern, the man at the helm looked round, and with a start of surprise I recognized my old acquaintance Hearn. The recognition, however, was not mutual, for I had grown a beard in the interval, and I passed on without appearing to notice him; but when I overtook the other three men, and recognized, as I had feared, the other three members of the gang, I must have looked rather hard at Jezzard, for he suddenly halted, and exclaimed: 'Why, it's our old friend Ted! Our long-lost and lamented brother!' He held out his hand with effusive cordiality, and began to make inquiries as to my welfare; but I cut him short with the remark that I was not proposing to renew the acquaintance, and, turning off on to a footpath that led away from the river, strode off without looking back.

"Naturally this meeting exercised my mind a good deal, and when I thought of the two men whom I had seen in the town, I could hardly believe that their likeness to my quondam friends was a mere coincidence. And yet when I had met Leach and Jezzard by the river, I had found them little altered, and had particularly noticed that Jezzard had no mole on his face, and that Leach was clean-shaven as of old.

"But a day or two later all my doubts were resolved by a paragraph in the local paper. It appeared that on the day of my visit to Eastwich a number of forged cheques had been cashed at the three banks. They had been presented by three well-dressed, horsy-looking men who looked like well-to-do farmers. One of them had a mole on the left cheek, another was distinguished by a waxed moustache and a single eyeglass, while the description of the third I did not recognize. None of the cheques had been drawn for large amounts, though the total sum obtained by the forgers was nearly four hundred pounds; but the most interesting point was that the cheque-forms had been manufactured by photographic process, and the water-mark skilfully, though not quite perfectly, imitated. Evidently the swindlers were clever and careful men, and willing to take a good deal of trouble for the sake of security, and the result of their precautions was that the police could make no guess as to their identity.

"The very next day, happening to walk over to Port Marston, I came upon the *Otter* lying moored alongside the quay in the harbour. As soon as I recognized the yacht, I turned quickly and walked away, but a minute later I ran into Leach and Jezzard, who were returning to their craft. Jezzard greeted me with an air of surprise. 'What! Still hanging about here, Ted?' he exclaimed. 'That is not discreet of you, dear boy. I should earnestly advise you to clear out.'

" 'What do you mean?' I asked.

" 'Tut, tut!' said he. 'We read the papers like other people, and we know now what business took you to Eastwich. But it's foolish of you to hang about the neighbourhood where you might be spotted at any moment.'

"The implied accusation took me aback so completely that I stood staring at him in speechless astonishment, and at that unlucky moment a tradesman, from whom I had ordered some house-linen, passed along the quay. Seeing me, he stopped and touched his hat.

" 'Beg pardon, Mr Draper,' said he, 'but I shall be sending my cart up to Sundersley tomorrow morning if that will do for you.'

"I said that it would, and as the man turned away, Jezzard's face broke out into a cunning smile.

" 'So you are Mr Draper, of Sundersley, now, are you?' said he. 'Well, I hope you won't be too proud to come and look in on your old friends. We shall be staying here for some time.'

"That same night Hearn made his appearance at my house. He had come as an emissary from the gang, to ask me to do some work for them – to execute some forgeries, in fact. Of course I refused, and pretty bluntly, too, whereupon Hearn began to throw out vague hints as to what might happen if I made enemies of the gang, and to utter veiled, but quite intelligible, threats. You will say that I was an idiot not to send him packing, and threaten to hand over the whole gang to the police; but I was never a man of strong nerve, and I don't mind admitting that I was mortally afraid of that cunning devil, Jezzard.

"The next thing that happened was that Hearn came and took lodgings in Sundersley, and, in spite of my efforts to avoid him, he haunted me continually. The yacht, too, had evidently settled down for some time at a berth in the harbour, for I heard that a local smack-boy had been engaged as a deck-hand; and I frequently encountered Jezzard and the other members of the gang, who all professed to believe that I had committed the Eastwich forgeries. One day I was foolish enough to allow myself to be lured on to the yacht for a few minutes, and when I would have gone ashore, I found that the shore ropes had been cast off, and that the vessel was already moving out of the harbour. At first I was furious, but the three scoundrels were so jovial and good-natured, and so delighted with the joke of taking me for a sail against my will, that I presently cooled down, and having changed into a pair of rubber-soled shoes (so that I should not make dents in the smooth deck with my hobnails), bore a hand at sailing the yacht, and spent quite a pleasant day.

"From that time I found myself gradually drifting back into a state of intimacy with these agreeable scoundrels, and daily becoming more and more afraid of them. In a moment of imbecility I mentioned what I had seen from the shop-window at Eastwich, and, though they passed the matter off with a joke, I could see that they were mightily disturbed by it. Their efforts to induce me to join them were redoubled, and Hearn took to calling almost daily at my house – usually with documents and signatures which he tried to persuade me to copy.

"A few evenings ago he made a new and startling proposition. We were walking in my garden, and he had been urging me once more to rejoin the gang – unsuccessfully, I need not say. Presently he sat down on a seat against a yew-hedge at the bottom of the garden, and, after an interval of silence, said suddenly: 'Then you absolutely refuse to go in with us?'

" 'Of course I do,' I replied. 'Why should I mix myself up with a gang of crooks when I have ample means and a decent position?'

" 'Of course,' he agreed, 'you'd be a fool if you did. But, you see, you know all about this Eastwich job, to say nothing of our other little exploits, and you gave us away once before. Consequently, you can take it from me that, now Jezzard has run you to earth, he won't leave you in peace until you have given us some kind of a hold on you. You know too much, you see, and as long as you have a clean sheet you are a standing menace to us. That is the position. You know it, and Jezzard knows it, and he is a desperate man, and as cunning as the devil.'

" 'I know that,' I said gloomily.

" 'Very well,' continued Hearn. 'Now I'm going to make you an offer. Promise me a small annuity – you can easily afford it – or pay me a substantial sum down, and I will set you free for ever from Jezzard and the others.'

" 'How will you do that?' I asked.

" 'Very simply,' he replied. 'I am sick of them all, and sick of this risky, uncertain mode of life. Now I am ready to clean off my own slate and set you free at the same time; but I must have some means of livelihood in view.'

" 'You mean that you will turn King's evidence?' I asked.

" 'Yes, if you will pay me a couple of hundred a year, or, say, two thousand down on the conviction of the gang.'

"I was so taken aback that for some time I made no reply, and as I sat considering this amazing proposition, the silence was suddenly broken by a suppressed sneeze from the other side of the hedge.

"Hearn and I started to our feet. Immediately hurried footsteps were heard in the lane outside the hedge. We raced up the garden to the gate and out through a side alley, but when we reached the lane there was not a soul in sight. We made a brief and fruitless search in the immediate neighbourhood, and then turned back to the house. Hearn was deathly pale and very agitated, and I must confess that I was a good deal upset by the incident.

" 'This is devilish awkward,' said Hearn.

" 'It is rather,' I admitted; 'but I expect it was only some inquisitive yokel.'

" 'I don't feel so sure of that,' said he. 'At any rate, we were stark lunatics to sit up against a hedge to talk secrets.'

"He paced the garden with me for some time in gloomy silence, and presently, after a brief request that I would think over his proposal, took himself off.

"I did not see him again until I met him last night on the yacht. Pitford called on me in the morning, and invited me to come and dine with them. I at first declined, for my housekeeper was going to spend the evening with her sister at Eastwich, and stay there for the night, and I did not much like leaving the house empty. However, I agreed eventually, stipulating that I should be allowed to come home early, and I accordingly went. Hearn and Pitford were waiting in the boat by the steps – for the yacht had been moved out to a buoy – and we went on board and spent a very pleasant and lively evening. Pitford put me ashore at ten o'clock, and I walked straight home, and went to bed. Hearn would have come with me, but the others insisted on his remaining, saying that they had some matters of business to discuss."

"Which way did you walk home?" asked Thorndyke.

"I came through the town, and along the main road."

"And that is all you know about this affair?"

"Absolutely all," replied Draper. "I have now admitted you to secrets of my past life that I had hoped never to have to reveal to any human creature, and I still have some faint hope that it may not be necessary for you to divulge what I have told you."

"Your secrets shall not be revealed unless it is absolutely indispensable that they should be," said Thorndyke; "but you are placing your life in my hands, and you must leave me perfectly free to act as I think best."

With this he gathered his notes together, and we took our departure.

"A very singular history, this, Jervis," he said, when, having wished the sergeant "Good night," we stepped out on to the dark road. "What do you think of it?"

"I hardly know what to think," I answered, "but, on the whole, it seems rather against Draper than otherwise. He admits that he is an old criminal, and it appears that he was being persecuted and blackmailed by the man Hearn. It is true that he represents Jezzard as being the leading spirit and prime mover in the persecution, but we have only his word for that. Hearn was in lodgings near him, and was undoubtedly taking the most active part in the business, and it is quite possible, and indeed probable, that Hearn was the actual *deus ex machina*."

Thorndyke nodded. "Yes," he said, "that is certainly the line the prosecution will take if we allow the story to become known. Ha! what is this? We are going to have some rain."

"Yes, and wind too. We are in for an autumn gale, I think."

"And that," said Thorndyke, "may turn out to be an important factor in our case."

"How can the weather affect your case?" I asked in some surprise. But, as the rain suddenly descended in a pelting shower, my companion broke into a run, leaving my question unanswered.

On the following morning, which was fair and sunny after the stormy night, Dr Burrows called for my friend. He was on his way to the extemporized mortuary to make the *post-mortem* examination of the murdered man's body. Thorndyke, having notified the coroner that he was watching the case on behalf of the accused, had been authorized to be present at the autopsy; but the authorization did not include me, and, as Dr Burrows did not issue any invitation, I was not able to be present. I met them, however, as they were returning, and it seemed to me that Dr Burrows appeared a little huffy.

"Your friend," said he, in a rather injured tone, "is really the most outrageous stickler for forms and ceremonies that I have ever met."

Thorndyke looked at him with an amused twinkle, and chuckled indulgently.

"Here was a body," Dr Burrows continued irritably, "found under circumstances clearly indicative of murder, and bearing a knife-wound that nearly divided the arch of the aorta; in spite of which, I assure you that Dr Thorndyke insisted on weighing the body, and examining every organ — lungs, liver, stomach, and brain — yes, actually the brain! — as if there had been no clue whatever to the cause of death. And then, as a climax, he insisted on sending the contents of the stomach in a jar, sealed with our respective seals, in charge of a special messenger, to Professor Copland, for analysis and report. I thought he was going to demand an examination for the tubercle bacillus, but he didn't; which," concluded Dr Burrows, suddenly becoming sourly facetious, "was an oversight, for, after all, the fellow may have died of consumption."

Thorndyke chuckled again, and I murmured that the precautions appeared to have been somewhat excessive.

"Not at all," was the smiling response. "You are losing sight of our function. We are the expert and impartial umpires, and it is our business to ascertain, with scientific accuracy, the cause of death. The *prima facie* appearances in this case suggest that the deceased was murdered by Draper, and that is the hypothesis advanced. But that is no concern of ours. It is not our function to confirm an hypothesis suggested by outside circumstances, but rather, on the contrary, to make certain that no other explanation is possible. And that is my invariable practice. No matter how glaringly obvious the appearances may be, I refuse to take anything for granted."

Dr Burrows received this statement with a grunt of dissent, but the arrival of his dogcart put a stop to further discussion.

Thorndyke was not subpœnaed for the inquest. Dr Burrows and the sergeant having been present immediately after the finding of the body, his evidence was not considered necessary, and, moreover, he was known to be watching the case in the interests of the accused. Like myself, therefore, he was present as a spectator, but as a highly interested one, for he took very complete shorthand notes of the whole of the evidence and the coroner's comments.

I shall not describe the proceedings in detail. The jury, having been taken to view the body, trooped into the room on tiptoe, looking pale and awe-stricken, and took their seats; and thereafter, from time to time, directed glances of furtive curiosity at Draper as he stood, pallid and haggard, confronting the court, with a burly rural constable on either side.

The medical evidence was taken first. Dr Burrows, having been sworn, began, with sarcastic emphasis, to describe the condition of the lungs and liver, until he was interrupted by the coroner.

"Is all this necessary?" the latter inquired. "I mean, is it material to the subject of the inquiry?"

"I should say not," replied Dr Burrows. "It appears to me to be quite irrelevant, but Dr Thorndyke, who is watching the case for the defence, thought it necessary."

"I think," said the coroner, "you had better give us only the facts that are material. The jury want you to tell them what you consider to have been the cause of death. They don't want a lecture on pathology."

"The cause of death," said Dr Burrows, "was a penetrating wound of the chest, apparently inflicted with a large knife. The weapon entered between the second and third ribs on the left side close to the sternum or breast-bone. It wounded the left lung, and partially divided both the pulmonary artery and the aorta – the two principal arteries of the body."

"Was this injury alone sufficient to cause death?" the coroner asked.

"Yes," was the reply; "and death from injury to these great vessels would be practically instantaneous."

"Could the injury have been self-inflicted?"

"So far as the position and nature of the wound are concerned," replied the witness, "self-infliction would be quite possible. But since death would follow in a few seconds at the most, the weapon would be found either in the wound, or grasped in the hand, or, at least, quite close to the body. But in this case no weapon was found at all, and the wound must therefore certainly have been homicidal."

"Did you see the body before it was moved?"

"Yes. It was lying on its back, with the arms extended and the legs nearly straight; and the sand in the neighbourhood of the body was trampled as if a furious struggle had taken place."

"Did you notice anything remarkable about the footprints in the sand?"

"I did," replied Dr Burrows. "They were the footprints of two persons only. One of these was evidently the deceased, whose footmarks could be easily identified by the circular rubber heels. The other footprints were those of a person – apparently a man – who wore shoes, or boots, the soles of which were studded with nails; and these nails were arranged in a very peculiar and unusual manner, for those on the soles formed a lozenge or diamond shape, and those on the heel were set out in the form of a cross."

"Have you ever seen shoes or boots with the nails arranged in this manner?"

"Yes. I have seen a pair of shoes which I am informed belong to the accused; the nails in them are arranged as I have described."

"Would you say that the footprints of which you have spoken were made by those shoes?"

"No; I could not say that. I can only say that, to the best of my belief, the pattern on the shoes is similar to that in the footprints."

This was the sum of Dr Burrows' evidence, and to all of it Thorndyke listened with an immovable countenance, though with the closest attention. Equally attentive was the accused man, though not equally impassive; indeed, so great was his agitation that presently one of the constables asked permission to get him a chair.

The next witness was Arthur Jezzard. He testified that he had viewed the body, and identified it as that of Charles Hearn; that he had been acquainted with deceased for some years, but knew practically nothing of his affairs. At the time of his death deceased was lodging in the village.

"Why did he leave the yacht?" the coroner inquired. "Was there any kind of disagreement?"

"Not in the least," replied Jezzard. "He grew tired of the confinement of the yacht, and came to live ashore for a change. But we were the best of friends, and he intended to come with us when we sailed."

"When did you see him last?"

"On the night before the body was found – that is, last Monday. He had been dining on the yacht, and we put him ashore about midnight. He said as we were rowing him ashore that he intended to walk home along the sands as the tide was out. He went up the stone steps by the watch-house, and turned at the top to wish us good night. That was the last time I saw him alive."

"Do you know anything of the relations between the accused and the deceased?" the coroner asked.

"Very little," replied Jezzard. "Mr Draper was introduced to us by the deceased about a month ago. I believe they had been acquainted some years, and they appeared to be on excellent terms. There was no indication of any quarrel or disagreement between them."

"What time did the accused leave the yacht on the night of the murder?"

"About ten o'clock. He said that he wanted to get home early, as his housekeeper was away and he did not like the house to be left with no one in it."

This was the whole of Jezzard's evidence, and was confirmed by that of Leach and Pitford. Then, when the fisherman had deposed to the discovery of the body, the sergeant was called, and stepped forward grasping a carpet-bag, and looking as uncomfortable as if he had been the accused instead of a witness. He described the circumstances under which he saw the body, giving the exact time and place with official precision.

"You have heard Dr Burrows' description of the footprints?" the coroner inquired.

"Yes. There were two sets. One set were evidently made by deceased. They showed that he entered St Bridget's Bay from the direction of Port Marston. He had been walking along the shore just about high-water mark, sometimes above and sometimes below. Where he had walked below high-water mark the foot-prints had of course been washed away by the sea."

"How far back did you trace the footprints of deceased?"

"About two-thirds of the way to Sundersley Gap. Then they disappeared below high-water mark. Later in the evening I walked from the Gap into Port Marston, but could not find any further traces of deceased. He must have walked between the tide-marks all the way from Port Marston to beyond Sundersley. When these footprints entered St Bridget's Bay they became mixed up with the footprints of another man, and the shore was trampled for a space of a dozen yards as if a furious struggle had taken place. The strange man's tracks came down from the Shepherd's Path, and went up it again; but, owing to the hardness of the ground from the dry weather, the tracks disappeared a short distance up the path, and I could not find them again."

"What were these strange footprints like?" inquired the coroner.

"They were very peculiar," replied the sergeant. "They were made by shoes armed with smallish hobnails, which were arranged in a diamond-shaped pattern on the soles and in a cross on the heels. I measured the footprints carefully, and made a drawing of each foot at the time." Here the sergeant produced a long note-book of funereal aspect, and, having opened it at a marked place, handed it to the coroner, who examined it attentively, and then

Extreme length, 11¾ inches   Length of heel, 3⅛ inches
Width at A, 4½ inches   Width of heel at cross, 3 inches

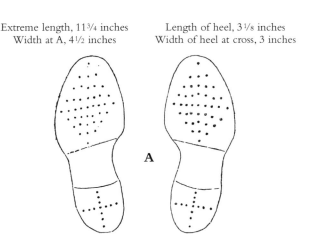

THE SERGENT'S SKETCH

passed it on to the jury. From the jury it was presently transferred to Thorndyke, and, looking over his shoulder, I saw a very workmanlike sketch of a pair of footprints with the principal dimensions inserted.

Thorndyke surveyed the drawing critically, jotted down a few brief notes, and returned the sergeant's notebook to the coroner, who, as he took it, turned once more to the officer.

"Have you any clue, sergeant, to the person who made these footprints?" he asked.

By way of reply the sergeant opened his carpet-bag, and, extracting therefrom a pair of smart but stoutly made shoes, laid them on the table.

"These shoes," he said, "are the property of the accused; he was wearing them when I arrested him. They appear to correspond exactly to the footprints of the murderer. The measurements are the same, and the nails with which they are studded are arranged in a similar pattern."

"Would you swear that the footprints were made with these shoes?" asked the coroner.

"No, sir, I would not," was the decided answer. "I would only swear to the similarity of size and pattern."

"Had you ever seen these shoes before you made the drawing?"

"No, sir," replied the sergeant; and he then related the incident of the footprints in the soft earth by the pond which led him to make the arrest.

The coroner gazed reflectively at the shoes which he held in his hand, and from them to the drawing; then, passing them to the foreman of the jury, he remarked: "Well, gentlemen, it is not for me to tell you whether these shoes answer to the description given by Dr Burrows and the sergeant, or whether they resemble the drawing which, as you have heard, was made by the officer on the spot and before he had seen the shoes; that is a matter for you to decide. Meanwhile, there is another question that we must consider." He turned to the sergeant and asked: "Have you made any inquiries as to the movements of the accused on the night of the murder?"

"I have," replied the sergeant, "and I find that, on that night, the accused was alone in the house, his housekeeper having gone over to Eastwich. Two men saw him in the town about ten o'clock, apparently walking in the direction of Sundersley."

This concluded the sergeant's evidence, and when one or two more witnesses had been examined without eliciting any fresh facts, the coroner briefly recapitulated the evidence, and requested the jury to consider their verdict. Thereupon a solemn hush fell upon the court, broken only by the whispers of the jurymen, as they consulted together; and the spectators gazed in awed expectancy from the accused to the whispering jury. I glanced at Draper, sitting huddled in his chair, his clammy face as pale as that of the corpse in the mortuary hard by, his hands tremulous and restless; and, scoundrel as I believed him to be, I could not but pity the abject misery that was written large all over him, from his damp hair to his incessantly shifting feet.

The jury took but a short time to consider their verdict. At the end of five minutes the foreman announced that they were agreed, and, in answer to the coroner's formal inquiry, stood up and replied: "We find that the deceased met his death by being stabbed in the chest by the accused man, Alfred Draper."

"That is a verdict of wilful murder," said the coroner, and he entered it accordingly in his notes. The Court now rose. The spectators reluctantly trooped out, the jurymen stood up and stretched themselves, and the two constables, under the guidance of the sergeant, carried the wretched Draper in a fainting condition to a closed fly that was waiting outside.

"I was not greatly impressed by the activity of the defence," I remarked maliciously as we walked home.

Thorndyke smiled. "You surely did not expect me to cast my pearls of forensic learning before a coroner's jury," said he.

"I expected that you would have something to say on behalf of your client," I replied. "As it was, his accusers had it all their own way."

"And why not?" he asked. "Of what concern to us is the verdict of the coroner's jury?"

"It would have seemed more decent to make some sort of defence," I replied.

"My dear Jervis," he rejoined, "you do not seem to appreciate the great virtue of what Lord Beaconsfield so felicitously called 'a policy of masterly inactivity'; and yet that is one of the great lessons that a medical training impresses on the student."

"That may be so," said I. "But the result, up to the present, of your masterly policy is that a verdict of wilful murder stands against your client, and I don't see what other verdict the jury could have found."

"Neither do I," said Thorndyke.

I had written to my principal, Dr Cooper, describing the stirring events that were taking place in the village, and had received a reply from him instructing me to place the house at Thorndyke's disposal, and to give him every facility for his work. In accordance with which edict my colleague took possession of a well-lighted, disused stable-loft, and announced his intention of moving his things into it. Now, as these "things" included the mysterious contents of the hamper that the housemaid had seen, I was possessed with a consuming desire to be present at the "flitting", and I do not mind confessing that I purposely lurked about the stairs in the hopes of thus picking up a few crumbs of information.

But Thorndyke was one too many for me. A misbegotten infant in the village having been seized with inopportune convulsions, I was compelled, most reluctantly, to hasten to its relief; and I returned only in time to find Thorndyke in the act of locking the door of the loft.

"A nice light, roomy place to work in," he remarked, as he descended the steps, slipping the key into his pocket.

"Yes," I replied, and added boldly: "What do you intend to do up there?"

"Work up the case for the defence," he replied, "and, as I have now heard all that the prosecution have to say, I shall be able to forge ahead."

This was vague enough, but I consoled myself with the reflection that in a very few days I should, in common with the rest of the world, be in possession of the results of his mysterious proceedings. For, in view of the approaching assizes, preparations were being made to push the case through the magistrate's court as quickly as possible in order to obtain a committal in time for the ensuing sessions. Draper had, of course, been already charged before a justice of the peace and evidence of arrest taken, and it was expected that the adjourned hearing would commence before the local magistrates on the fifth day after the inquest.

The events of these five days kept me in a positive ferment of curiosity. In the first place an inspector of the Criminal Investigation Department came down and browsed about the place in company with the sergeant. Then Mr Bashfield, who was to conduct the prosecution, came and took up his abode at the "Cat and Chicken". But the most surprising visitor was Thorndyke's laboratory assistant, Polton, who appeared one evening with a large trunk and a sailor's hammock, and announced that he was going to take up his quarters in the loft.

As to Thorndyke himself, his proceedings were beyond speculation. From time to time he made mysterious appearances at the windows of the loft, usually arrayed in what looked suspiciously like a nightshirt. Sometimes I would see him holding a negative up to the light, at others manipulating a photographic printing-frame; and once I observed him with a paintbrush and a large gallipot; on which I turned away in despair, and nearly collided with the inspector.

"Dr Thorndyke is staying with you, I hear," said the latter, gazing earnestly at my colleague's back, which was presented for his inspection at the window.

"Yes," I answered. "Those are his temporary premises."

"That is where he does his bedevilments, I suppose?" the officer suggested.

"He conducts his experiments there," I corrected haughtily.

"That's what I mean," said the inspector; and, as Thorndyke at this moment turned and opened the window, our visitor began to ascend the steps.

"I've just called to ask if I could have a few words with you, Doctor," said the inspector, as he reached the door.

"Certainly," Thorndyke replied blandly. "If you will go down and wait with Dr Jervis, I will be with you in five minutes."

The officer came down the steps grinning, and I thought I heard him murmur "Sold!" But this may have been an illusion. However, Thorndyke presently emerged, and he and the officer strode away into the shrubbery. What the inspector's business was, or whether he had any business at all, I never learned; but the incident seemed to throw some light on the presence of Polton and the sailor's hammock. And this reference to Polton reminds me of a very singular change that took place about this time in the habits of this usually staid and sedate little man; who, abandoning the somewhat clerical style of dress that he ordinarily affected, broke out into a semi-nautical costume, in which he would sally forth every morning in the direction of Port Marston. And there, on more than one occasion, I saw him leaning against a post by the harbour, or lounging outside a waterside tavern in earnest and amicable conversation with sundry nautical characters.

On the afternoon of the day before the opening of the proceedings we had two new visitors. One of them, a grey-haired spectacled man, was a stranger to me, and for some reason I failed to recall his name, Copland, though I was sure I had heard it before. The other was Anstey, the barrister who usually worked with Thorndyke in cases that went into Court. I saw very little of either of them, however, for they retired almost immediately to the loft, where, with short intervals for meals, they remained for the rest of the day, and, I believe, far into the night. Thorndyke requested me not to mention the names of his visitors to anyone, and at the same time apologized for the secrecy of his proceedings.

"But you are a doctor, Jervis," he concluded, "and you know what professional confidences are; and you will understand how greatly it is in our favour that we know exactly what the prosecution can do, while they are absolutely in the dark as to our line of defence."

I assured him that I fully understood his position, and with this assurance he retired, evidently relieved, to the council chamber.

The proceedings, which opened on the following day, and at which I was present throughout, need not be described in detail. The evidence for the prosecution was, of course, mainly a repetition of that given at the inquest. Mr Bashfield's opening statement, however, I shall give at length, inasmuch as it summarized very clearly the whole of the case against the prisoner.

"The case that is now before the Court," said the counsel, "involves a charge of wilful murder against the prisoner Alfred Draper, and the facts, in so far as they are known, are briefly these: On the night of Monday, the 27th of September, the deceased, Charles Hearn, dined with some friends on board the yacht *Otter*. About midnight he came ashore, and proceeded to walk towards Sundersley along the beach. As he entered St Bridget's Bay, a man, who appears to have been lying in wait, and who came down the Shepherd's Path, met him, and a deadly struggle seems to have taken place. The deceased received a wound of a kind calculated to cause almost instantaneous death, and apparently fell down dead.

"And now, what was the motive of this terrible crime? It was not robbery, for nothing appears to have been taken from the corpse. Money and valuables were found, as far as is known, intact. Nor, clearly, was it a case of a casual affray. We are, consequently, driven to the conclusion that the motive was a personal one, a motive of interest or revenge, and with this view the time, the place, and the evident deliberateness of the murder are in full agreement.

"So much for the motive. The next question is, Who was the perpetrator of this shocking crime? And the answer to that question is given in a very singular and dramatic circumstance, a circumstance that illustrates once more the amazing lack of precaution shown by persons who commit such crimes. The murderer was wearing a very remarkable pair of shoes, and those shoes left very remarkable footprints in the smooth sand, and those footprints were seen and examined by a very acute and painstaking police-officer, Sergeant Payne, whose evidence you will hear presently. The sergeant not only examined the footprints, he made careful drawings of them on the spot – on the spot, mind you, not from memory – and he made very exact measurements of them, which he duly noted down. And from those drawings and those measurements, those tell-tale shoes have been identified, and are here for your inspection.

"And now, who is the owner of those very singular, those almost unique shoes? I have said that the motive of this murder must have been a personal one, and, behold! the owner of those shoes happens to be the one person in the whole of this district who could have had a motive for compassing the murdered man's death. Those shoes belong to, and were taken from the feet of, the prisoner, Alfred Draper, and the prisoner, Alfred Draper, is the only person living in this neighbourhood who was acquainted with the deceased.

"It has been stated in evidence at the inquest that the relations of these two men, the prisoner and the deceased, were entirely friendly; but I shall prove to you that they were not so friendly as has been supposed. I shall prove to you, by the evidence of the prisoner's housekeeper, that the deceased was often an unwelcome visitor at the house, that the prisoner often denied himself when he was really at home and disengaged, and, in short, that he appeared constantly to shun and avoid the deceased.

"One more question and I have finished. Where was the prisoner on the night of the murder? The answer is that he was in a house little more than half a mile from the scene of the crime.

And who was with him in that house? Who was there to observe and testify to his going forth and his coming home? No one. He was alone in the house. On that night, of all nights, he was alone. Not a soul was there to rouse at the creak of a door or the tread of a shoe – to tell us whether he slept or whether he stole forth in the dead of the night.

"Such are the facts of this case. I believe that they are not disputed, and I assert that, taken together, they are susceptible of only one explanation, which is that the prisoner, Alfred Draper, is the man who murdered the deceased, Charles Hearn."

Immediately on the conclusion of this address, the witnesses were called, and the evidence given was identical with that at the inquest. The only new witness for the prosecution was Draper's housekeeper, and her evidence fully bore out Mr Bashfield's statement. The sergeant's account of the footprints was listened to with breathless interest, and at its conclusion the presiding magistrate – a retired solicitor, once well known in criminal practice – put a question which interested me as showing how clearly Thorndyke had foreseen the course of events, recalling, as it did, his remark on the night when we were caught in the rain.

"Did you," the magistrate asked, "take these shoes down to the beach and compare them with the actual footprints?"

"I obtained the shoes at night," replied the sergeant, "and I took them down to the shore at daybreak the next morning. But, unfortunately, there had been a storm in the night, and the footprints were almost obliterated by the wind and rain."

When the sergeant had stepped down, Mr Bashfield announced that that was the case for the prosecution. He then resumed his seat, turning an inquisitive eye on Anstey and Thorndyke.

The former immediately rose and opened the case for the defence with a brief statement.

"The learned counsel for the prosecution," said he, "has told us that the facts now in the possession of the Court admit of but one explanation – that of the guilt of the accused. That may or may not be; but I shall now proceed to lay before the Court certain fresh facts − facts, I may say, of the most singular and startling character, which will, I think, lead to a very different conclusion. I shall say no more, but call the witnesses forthwith, and let the evidence speak for itself."

The first witness for the defence was Thorndyke; and as he entered the box I observed Polton take up a position close behind him with a large wicker trunk. Having been sworn, and requested by Anstey to tell the Court what he knew about the case, he commenced without preamble: "About half-past four in the afternoon of the 28th of September I walked down Sundersley Gap with Dr Jervis. Our attention was attracted by certain footprints in the sand, particularly those of a man who had landed from a boat, had walked up the Gap, and presently returned, apparently to the boat.

"As we were standing there Sergeant Payne and Dr Burrows passed down the Gap with two constables carrying a stretcher. We followed at a distance, and as we walked along the shore we encountered another set of footprints − those which the sergeant has described as the footprints of the deceased. We examined these carefully, and endeavoured to frame a description of the person by whom they had been made."

"And did your description agree with the characters of the deceased?" the magistrate asked.

"Not in the least," replied Thorndyke, whereupon the magistrate, the inspector, and Mr Bashfield laughed long and heartily.

"When we turned into St Bridget's Bay, I saw the body of deceased lying on the sand close to the cliff. The sand all round was covered with footprints, as if a prolonged, fierce struggle had taken place. There were two sets of footprints, one set being apparently those of the deceased and the other those of a man with nailed shoes of a very peculiar and conspicuous pattern. The incredible folly that the wearing of such shoes indicated caused me to look more closely at the footprints, and then I made the surprising discovery that there had in reality been no struggle; that, in fact, the two sets of footprints had been made at different times."

"At different times!" the magistrate exclaimed in astonishment.
"Yes. The interval between them may have been one of hours
or one only of seconds, but the undoubted fact is that the two sets
of footprints were made, not simultaneously, but in succession."
"But how did you arrive at that fact?" the magistrate asked.
"It was very obvious when one looked," said Thorndyke. "The
marks of the deceased man's shoes showed that he repeatedly trod
in his own footprints; but never in a single instance did he tread in
the footprints of the other man, although they covered the same
area. The man with the nailed shoes, on the contrary, not only trod
in his own footprints, but with equal frequency in those of the
deceased. Moreover, when the body was removed, I observed that
the footprints in the sand on which it was lying were exclusively
those of the deceased. There was not a sign of any nail-marked
footprint under the corpse, although there were many close
around it. It was evident, therefore, that the footprints of the
deceased were made first and those of the nailed shoes
afterwards."

As Thorndyke paused the magistrate rubbed his nose
thoughtfully, and the inspector gazed at the witness with a puzzled
frown.

"The singularity of this fact," my colleague resumed, "made me
look at the footprints yet more critically, and then I made another
discovery. There was a double track of the nailed shoes, leading
apparently from and back to the Shepherd's Path. But on examining
these tracks more closely, I was astonished to find that the man who
had made them had been walking backwards; that, in fact, he had
walked backwards from the body to the Shepherd's Path, had
ascended it for a short distance, had turned round, and returned, still
walking backwards, to the face of the cliff near the corpse, and there
the tracks vanished altogether. On the sand at this spot were some
small, inconspicuous marks which might have been made by the
end of a rope, and there were also a few small fragments which had
fallen from the cliff above. Observing these, I examined the surface
of the cliff, and at one spot, about six feet above the beach, I found

a freshly rubbed spot on which were parallel scratches such as might have been made by the nailed sole of a boot. I then ascended the Shepherd's Path, and examined the cliff from above, and here I found on the extreme edge a rather deep indentation, such as would be made by a taut rope, and, on lying down and looking over, I could see, some five feet from the top, another rubbed spot with very distinct parallel scratches."

"You appear to infer," said the chairman, "that this man performed these astonishing evolutions and was then hauled up the cliff?"

"That is what the appearances suggested," replied Thorndyke.

The chairman pursed up his lips, raised his eyebrows, and glanced doubtfully at his brother magistrates. Then, with a resigned air, he bowed to the witness to indicate that he was listening.

"That same night," Thorndyke resumed, "I cycled down to the shore, through the Gap, with a supply of plaster of Paris, and proceeded to take plaster moulds of the more important of the footprints." (Here the magistrates, the inspector, and Mr Bashfield with one accord sat up at attention; Sergeant Payne swore quite audibly; and I experienced a sudden illumination respecting a certain basin and kitchen spoon which had so puzzled me on the night of Thorndyke's arrival.) "As I thought that liquid plaster might confuse or even obliterate the prints in sand, I filled up the respective footprints with dry plaster, pressed it down lightly, and then cautiously poured water on to it. The moulds, which are excellent impressions, of course show the appearance of the boots which made the footprints, and from these moulds I have prepared casts which reproduce the footprints themselves.

"The first mould that I made was that of one of the tracks from the boat up to the Gap, and of this I shall speak presently. I next made a mould of one of the footprints which have been described as those of the deceased."

"Have been described!" exclaimed the chairman. "The deceased was certainly there, and there were no other footprints, so, if they were not his, he must have flown to where he was found."

"I will call them the footprints of the deceased," replied Thorndyke imperturbably. "I took a mould of one of them, and with it, on the same mould, one of my own footprints. Here is the mould, and here is a cast from it." (He turned and took them from the triumphant Polton, who had tenderly lifted them out of the trunk in readiness.) "On looking at the cast, it will be seen that the appearances are not such as would be expected. The deceased was five feet nine inches high, but was very thin and light, weighing only nine stone six pounds, as I ascertained by weighing the body, whereas I am five feet eleven and weigh nearly thirteen stone. But yet the footprint of the deceased is nearly twice as deep as mine – that is to say, the lighter man has sunk into the sand nearly twice as deeply as the heavier man."

The magistrates were now deeply attentive. They were no longer simply listening to the despised utterances of a mere scientific expert. The cast lay before them with the two footprints side by side; the evidence appealed to their own senses and was proportionately convincing. "This is very singular," said the chairman; "but perhaps you can explain the discrepancy?"

"I think I can," replied Thorndyke; "but I should prefer to place all the facts before you first."

"Undoubtedly that would be better," the chairman agreed. "Pray proceed."

"There was another remarkable peculiarity about these footprints," Thorndyke continued, "and that was their distance apart – the length of the stride, in fact. I measured the steps carefully from heel to heel, and found them only nineteen and a half inches. But a man of Hearn's height would have an ordinary stride of about thirty-six inches – more if he was walking fast. Walking with a stride of nineteen and a half inches he would look as if his legs were tied together.

"I next proceeded to the Bay, and took two moulds from the footprints of the man with the nailed shoes, a right and a left. Here is a cast from the mould, and it shows very clearly that the man was walking backwards."

"How does it show that?" asked the magistrate.

"There are several distinctive points. For instance, the absence of the usual 'kick off' at the toe, the slight drag behind the heel, showing the direction in which the foot was lifted, and the undisturbed impression of the sole."

"You have spoken of moulds and casts. What is the difference between them?"

"A mould is a direct, and therefore reversed, impression. A cast is the impression of a mould, and therefore a facsimile of the object. If I pour liquid plaster on a coin, when it sets I have a mould, a sunk impression, of the coin. If I pour melted wax into the mould I obtain a cast, a facsimile of the coin. A footprint is a mould of the foot. A mould of the footprint is a cast of the foot, and a cast from the mould reproduces the footprint."

"Thank you," said the magistrate. "Then your moulds from these two footprints are really facsimiles of the murderer's shoes, and can be compared with these shoes which have been put in evidence?"

"Yes, and when we compare them they demonstrate a very important fact."

"What is that?"

"It is that the prisoner's shoes were not the shoes that made those footprints." A buzz of astonishment ran through the court, but Thorndyke continued stolidly: "The prisoner's shoes were not in my possession, so I went on to Barker's pond, on the clay margin of which I had seen footprints actually made by the prisoner. I took moulds of those footprints, and compared them with these from the sand. There are several important differences, which you will see if you compare them. To facilitate the comparison I have made transparent photographs of both sets of moulds to the same scale. Now, if we put the photograph of the mould of the prisoner's right shoe over that of the murderer's right shoe, and hold the two superposed photographs up to the light, we cannot make the two pictures coincide. They are exactly of the same length, but the shoes are of different shape. Moreover, if we put one of the nails in one photograph over the corresponding nail in the other photograph, we cannot make the rest of the nails coincide. But the most conclusive fact of all – from which there is no possible escape – is that the number of nails in the two shoes is not the same. In the sole of the prisoner's right shoe there are forty nails; in that of the murderer there are forty-one. The murderer has one nail too many."

There was a deathly silence in the court as the magistrates and Mr Bashfield pored over the moulds and the prisoner's shoes, and examined the photographs against the light. Then the chairman asked: "Are these all the facts, or have you something more to tell us?" He was evidently anxious to get the key to this riddle.

"There is more evidence, your Worship," said Anstey. "The witness examined the body of deceased." Then, turning to Thorndyke, he asked: "You were present at the *post-mortem* examination?"

"I was."

"Did you form any opinion as to the cause of death?"

"Yes. I came to the conclusion that death was occasioned by an overdose of morphia."

A universal gasp of amazement greeted this statement. Then the presiding magistrate protested breathlessly: "But there was a wound, which we have been told was capable of causing instantaneous death. Was that not the case?"

"There was undoubtedly such a wound," replied Thorndyke. "But when that wound was inflicted the deceased had already been dead from a quarter to half an hour."

"This is incredible!" exclaimed the magistrate. "But, no doubt, you can give us your reasons for this amazing conclusion?"

"My opinion," said Thorndyke, "was based on several facts. In the first place, a wound inflicted on a living body gapes rather widely, owing to the retraction of the living skin. The skin of a dead body does not retract, and the wound, consequently, does not gape. This wound gaped very slightly, showing that death was recent, I should say, within half an hour. Then a wound on the living body becomes filled with blood, and blood is shed freely on the clothing. But the wound on the deceased contained only a little blood-clot. There was hardly any blood on the clothing, and I had already noticed that there was none on the sand where the body had lain."

"And you consider this quite conclusive?" the magistrate asked doubtfully.

"I do," answered Thorndyke. "But there was other evidence which was beyond all question. The weapon had partially divided both the aorta and the pulmonary artery – the main arteries of the body. Now, during life, these great vessels are full of blood at a high internal pressure, whereas after death they become almost empty. It follows that, if this wound had been inflicted during life, the cavity in which those vessels lie would have become filled with blood. As a matter of fact, it contained practically no blood, only the merest oozing from some small veins, so that it is certain that the wound was inflicted after death. The presence and nature of the poison I ascertained by analysing certain secretions from the body, and the analysis enabled me to judge that the quantity of the poison was large; but the contents of the stomach were sent to Professor Copland for more exact examination."

"Is the result of Professor Copland's analysis known?" the magistrate asked Anstey.

"The professor is here, your Worship," replied Anstey, "and is prepared to swear to having obtained over one grain of morphia from the contents of the stomach; and as this, which is in itself a poisonous dose, is only the unabsorbed residue of what was actually swallowed, the total quantity taken must have been very large indeed."

"Thank you," said the magistrate. "And now, Dr Thorndyke, if you have given us all the facts, perhaps you will tell us what conclusions you have drawn from them."

"The facts which I have stated," said Thorndyke, "appear to me to indicate the following sequence of events. The deceased died about midnight on September 27, from the effects of a poisonous dose of morphia, how or by whom administered I offer no opinion. I think that his body was conveyed in a boat to Sundersley Gap. The boat probably contained three men, of whom one remained in charge of it, one walked up the Gap and along the cliff towards St Bridget's Bay, and the third, having put on the shoes of the deceased, carried the body along the shore to the Bay. This would account for the great depth and short stride of the tracks that have been spoken of as those of the deceased. Having reached the Bay, I believe that this man laid the corpse down on his tracks, and then trampled the sand in the neighbourhood. He next took off deceased's shoes and put them on the corpse; then he put on a pair of boots or shoes which he had been carrying – perhaps hung round his neck – and which had been prepared with nails to imitate Draper's shoes. In these shoes he again trampled over the area near the corpse. Then he walked backwards to the Shepherd's Path, and from it again, still backwards, to the face of the cliff. Here his accomplice had lowered a rope, by which he climbed up to the top. At the top he took off the nailed shoes, and the two men walked back to the Gap, where the man who had carried the rope took his confederate on his back, and carried him down to the boat to avoid leaving the tracks of stockinged feet. The tracks that I saw at the Gap certainly indicated that the man was carrying something very heavy when he returned to the boat."

"But why should the man have climbed a rope up the cliff when he could have walked up the Shepherd's Path?" the magistrate asked.

"Because," replied Thorndyke, "there would then have been a set of tracks leading out of the Bay without a corresponding set leading into it; and this would have instantly suggested to a smart police-officer – such as Sergeant Payne – a landing from a boat."

"Your explanation is highly ingenious," said the magistrate, "and appears to cover all the very remarkable facts. Have you anything more to tell us?"

"No, your Worship," was the reply, "excepting" (here he took from Polton the last pair of moulds and passed them up to the magistrate) "that you will probably find these moulds of importance presently."

As Thorndyke stepped from the box – for there was no cross-examination – the magistrates scrutinized the moulds with an air of perplexity; but they were too discreet to make any remark. When the evidence of Professor Copland (which showed that an unquestionably lethal dose of morphia must have been swallowed) had been taken, the clerk called out the – to me – unfamiliar name of Jacob Gummer. Thereupon an enormous pair of brown dreadnought trousers, from the upper end of which a smack-boy's head and shoulders protruded, walked into the witness-box.

Jacob admitted at the outset that he was a smack-master's apprentice, and that he had been "hired out" by his master to one Mr Jezzard as deck-hand and cabin-boy of the yacht *Otter*.

"Now, Gummer," said Anstey, "do you remember the prisoner coming on board the yacht?"

"Yes. He has been on board twice. The first time was about a month ago. He went for a sail with us then. The second time was on the night when Mr Hearn was murdered."

"Do you remember what sort of boots the prisoner was wearing the first time he came?"

"Yes. They were shoes with a lot of nails in the soles. I remember them because Mr Jezzard made him take them off and put on a canvas pair."

"What was done with the nailed shoes?"

"Mr Jezzard took 'em below to the cabin."

"And did Mr Jezzard come up on deck again directly?"

"No. He stayed down in the cabin about ten minutes."

"Do you remember a parcel being delivered on board from a London boot-maker?"

"Yes. The postman brought it about four or five days after Mr Draper had been on board. It was labelled 'Walker Bros., Boot and Shoe Makers, London.' Mr Jezzard took a pair of shoes from it, for I saw them on the locker in the cabin the same day."

50

"Did you ever see him wear them?"

"No. I never see 'em again."

"Have you ever heard sounds of hammering on the yacht?"

"Yes. The night after the parcel came I was on the quay alongside, and I heard someone a-hammering in the cabin."

"What did the hammering sound like?"

"It sounded like a cobbler a-hammering in nails."

"Have you ever seen any boot-nails on the yacht?"

"Yes. When I was a-clearin' up the cabin the next mornin', I found a hobnail on the floor in a corner by the locker."

"Were you on board on the night when Mr Hearn died?"

"Yes. I'd been ashore, but I came aboard about half-past nine."

"Did you see Mr Hearn go ashore?"

"I see him leave the yacht. I had turned into my bunk and gone to sleep, when Mr Jezzard calls down to me: 'We're putting Mr Hearn ashore,' says he; 'and then,' he says, 'we're a-going for an hour's fishing. You needn't sit up,' he says, and with that he shuts the scuttle. Then I got up and slid back the scuttle and put my head out, and I see Mr Jezzard and Mr Leach a-helpin' Mr Hearn acrost the deck. Mr Hearn he looked as if he was drunk. They got him into the boat – and a rare job they had – and Mr Pitford, what was in the boat already, he pushed off. And then I popped my head in again, 'cause I didn't want them to see me."

"Did they row to the steps?"

"No. I put my head out again when they were gone, and I heard 'em row round the yacht, and then pull out towards the mouth of the harbour. I couldn't see the boat, 'cause it was a very dark night."

"Very well. Now I am going to ask you about another matter. Do you know anyone of the name of Polton?"

"Yes," replied Gummer, turning a dusky red. "I've just found out his real name. I thought he was called Simmons."

"Tell us what you know about him," said Anstey, with a mischievous smile.

"Well," said the boy, with a ferocious scowl at the bland and smiling Polton, "one day he come down to the yacht when the gentlemen had gone ashore. I believe he'd seen 'em go. And he offers me ten shillin' to let him see all the boots and shoes we'd got on board. I didn't see no harm, so I turns out the whole lot in the cabin for him to look at. While he was lookin' at 'em he asks me to fetch a pair of mine from the fo'c'sle, so I fetches 'em. When I come back he was pitchin' the boots and shoes back into the locker. Then, presently, he nips off, and when he was gone I looked over the shoes, and then I found there was a pair missing. They was an old pair of Mr Jezzard's, and what made him nick 'em is more than I can understand."

"Would you know those shoes if you saw them?"

"Yes, I should," replied the lad.

"Are these the pair?" Anstey handed the boy a pair of dilapidated canvas shoes, which he seized eagerly.

"Yes, these is the ones what he stole!" he exclaimed.

Anstey took them back from the boy's reluctant hands, and passed them up to the magistrate's desk. "I think," said he, "that if your Worship will compare these shoes with the last pair of moulds, you will have no doubt that these are the shoes which made the footprints from the sea to Sundersley Gap and back again."

The magistrates together compared the shoes and the moulds amidst a breathless silence. At length the chairman laid them down on the desk. "It is impossible to doubt it," said he. "The broken heel and the tear in the rubber sole, with the remains of the chequered pattern, make the identity practically certain."

As the chairman made this statement I involuntarily glanced round to the place where Jezzard was sitting. But he was not there; neither he, nor Pitford, nor Leach. Taking advantage of the preoccupation of the Court, they had quietly slipped out of the door. But I was not the only person who had noted their absence. The inspector and the sergeant were already in earnest consultation, and a minute later they, too, hurriedly departed.

The proceedings now speedily came to an end. After a brief discussion with his brother-magistrates, the chairman addressed the Court. "The remarkable and I may say startling evidence, heard in this court today, if it has not fixed the guilt of this crime on any individual, has, at any rate, made it clear to our satisfaction the prisoner is not the guilty person, and he is accordingly discharged. Mr Draper, I have great pleasure in informing you that you are at liberty to leave the court, and do so entirely clear of all suspicion; and congratulate you very heartily on the skill and ingenuity of your legal advisers, but for which the decision of the Court would, I am afraid, have been very different."

That evening, lawyers, witnesses, and the jubilant and grateful client gathered round a truly festive board to dine, and fight over again the battle of the day. But we were scarcely halfway through our meal when, to the indignation of the servants, Sergeant Payne burst breathlessly into the room. "They've gone, sir!" he exclaimed, addressing Thorndyke. "They've given us the slip for good."

"Why, how can that be?" asked Thorndyke.

"They're dead, sir! All three of them!"

"Dead!" we all exclaimed.

"Yes. They made a burst for the yacht when they left the court, and they got on board and put out to sea at once, hoping, no doubt, to get clear as the light was failing. But they were in such a hurry they did not see a steam trawler entering, hidden by the pier. Then, just at the entrance, as the yacht was creeping out, the trawler hit her amidships, and fairly cut her in two. The three men were in the water in an instant, and were swept away in the eddy behind the north pier; and before any boat could put out to them they had all gone under. Jezzard's body came up on the beach just as I was coming away."

We were all silent and a little awed, but if any of us felt regret at the catastrophe, it was at the thought that three such cold-blooded villains should have made so easy an exit; and to one of us, at least, the news came as a blessed relief.

TWO

The Stranger's Latchkey

The contrariety of human nature is a subject that has given a surprising amount of occupation to makers of proverbs and to those moral philosophers who make it their province to discover and expound the glaringly obvious; and especially have they been concerned to enlarge upon that form of perverseness which engenders dislike of things offered under compulsion, and arouses desire of them as soon as their attainment becomes difficult or impossible. They assure us that a man who has had a given thing within his reach and put it by, will, as soon as it is beyond his reach, find it the one thing necessary and desirable; even as the domestic cat which has turned disdainfully from the proffered saucer, may presently be seen with her head jammed hard in the milk-jug, or, secretly and with horrible relish, slaking her thirst at the scullery sink.

To this peculiarity of the human mind was due, no doubt, the fact that no sooner had I abandoned the clinical side of my profession in favour of the legal, and taken up my abode in the chambers of my friend Thorndyke, the famous medico-legal expert, to act as his assistant or junior, than my former mode of life – that of a *locum tenens*, or minder of other men's practices – which had, when I was following it, seemed intolerably irksome, now appeared to possess many desirable features; and I found myself occasionally hankering to sit once more by the bedside, to puzzle out the perplexing train of symptoms, and to wield that power – the greatest, after all, possessed by man – the power to banish suffering and ward off the approach of death itself.

Hence it was that on a certain morning of the long vacation I found myself installed at The Larches, Burling, in full charge of the practice of my old friend Dr Hanshaw, who was taking a fishing holiday in Norway. I was not left desolate, however, for Mrs Hanshaw remained at her post, and the roomy, old-fashioned house accommodated three visitors in addition. One of these was Dr Hanshaw's sister, a Mrs Haldean, the widow of a wealthy Manchester cotton factor; the second was her niece by marriage, Miss Lucy Haldean, a very handsome and charming girl of twenty-three; while the third was no less a person than Master Fred, the only child of Mrs Haldean, and a strapping boy of six.

"It is quite like old times – and very pleasant old times, too – to see you sitting at our breakfast-table, Dr Jervis." With these gracious words and a friendly smile, Mrs Hanshaw handed me my tea-cup.

I bowed. "The highest pleasure of the altruist," I replied, "is in contemplating the good fortune of others."

Mrs Haldean laughed. "Thank you," she said. "You are quite unchanged, I perceive. Still as suave and as – shall I say oleaginous?"

"No, please don't!" I exclaimed in a tone of alarm.

"Then I won't. But what does Dr Thorndyke say to this backsliding on your part? How does he regard this relapse from medical jurisprudence to common general practice?"

"Thorndyke," said I, "is unmoved by any catastrophe; and he not only regards the 'Decline and Fall-off of the Medical Jurist' with philosophic calm, but he even favours the relapse, as you call it. He thinks it may be useful to me to study the application of medico-legal methods to general practice."

"That sounds rather unpleasant – for the patients, I mean," remarked Miss Haldean.

"Very," agreed her aunt. "Most cold-blooded. What sort of man is Dr Thorndyke? I feel quite curious about him. Is he at all human, for instance?"

"He is entirely human," I replied; "the accepted tests of humanity being, as I understand, the habitual adoption of the erect posture in locomotion, and the relative position of the end of the thumb – "

"I don't mean that," interrupted Mrs Haldean. "I mean human in things that matter."

"I think those things matter," I rejoined. "Consider, Mrs Haldean, what would happen if my learned colleague were to be seen in wig and gown, walking towards the Law Courts in any posture other than the erect. It would be a public scandal."

"Don't talk to him, Mabel," said Mrs Hanshaw; "he is incorrigible. What are you doing with yourself this morning, Lucy?"

Miss Haldean (who had hastily set down her cup to laugh at my imaginary picture of Dr Thorndyke in the character of a quadruped) considered a moment.

"I think I shall sketch that group of birches at the edge of Bradham Wood," she said.

"Then, in that case," said I, "I can carry your traps for you, for I have to see a patient in Bradham."

"He is making the most of his time," remarked Mrs Haldean maliciously to my hostess. "He knows that when Mr Winter arrives he will retire into the extreme background."

Douglas Winter, whose arrival was expected in the course of the week, was Miss Haldean's fiancé. Their engagement had been somewhat protracted, and was likely to be more so, unless one of them received some unexpected accession of means; for Douglas was a subaltern in the Royal Engineers, living, with great difficulty, on his pay, while Lucy Haldean subsisted on an almost invisible allowance left her by an uncle.

I was about to reply to Mrs Haldean when a patient was announced, and, as I had finished my breakfast, I made my excuses and left the table.

Half an hour later, when I started along the road to the village of Bradham, I had two companions. Master Freddy had joined the party, and he disputed with me the privilege of carrying the "traps", with the result that a compromise was effected, by which he carried the camp-stool, leaving me in possession of the easel, the bag, and a large bound sketching-block.

"Where are you going to work this morning?" I asked, when we had trudged on some distance.

"Just off the road to the left there, at the edge of the wood. Not very far from the house of the mysterious stranger." She glanced at me mischievously as she made this reply, and chuckled with delight when I rose at the bait.

"What house do you mean?" I inquired.

"Ha!" she exclaimed, "the investigator of mysteries is aroused. He saith, 'Ha! ha!' amidst the trumpets; he smelleth the battle afar off."

"Explain instantly," I commanded, "or I drop, your sketch-block into the very next puddle."

"You terrify me," said she. "But I will explain, only there isn't any mystery except to the bucolic mind. The house is called Lavender Cottage, and it stands alone in the fields behind the wood. A fortnight ago it was let furnished to a stranger named Whitelock, who has taken it for the purpose of studying the botany of the district; and the only really mysterious thing about him is that no one has seen him. All arrangements with the house-agent were made by letter, and, as far as I can make out, none of the local tradespeople supply him, so he must get his things from a distance – even his bread, which really is rather odd. Now say I am an inquisitive, gossiping country bumpkin."

"I was going to," I answered, "but it is no use now."

She relieved me of her sketching appliances with pretended indignation, and crossed into the meadow, leaving me to pursue my way alone; and when I presently looked back, she was setting up her easel and stool, gravely assisted by Freddy.

My "round", though not a long one, took up more time than I had anticipated, and it was already past the luncheon hour when I passed the place where I had left Miss Haldean. She was gone, as I had expected, and I hurried homewards, anxious to be as nearly punctual as possible. When I entered the dining-room, I found Mrs Haldean and our hostess seated at the table, and both looked up at me expectantly.

"Have you seen Lucy?" the former inquired.

"No," I answered. "Hasn't she come back? I expected to find her here. She had left the wood when I passed just now."

Mrs Haldean knitted her brows anxiously. "It is very strange," she said, "and very thoughtless of her. Freddy will be famished."

I hurried over my lunch, for two fresh messages had come in from outlying hamlets, effectually dispelling my visions of a quiet afternoon; and as the minutes passed without bringing any signs of the absentees, Mrs Haldean became more and more restless and anxious. At length her suspense became unbearable; she rose suddenly, announcing her intention of cycling up the road to look for the defaulters, but as she was moving towards the door, it burst open, and Lucy Haldean staggered into the room.

Her appearance filled us with alarm. She was deadly pale, breathless, and wild-eyed; her dress was draggled and torn, and she trembled from head to foot.

"Good God, Lucy!" gasped Mrs Haldean. "What has happened? And where is Freddy?" she added in a sterner tone.

"He is lost!" replied Miss Haldean in a faint voice, and with a catch in her breath. "He strayed away while I was painting. I have searched the wood through, and called to him, and looked in all the meadows. Oh! where can he have gone?" Her sketching "kit", with which she was loaded, slipped from her grasp and rattled on to the floor, and she buried her face in her hands and sobbed hysterically.

"And you have dared to come back without him?" exclaimed Mrs Haldean.

"I was getting exhausted. I came back for help," was the faint reply.

"Of course she was exhausted," said Mrs Hanshaw. "Come, Lucy: come, Mabel; don't make mountains out of molehills. The little man is safe enough. We shall find him presently, or he will come home by himself. Come and have some food, Lucy."

Miss Haldean shook her head. "I can't, Mrs Hanshaw – really I can't," she said; and, seeing that she was in a state of utter exhaustion, I poured out a glass of wine and made her drink it.

Mrs Haldean darted from the room, and returned immediately, putting on her hat. "You have got to come with me and show me where you lost him," she said.

"She can't do that, you know," I said rather brusquely. "She will have to lie down for the present. But I know the place, and will cycle up with you."

"Very well," replied Mrs Haldean, "that will do. What time was it," she asked, turning to her niece, "when you lost the child? and which way – "

She paused abruptly, and I looked at her in surprise. She had suddenly turned ashen and ghastly; her face had set like a mask of stone, with parted lips and staring eyes that were fixed in horror on her niece.

There was a deathly silence for a few seconds. Then, in a terrible voice, she demanded: "What is that on your dress, Lucy?" And, after a pause, her voice rose into a shriek. "What have you done to my, boy?"

I glanced in astonishment at the dazed and terrified girl, and then I saw what her aunt had seen – a good-sized blood-stain halfway down the front of her skirt, and another smaller one on her right sleeve. The girl herself looked down at the sinister patch of red and then up at her aunt. "It looks like – like blood," she stammered. "Yes, it is – I think – of course it is. He struck his nose – and it bled – "

"Come," interrupted Mrs Haldean, "let us go," and she rushed from the room, leaving me to follow.

I lifted Miss Haldean, who was half fainting with fatigue and agitation, on to the sofa, and, whispering a few words of encouragement into her ear, turned to Mrs Hanshaw.

"I can't stay with Mrs Haldean," I said. "There are two visits to be made at Rebworth. Will you send the dogcart up the road with somebody to take my place?"

"Yes," she answered. "I will send Giles, or come myself if Lucy is fit to be left."

I ran to the stables for my bicycle, and as I pedalled out into the road I could see Mrs Haldean already far ahead, driving her machine at frantic speed. I followed at a rapid pace, but it was not until we approached the commencement of the wood, when she slowed down somewhat, that I overtook her.

"This is the place," I said, as we reached the spot where I had parted from Miss Haldean. We dismounted and wheeled our bicycles through the gate, and, laying them down beside the hedge, crossed the meadow and entered the wood.

It was a terrible experience, and one that I shall never forget – the white-faced, distracted woman, tramping in her flimsy house-shoes over the rough ground, bursting through the bushes, regardless of the thorny branches that dragged at skin and hair and dainty clothing, and sending forth from time to time a tremulous cry, so dreadfully pathetic in its mingling of terror and coaxing softness, that a lump rose in my throat, and I could barely keep my self-control.

"Freddy! Freddy-boy! Mummy's here, darling!" The wailing cry sounded through the leafy solitude; but no answer came save the whirr of wings or the chatter of startled birds. But even more shocking than that terrible cry – more disturbing and eloquent with dreadful suggestion – was the way in which she peered, furtively, but with fearful expectation, among the roots of the bushes, or halted to gaze upon every molehill and hummock, every depression or disturbance of the ground.

So we stumbled on for a while, with never a word spoken, until we came to a beaten track or footpath leading across the wood. Here I paused to examine the footprints, of which several were visible in the soft earth, though none seemed very recent; but, proceeding a little way down the track, I perceived, crossing it, a set of fresh imprints, which I recognized at once as Miss Haldean's. She was wearing, as I knew, a pair of brown golf-boots, with rubber pads in the leather soles, and the prints made by them were unmistakable.

"Miss Haldean crossed the path here," I said, pointing to the footprints.

"Don't speak of her before me!" exclaimed Mrs Haldean; but she gazed eagerly at the footprints, nevertheless, and immediately plunged into the wood to follow the tracks.

"You are very unjust to your niece, Mrs Haldean," I ventured to protest.

She halted and faced me with an angry frown.

"You don't understand!" she exclaimed. "You don't know, perhaps, that if my poor child is really dead, Lucy Haldean will be a rich woman, and may marry tomorrow if she chooses?"

"I did not know that," I answered, "but if I had, I should have said the same."

"Of course you would," she retorted bitterly. "A pretty face can muddle any man's judgment."

She turned away abruptly to resume her pursuit, and I followed in silence. The trail which we were following zigzagged through the thickest part of the wood, but its devious windings eventually brought us out on to an open space on the farther side. Here we at once perceived traces of another kind. A litter of dirty rags, pieces of paper, scraps of stale bread, bones and feathers, with hoof-marks, wheel ruts, and the ashes of a large wood fire, pointed clearly to a gipsy encampment recently broken up. I laid my hand on the heap of ashes, and found it still warm, and on scattering it with my foot a layer of glowing cinders appeared at the bottom.

"These people have only been gone an hour or two," I said. "It would be well to have them followed without delay."

A gleam of hope shone on the drawn, white face as the bereaved mother caught eagerly at my suggestion.

"Yes," she exclaimed breathlessly; "she may have bribed them to take him away. Let us see which way they went."

We followed the wheel tracks down to the road, and found that they turned towards London. At the same time I perceived the dogcart in the distance, with Mrs Hanshaw standing beside it; and, as the coachman observed me, he whipped up his horse and approached.

"I shall have to go," I said, "but Mrs Hanshaw will help you to continue the search."

"And you will make inquiries about the gipsies, won't you?" she said.

I promised to do so, and as the dogcart now came up, I climbed to the seat, and drove off briskly up the London Road.

The extent of a country doctor's round is always an unknown quantity. On the present occasion I picked up three additional patients, and as one of them was a case of incipient pleurisy, which required to have the chest strapped, and another was a neglected dislocation of the shoulder, a great deal of time was taken up. Moreover, the gipsies, whom I ran to earth on Rebworth Common, delayed me considerably, though I had to leave the rural constable to carry out the actual search, and, as a result, the clock of Burling Church was striking six as I drove through the village on my way home.

I got down at the front gate, leaving the coachman to take the dogcart round, and walked up the drive; and my astonishment may be imagined when, on turning the corner, I came suddenly upon the inspector of the local police in earnest conversation with no less a person than John Thorndyke.

"What on earth has brought you here?" I exclaimed, my surprise getting the better of my manners.

"The ultimate motive-force," he replied, "was an impulsive lady named Mrs Haldean. She telegraphed for me – in your name."

"She oughtn't to have done that," I said.

"Perhaps not. But the ethics of an agitated woman are not worth discussing, and she has done something much worse – she has applied to the local JP (a retired Major-General), and our gallant and unlearned friend has issued a warrant for the arrest of Lucy Haldean on the charge of murder."

"But there has been no murder!" I exclaimed.

"That," said Thorndyke, "is a legal subtlety that he does not appreciate. He has learned his law in the orderly-room, where the qualifications to practise are an irritable temper and a loud voice. However, the practical point is, inspector, that the warrant is irregular. You can't arrest people for hypothetical crimes."

The officer drew a deep breath of relief. He knew all about the irregularity, and now joyfully took refuge behind Thorndyke's great reputation.

When he had departed – with a brief note from my colleague to the General – Thorndyke slipped his arm through mine, and we strolled towards the house.

"This is a grim business, Jervis," said he. "That boy has got to be found for everybody's sake. Can you come with me when you have had some food?"

"Of course I can. I have been saving myself all the afternoon with a view to continuing the search."

"Good," said Thorndyke. "Then come in and feed."

A nondescript meal, half tea and half dinner, was already prepared, and Mrs Hanshaw, grave but self-possessed, presided at the table.

"Mabel is still out with Giles, searching for the boy," she said. "You have heard what she has done?"

I nodded.

"It was dreadful of her," continued Mrs Hanshaw, "but she is half mad, poor thing. You might run up and say a few kind words to poor Lucy while I make the tea."

I went up at once and knocked at Miss Haldean's door, and, being bidden to enter, found her lying on the sofa, red-eyed and pale, the very ghost of the merry, laughing girl who had gone out with me in the morning. I drew up a chair, and sat down by her side, and as I took the hand she held out to me, she said: "It is good of you to come and see a miserable wretch like me. And Jane has been so sweet to me, Dr Jervis; but Aunt Mabel thinks I have killed Freddy — you know she does — and it was really my fault that he was lost. I shall never forgive myself!"

She burst into a passion of sobbing, and I proceeded to chide her gently.

"You are a silly little woman," I said, "to take this nonsense to heart as you are doing. Your aunt is not responsible just now, as you must know; but when we bring the boy home she shall make you a handsome apology. I will see to that."

She pressed my hand gratefully, and as the bell now rang for tea, I bade her have courage and went downstairs.

"You need not trouble about the practice," said Mrs Hanshaw, as I concluded my lightning repast, and Thorndyke went off to get our bicycles. "Dr Symons has heard of our trouble, and has called to say that he will take anything that turns up; so we shall expect you when we see you."

"How do you like Thorndyke?" I asked.

"He is quite charming," she replied enthusiastically; "so tactful and kind, and so handsome, too. You didn't tell us that. But here he is. Goodbye, and good luck."

She pressed my hand, and I went out into the drive, where Thorndyke and the coachman were standing with three bicycles.

"I see you have brought your outfit," I said as we turned into the road; for Thorndyke's machine bore a large canvas-covered case strapped on to a strong bracket.

"Yes; there are many things that we may want on a quest of this kind. How did you find Miss Haldean?"

"Very miserable, poor girl. By the way, have you heard anything about her pecuniary interest in the child's death?"

"Yes," said Thorndyke. "It appears that the late Mr Haldean used up all his brains on his business, and had none left for the making of his will – as often happens. He left almost the whole of his property – about eighty thousand pounds – to his son, the widow to have a life-interest in it. He also left to his late brother's daughter, Lucy, fifty pounds a year, and to his surviving brother Percy, who seems to have been a good-for-nothing, a hundred a year for life. But – and here is the utter folly of the thing – if the son should die, the property was to be equally divided between the brother and the niece, with the exception of five hundred a year for life to the widow. It was an insane arrangement."

"Quite," I agreed, "and a very dangerous one for Lucy Haldean, as things are at present."

"Very; especially if anything should have happened to the child."

"What are you going to do now?" I inquired, seeing that Thorndyke rode on as if with a definite purpose.

"There is a footpath through the wood," he replied. "I want to examine that. And there is a house behind the wood which I should like to see."

"The house of the mysterious stranger," I suggested.

"Precisely. Mysterious and solitary strangers invite inquiry."

We drew up at the entrance to the footpath, leaving Willett the coachman in charge of the three machines, and proceeded up the narrow track. As we went, Thorndyke looked back at the prints of our feet, and nodded approvingly.

"This soft loam," he remarked, "yields beautifully clear impressions, and yesterday's rain has made it perfect."

We had not gone far when we perceived a set of footprints which I recognized, as did Thorndyke also, for he remarked: "Miss Haldean – running, and alone." Presently we met them again, crossing in the opposite direction, together with the prints of small shoes with very high heels. "Mrs Haldean on the track of her niece," was Thorndyke's comment; and a minute later we encountered them both again, accompanied by my own footprints.

"The boy does not seem to have crossed the path at all," I remarked as we walked on, keeping off the track itself to avoid confusing the footprints.

"We shall know when we have examined the whole length," replied Thorndyke, plodding on with his eyes on the ground. "Ha! here is something new," he added, stopping short and stooping down eagerly – "a man with a thick stick – a smallish man, rather lame. Notice the difference between the two feet, and the peculiar way in which he uses his stick. Yes, Jervis, there is a great deal to interest us in these footprints. Do you notice anything very suggestive about them?"

"Nothing but what you have mentioned," I replied. "What do you mean?"

"Well, first there is the very singular character of the prints themselves, which we will consider presently. You observe that this man came down the path, and at this point turned off into the wood; then he returned from the wood and went up the path again. The imposition of the prints makes that clear. But now look at the two sets of prints, and compare them. Do you notice any difference?"

"The returning footprints seem more distinct – better impressions."

"Yes; they are noticeably deeper. But there is something else." He produced a spring tape from his pocket, and took half a dozen measurements. "You see," he said, "the first set of footprints have a stride of twenty-one inches from heel to heel – a short stride; but he is a smallish man, and lame; the returning ones have a stride of only nineteen and a half inches; hence the returning footprints are deeper than the others, and the steps are shorter. What do you make of that?"

"It would suggest that he was carrying a burden when he returned," I replied.

"Yes; and a heavy one, to make that difference in the depth. I think I will get you to go and fetch Willett and the bicycles."

I strode off down the path to the entrance, and, taking possession of Thorndyke's machine, with its precious case of instruments, bade Willett follow with the other two.

When I returned, my colleague was standing with his hands behind him, gazing with intense preoccupation at the footprints. He looked up sharply as we approached, and called out to us to keep off the path if possible.

"Stay here with the machines, Willett," said he. "You and I, Jervis, must go and see where our friend went to when he left the path, and what was the burden that he picked up."

We struck off into the wood, where last year's dead leaves made the footprints almost indistinguishable, and followed the faint double track for a long distance between the dense clumps of bushes. Suddenly my eye caught, beside the double trail, a third row of tracks, smaller in size and closer together. Thorndyke had seen them, too, and already his measuring-tape was in his hand.

"Eleven and a half inches to the stride," said he. "That will be the boy, Jervis. But the light is getting weak. We must press on quickly, or we shall lose it."

Some fifty yards farther on, the man's tracks ceased abruptly, but the small ones continued alone; and we followed them as rapidly as we could in the fading light.

"There can be no reasonable doubt that these are the child's tracks," said Thorndyke; "but I should like to find a definite footprint to make the identification absolutely certain."

A few seconds later he halted with an exclamation, and stooped on one knee. A little heap of fresh earth from the surface-burrow of a mole had been thrown up over the dead leaves; and fairly planted on it was the clean and sharp impression of a diminutive foot, with a rubber heel showing a central star. Thorndyke drew from his pocket a tiny shoe, and pressed it on the soft earth beside the footprint; and when he raised it the second impression was identical with the first.

"The boy had two pairs of shoes exactly alike," he said, "so I borrowed one of the duplicate pair."

He turned, and began to retrace his steps rapidly, following our own fresh tracks, and stopping only once to point out the place where the unknown man had picked the child up. When we regained the path we proceeded without delay until we emerged from the wood within a hundred yards of the cottage.

"I see Mrs Haldean has been here with Giles," remarked Thorndyke, as he pushed open the garden-gate. "I wonder if they saw anybody."

He advanced to the door, and having first rapped with his knuckles and then kicked at it vigorously, tried the handle.

"Locked," he observed, "but I see the key is in the lock, so we can get in if we want to. Let us try the back."

The back door was locked, too, but the key had been removed.

"He came out this way, evidently," said Thorndyke, "though he went in at the front, as I suppose you noticed. Let us see where he went."

The back garden was a small, fenced patch of ground, with an earth path leading down to the back gate. A little way beyond the gate was a small barn or outhouse.

"We are in luck," Thorndyke remarked, with a glance at the path. "Yesterday's rain has cleared away all old footprints, and prepared the surface for new ones. You see there are three sets of excellent impressions – two leading away from the house, and one set towards it. Now, you notice that both of the sets leading *from* the house are characterized by deep impressions and short steps, while the set leading *to* the house has lighter impressions and longer steps. The obvious inference is that he went down the path with a heavy burden, came back empty-handed, and went down again – and finally – with another heavy burden. You observe, too, that he walked with his stick on each occasion."

By this time we had reached the bottom of the garden. Opening the gate, we followed the tracks towards the outhouse, which stood beside a cart-track; but as we came round the corner we both stopped short and looked at one another. On the soft earth were the very distinct impressions of the tyres of a motorcar leading from the wide door of the outhouse. Finding that the door was unfastened, Thorndyke opened it, and looked in, to satisfy himself that the place was empty. Then he fell to studying the tracks.

"The course of events is pretty plain," he observed. "First the fellow brought down his luggage, started the engine, and got the car out – you can see where it stood, both by the little pool of oil, and by the widening and blurring of the wheel-tracks from the vibration of the free engine; then he went back and fetched the boy – carried him pick-a-back, I should say, judging by the depth of the toe-marks in the last set of footprints. That was a tactical mistake. He should have taken the boy straight into the shed."

He pointed as he spoke to one of the footprints beside the wheel-tracks, from the toe of which projected a small segment of the print of a little rubber heel.

We now made our way back to the house, where we found Willett pensively rapping at the front door with a cycle-spanner. Thorndyke took a last glance, with his hand in his pocket, at an open window above, and then, to the coachman's intense delight, brought forth what looked uncommonly like a small bunch of skeleton keys. One of these he inserted into the keyhole, and as he gave it a turn, the lock clicked, and the door stood open.

The little sitting-room, which we now entered, was furnished with the barest necessaries. Its centre was occupied by an oilcloth-covered table, on which I observed with surprise a dismembered "Bee" clock (the works of which had been taken apart with a tin-opener that lay beside them) and a box-wood bird-call. At these objects Thorndyke glanced and nodded, as though they fitted into some theory that he had formed; examined carefully the oilcloth around the litter of wheels and pinions, and then proceeded on a tour of inspection round the room, peering inquisitively into the kitchen and store-cupboard.

"Nothing very distinctive or personal here," he remarked. "Let us go upstairs."

There were three bedrooms on the upper floor, of which two were evidently disused, though the windows were wide open. The third bedroom showed manifest traces of occupation, though it was as bare as the others, for the water still stood in the wash-hand basin, and the bed was unmade. To the latter Thorndyke advanced, and, having turned back the bedclothes, examined the interior attentively, especially at the foot and the pillow. The latter was soiled – not to say grimy – though the rest of the bed-linen was quite clean.

"Hair-dye," remarked Thorndyke, noting my glance at it; then he turned and looked out of the open window. "Can you see the place where Miss Haldean was sitting to sketch?" he asked.

"Yes," I replied; "there is the place well in view, and you can see right up the road. I had no idea this house stood so high. From the three upper windows you can see all over the country excepting through the wood."

"Yes," Thorndyke rejoined, "and he has probably been in the habit of keeping watch up here with a telescope or a pair of field-glasses. Well, there is not much of interest in this room. He kept his effects in a cabin trunk which stood there under the window. He shaved this morning. He has a white beard, to judge by the stubble on the shaving-paper, and that is all. Wait, though. There is a key hanging on that nail. He must have overlooked that, for it evidently does not belong to this house. It is an ordinary town latchkey."

He took the key down, and having laid a sheet of notepaper, from his pocket, on the dressing-table, produced a pin, with which he began carefully to probe the interior of the key-barrel. Presently there came forth, with much coaxing, a large ball of grey fluff, which Thorndyke folded up in the paper with infinite care.

"I suppose we mustn't take away the key," he said, "but I think we will take a wax mould of it."

He hurried downstairs, and, unstrapping the case from his bicycle, brought it in and placed it on the table. As it was now getting dark, he detached the powerful acetylene lamp from his machine, and, having lighted it, proceeded to open the mysterious case. First he took from it a small insufflator, or powder-blower, with which he blew a cloud of light yellow powder over the table around the remains of the clock. The powder settled on the table in an even coating, but when he blew at it smartly with his breath, it cleared off, leaving, however, a number of smeary impressions which stood out in strong yellow against the black oilcloth. To one of these impressions he pointed significantly. It was the print of a child's hand.

He next produced a small, portable microscope and some glass slides and cover-slips, and having opened the paper and tipped the ball of fluff from the key-barrel on to a slide, set to work with a pair of mounted needles to tease it out into its component parts. Then he turned the light of the lamp on to the microscope mirror and proceeded to examine the specimen.

"A curious and instructive assortment this, Jervis," he remarked, with his eye at the microscope: "woollen fibres – no cotton or linen; he is careful of his health to have woollen pockets – and two hairs; very curious ones, too. Just look at them, and observe the root bulbs."

I applied my eye to the microscope, and saw, among other things, two hairs – originally white, but encrusted with a black, opaque, glistening stain. The root bulbs, I noticed, were shrivelled and atrophied.

"But how on earth," I exclaimed, "did the hairs get into his pocket?"

"I think the hairs themselves answer that question," he replied, "when considered with the other curios. The stain is obviously lead sulphide; but what else do you see?"

"I see some particles of metal – a white metal apparently – and a number of fragments of woody fibre and starch granules, but I don't recognize the starch. It is not wheat-starch, nor rice, nor potato. Do you make out what it is?"

Thorndyke chuckled. "Experientia does it," said he. "You will have, Jervis, to study the minute properties of dust and dirt. Their evidential value is immense. Let us have another look at that starch; it is all alike, I suppose."

It was; and Thorndyke had just ascertained the fact when the door burst open and Mrs Haldean entered the room, followed by Mrs Hanshaw and the police inspector. The former lady regarded my colleague with a glance of extreme disfavour.

"We heard that you had come here, sir," said she, "and we supposed you were engaged in searching for my poor child. But it seems we were mistaken, since we find you here amusing yourselves fiddling with these nonsensical instruments."

"Perhaps, Mabel," said Mrs Hanshaw stiffly, "it would be wiser, and infinitely more polite, to ask if Dr Thorndyke has any news for us."

"That is undoubtedly so, madam," agreed the inspector, who had apparently suffered also from Mrs Haldean's impulsiveness.

"Then perhaps," the latter lady suggested, "you will inform us if you have discovered anything."

"I will tell you," replied Thorndyke, "all that we know. The child was abducted by the man who occupied this house, and who appears to have watched him from an upper window, probably through a glass. This man lured the child into the wood by blowing this bird-call; he met him in the wood, and induced him – by some promises, no doubt – to come with him. He picked the child up and carried him – on his back, I think – up to the house, and brought him in through the front door, which he locked after him. He gave the boy this clock and the bird-call to amuse him while he went upstairs and packed his trunk. He took the trunk out through the back door and down the garden to the shed there, in which he had a motorcar. He got the car out and came back for the boy, whom he carried down to the car, locking the back door after him. Then he drove away."

"You know he has gone," cried Mrs Haldean, "and yet you stay here playing with these ridiculous toys. Why are you not following him?"

"We have just finished ascertaining the facts," Thorndyke replied calmly, "and should by now be on the road if you had not come."

Here the inspector interposed anxiously. "Of course, sir, you can't give any description of the man. You have no clue to his identity, I suppose?"

"We have only his footprints," Thorndyke answered, "and this fluff which I raked out of the barrel of his latchkey, and have just been examining. From these data I conclude that he is a rather short and thin man, and somewhat lame. He walks with the aid of a thick stick, which has a knob, not a crook, at the top, and which he carries in his left hand. I think that his left leg has been amputated above the knee, and that he wears an artificial limb. He is elderly, he shaves his beard, has white hair dyed a greyish black, is partly bald, and probably combs a wisp of hair over the bald place; he takes snuff, and carries a leaden comb in his pocket."

As Thorndyke's description proceeded, the inspector's mouth gradually opened wider and wider, until he appeared the very type and symbol of astonishment. But its effect on Mrs Haldean was much more remarkable. Rising from her chair, she leaned on the table and stared at Thorndyke with an expression of awe – even of terror; and as he finished she sank back into her chair, with her hands clasped, and turned to Mrs Hanshaw.

"Jane!" she gasped, "it is Percy – my brother-in-law! He has described him exactly, even to his stick and his pocket-comb. But I thought he was in Chicago."

"If that is so," said Thorndyke, hastily repacking his case, "we had better start at once."

"We have the dogcart in the road," said Mrs Hanshaw.

"Thank you," replied Thorndyke. "We will ride on our bicycles, and the inspector can borrow Willett's. We go out at the back by the cart-track, which joins the road farther on."

"Then we will follow in the dogcart," said Mrs Haldean. "Come, Jane."

The two ladies departed down the path, while we made ready our bicycles and lit our lamps.

"With your permission, inspector," said Thorndyke, "we will take the key with us."

"It's hardly legal, air," objected the officer. "We have no authority."

"It is quite illegal," answered Thorndyke; "but it is necessary; and necessity — like your military JP — knows no law."

The inspector grinned and went out, regarding me with a quivering eyelid as Thorndyke locked the door with his skeleton key. As we turned into the road, I saw the lights of the dogcart behind us, and we pushed forward at a swift pace, picking up the trail easily on the soft, moist road.

"What beats me," said the inspector confidentially, as we rode along, "is how he knew the man was bald. Was it the footprints or the latchkey? And that comb, too, that was a regular knock-out."

These points were, by now, pretty clear to me. I had seen the hairs with their atrophied bulbs — such as one finds at the margin of a bald patch; and the comb was used, evidently, for the double purpose of keeping the bald patch covered and blackening the sulphur-charged hair. But the knobbed stick and the artificial limb puzzled me so completely that I presently overtook Thorndyke to demand an explanation.

"The stick," said he, "is perfectly simple. The ferrule of a knobbed stick wears evenly all round; that of a crooked stick wears on one side — the side opposite the crook. The impressions showed that the ferrule of this one was evenly convex; therefore it had no crook. The other matter is more complicated. To begin with, an artificial foot makes a very characteristic impression, owing to its purely passive elasticity, as I will show you tomorrow. But an artificial leg fitted below the knee is quite secure, whereas one fitted above the knee — that is, with an artificial knee-joint worked by a spring — is much less reliable. Now, this man had an artificial foot, and he evidently distrusted his knee-joint, as is shown by his steadying it with his stick on the same side. If he had merely had a weak leg, he would have used the stick with his right hand – with the natural swing of the arm, in fact – unless he had been very lame, which he evidently was not. Still, it was only a question of probability, though the probability was very great. Of course, you understand that those particles of woody fibre and starch granules were disintegrated snuff-grains."

This explanation, like the others, was quite simple when one had heard it, though it gave me material for much thought as we pedalled on along the dark road, with Thorndyke's light flickering in front, and the dogcart pattering in our wake. But there was ample time for reflection; for our pace rather precluded conversation, and we rode on, mile after mile, until my legs ached with fatigue. On and on we went through village after village, now losing the trail in some frequented street, but picking it up again unfailingly as we emerged on to the country road, until at last, in the paved High Street of the little town of Horsefield, we lost it for good. We rode on through the town out on to the country road; but although there were several tracks of motors, Thorndyke shook his head at them all. "I have been studying those tyres until I know them by heart," he said. "No; either he is in the town, or he has left it by a side road."

There was nothing for it but to put up the horse and the machines at the hotel, while we walked round to reconnoitre; and this we did, tramping up one street and down another, with eyes bent on the ground, fruitlessly searching for a trace of the missing car.

Suddenly, at the door of a blacksmith's shop, Thorndyke halted. The shop had been kept open late for the shoeing of a carriage horse, which was just being led away, and the smith had come to the door for a breath of air. Thorndyke accosted him genially.

"Good evening. You are just the man I wanted to see. I have mislaid the address of a friend of mine, who, I think, called on you this afternoon – a lame gentleman who walks with a stick. I expect he wanted you to pick a lock or make him a key."

"Oh, I remember him!" said the man. "Yes, he had lost his latchkey, and wanted the lock picked before he could get into his house. Had to leave his motorcar outside while he came here. But I took some keys round with me, and fitted one to his latch."

He then directed us to a house at the end of a street close by, and, having thanked him, we went off in high spirits.

"How did you know he had been there?" I asked.

"I didn't; but there was the mark of a stick and part of a left foot on the soft earth inside the doorway, and the thing was inherently probable, so I risked a false shot."

The house stood alone at the far end of a straggling street, and was enclosed by a high wall, in which, on the side facing the street, was a door and a wide carriage-gate. Advancing to the former, Thorndyke took from his pocket the purloined key, and tried it in the lock. It fitted perfectly, and when he had turned it and pushed open the door, we entered a small courtyard. Crossing this, we came to the front door of the house, the latch of which fortunately fitted the same key; and this having been opened by Thorndyke, we trooped into the hall. Immediately we heard the sound of an opening door above, and a reedy, nasal voice sang out: "Hello, there! Who's that below?"

The voice was followed by the appearance of a head projecting over the baluster rail.

"You are Mr Percy Haldean, I think," said the inspector.

At the mention of this name, the head was withdrawn, and a quick tread was heard, accompanied by the tapping of a stick on the floor. We started to ascend the stairs, the inspector leading, as the authorized official; but we had only gone up a few steps, when a fierce, wiry little man danced out on to the landing, with a thick stick in one hand and a very large revolver in the other.

"Move another step, either of you," he shouted, pointing the weapon at the inspector, "and I let fly; and, mind you, when I shoot I hit."

He looked as if he meant it, and we accordingly halted with remarkable suddenness, while the inspector proceeded to parley.

"Now, what's the good of this, Mr Haldean?" said he. "The game's up, and you know it."

"You clear out of my house, and clear out sharp," was the inhospitable rejoinder, "or you'll give me the trouble of burying you in the garden."

I looked round to consult with Thorndyke, when, to my amazement, I found that he had vanished – apparently through the open hall-door. I was admiring his discretion when the inspector endeavoured to reopen negotiations, but was cut short abruptly.

"I am going to count fifty," said Mr Haldean, "and if you aren't gone then, I shall shoot."

He began to count deliberately, and the inspector looked round at me in complete bewilderment. The flight of stairs was a long one, and well lighted by gas, so that to rush it was an impossibility. Suddenly my heart gave a bound and I held my breath, for out of an open door behind our quarry, a figure emerged slowly and noiselessly on to the landing. It was Thorndyke, shoeless, and in his shirt-sleeves.

Slowly and with cat-like stealthiness, he crept across the landing until he was within a yard of the unconscious fugitive, and still the nasal voice droned on, monotonously counting out the allotted seconds.

"Forty-one, forty-two, forty-three – "

"There was a lightning-like movement – a shout – a flash – a bang – a shower of falling plaster, and then the revolver came clattering down the stairs. The inspector and I rushed up, and in a moment the sharp click of the handcuffs told Mr Percy Haldean that the game was really up.

Five minutes later Freddy-boy, half asleep, but wholly cheerful, was borne on Thorndyke's shoulders into the private sitting-room of the Black Horse Hotel. A shriek of joy saluted his entrance, and a shower of maternal kisses brought him to the verge of suffocation.

Finally, the impulsive Mrs Haldean, turning suddenly to Thorndyke, seized both his hands, and for a moment I hoped that she was going to kiss him, too. But he was spared, and I have not yet recovered from the disappointment.

THREE

The Anthropologist at Large

Thorndyke was not a newspaper reader. He viewed with extreme disfavour all scrappy and miscellaneous forms of literature, which, by presenting a disorderly series of unrelated items of information, tended, as he considered, to destroy the habit of consecutive mental effort.

"It is most important," he once remarked to me, "habitually to pursue a definite train of thought, and to pursue it to a finish, instead of flitting indolently from one uncompleted topic to another, as the newspaper reader is so apt to do. Still, there is no harm in a daily paper – so long as you don't read it."

Accordingly, he patronized a morning paper, and his method of dealing with it was characteristic. The paper was laid on the table after breakfast, together with a blue pencil and a pair of office shears. A preliminary glance through the sheets enabled him to mark with the pencil those paragraphs that were to be read, and these were presently cut out and looked through, after which they were either thrown away or set aside to be pasted in an indexed book.

The whole proceeding occupied, on an average, a quarter of an hour.

On the morning of which I am now speaking he was thus engaged. The pencil had done its work, and the snick of the shears announced the final stage. Presently he paused with a newly-excised cutting between his fingers, and, after glancing at it for a moment, he handed it to me.

"Another art robbery," he remarked. "Mysterious affairs, these – as to motive, I mean. You can't melt down a picture or an ivory carving, and you can't put them on the market as they stand. The very qualities that give them their value make them totally unnegotiable."

"Yet I suppose," said I, "the really inveterate collector – the pottery or stamp maniac, for instance – will buy these contraband goods even though he dare not show them."

"Probably. No doubt the *cupiditas habendi*, the mere desire to possess, is the motive force rather than any intelligent purpose – "

The discussion was at this point interrupted by a knock at the door, and a moment later my colleague admitted two gentlemen. One of these I recognized as a Mr Marchmont, a solicitor, for whom we had occasionally acted; the other was a stranger – a typical Hebrew of the blonde type – good-looking, faultlessly dressed, carrying a bandbox, and obviously in a state of the most extreme agitation.

"Good morning to you, gentlemen," said Mr Marchmont, shaking hands cordially. "I have brought a client of mine to see you, and when I tell you that his name is Solomon Löwe, it will be unnecessary for me to say what our business is."

"Oddly enough," replied Thorndyke, "we were, at the very moment when you knocked, discussing the bearings of his case."

"It is a horrible affair!" burst in Mr Löwe. "I am distracted! I am ruined! I am in despair!"

He banged the bandbox down on the table, and flinging himself into a chair, buried his face in his hands.

"Come, come," remonstrated Marchmont, "we must be brave, we must be composed. Tell Dr Thorndyke your story, and let us hear what he thinks of it."

He leaned back in his chair, and looked at his client with that air of patient fortitude that comes to us all so easily when we contemplate the misfortunes of other people.

"You must help us, sir," exclaimed Löwe, starting up again –
"you must, indeed, or I shall go mad. But I shall tell you what has
happened, and then you must act at once. Spare no effort and no
expense. Money is no object – at least, not in reason," he added,
with native caution. He sat down once more, and in perfect
English, though with a slight German accent, proceeded volubly:
"My brother Isaac is probably known to you by name."

Thorndyke nodded.

"He is a great collector, and to some extent a dealer – that is to
say, he makes his hobby a profitable hobby."

"What does he collect?" asked Thorndyke.

"Everything," replied our visitor, flinging his hands apart with a
comprehensive gesture – "everything that is precious and beautiful
– pictures, ivories, jewels, watches, objects of art and *vertu* –
everything. He is a Jew, and he has that passion for things that are
rich and costly that has distinguished our race from the time of my
namesake Solomon onwards. His house in Howard Street,
Piccadilly, is at once a museum and an art gallery. The rooms are
filled with cases of gems, of antique jewellery, of coins and historic
relics – some of priceless value – and the walls are covered with
paintings, every one of which is a masterpiece. There is a fine
collection of ancient weapons and armour, both European and
Oriental; rare books, manuscripts, papyri, and valuable antiquities
from Egypt, Assyria, Cyprus, and elsewhere. You see, his taste
is quite catholic, and his knowledge of rare and curious things is
probably greater than that of any other living man. He is never
mistaken. No forgery deceives him, and hence the great prices that
he obtains; for a work of art purchased from Isaac Löwe is a work
certified as genuine beyond all cavil."

He paused to mop his face with a silk handkerchief, and then,
with the same plaintive volubility, continued: "My brother is
unmarried. He lives for his collection, and he lives with it. The
house is not a very large one, and the collection takes up most of
it; but he keeps a suite of rooms for his own occupation, and has
two servants – a man and wife – to look after him. The man, who

is a retired police-sergeant, acts as caretaker and watchman; the woman as housekeeper and cook, if required, but my brother lives largely at his club. And now I come to this present catastrophe."

He ran his fingers through his hair, took a deep breath, and continued: "Yesterday morning Isaac started for Florence by way of Paris, but his route was not certain, and he intended to break his journey at various points as circumstances determined. Before leaving, he put his collection in my charge, and it was arranged that I should occupy his rooms in his absence. Accordingly, I sent my things round and took possession.

"Now, Dr Thorndyke, I am closely connected with the drama, and it is my custom to spend my evenings at my club, of which most of the members are actors. Consequently, I am rather late in my habits; but last night I was earlier than usual in leaving my club, for I started for my brother's house before half-past twelve. I felt, as you may suppose, the responsibility of the great charge I had undertaken; and you may, therefore, imagine my horror, my consternation, my despair, when, on letting myself in with my latchkey, I found a police-inspector, a sergeant, and a constable in the hall. There had been a robbery, sir, in my brief absence, and the account that the inspector gave of the affair was briefly this:

"While taking the round of his district, he had noticed an empty hansom proceeding in leisurely fashion along Howard Street. There was nothing remarkable in this, but when, about ten minutes later, he was returning, and met a hansom, which he believed to be the same, proceeding along the same street in the same direction, and at the same easy pace, the circumstance struck him as odd, and he made a note of the number of the cab in his pocket-book. It was 72,863, and the time was 11.35.

"At 11.45 a constable coming up Howard Street noticed a hansom standing opposite the door of my brother's house, and, while he was looking at it, a man came out of the house carrying something, which he put in the cab. On this the constable quickened his pace, and when the man returned to the house and reappeared carrying what looked like a portmanteau, and closing the door softly behind him, the policeman's suspicions were aroused, and he hurried forward, hailing the cabman to stop. "The man put his burden into the cab, and sprang in himself. The cabman lashed his horse, which started off at a gallop, and the policeman broke into a run, blowing his whistle and flashing his lantern on to the cab. He followed it round the two turnings into Albemarle Street, and was just in time to see it turn into Piccadilly, where, of course, it was lost. However, he managed to note the number of the cab, which was 72,863, and he describes the man as short and thick-set, and thinks he was not wearing any hat.

"As he was returning, he met the inspector and the sergeant, who had heard the whistle, and on his report the three officers hurried to the house, where they knocked and rang for some minutes without any result. Being now more than suspicious, they went to the back of the house, through the mews, where, with great difficulty, they managed to force a window and effect an entrance into the house.

"Here their suspicions were soon changed to certainty, for, on reaching the first-floor, they heard strange muffled groans proceeding from one of the rooms, the door of which was locked, though the key had not been removed. They opened the door, and found the caretaker and his wife sitting on the floor, with their backs against the wall. Both were bound hand and foot, and the head of each was enveloped in a green-baize bag; and when the bags were taken off, each was found to be lightly but effectively gagged.

"Each told the same story. The caretaker, fancying he heard a noise, armed himself with a truncheon, and came downstairs to the first-floor, where he found the door of one of the rooms open, and a light burning inside. He stepped on tiptoe to the open door, and was peering in, when he was seized from behind, half suffocated by a pad held over his mouth, pinioned, gagged, and blindfolded with the bag.

"His assailant – whom he never saw – was amazingly strong and skilful, and handled him with perfect ease, although he – the caretaker – is a powerful man, and a good boxer and wrestler. The same thing happened to the wife, who had come down to look for her husband. She walked into the same trap, and was gagged, pinioned, and blindfolded without ever having seen the robber. So the only description that we have of this villain is that furnished by the constable."

"And the caretaker had no chance of using his truncheon?" said Thorndyke.

"Well, he got in one backhanded blow over his right shoulder, which he thinks caught the burglar in the face; but the fellow caught him by the elbow, and gave his arm such a twist that he dropped the truncheon on the floor."

"Is the robbery a very extensive one?"

"Ah!" exclaimed Mr Löwe, "that is just what we cannot say. But I fear it is. It seems that my brother had quite recently drawn out of his bank four thousand pounds in notes and gold. These little transactions are often carried out in cash rather than by cheque" – here I caught a twinkle in Thorndyke's eye – "and the caretaker says that a few days ago Isaac brought home several parcels, which were put away temporarily in a strong cupboard. He seemed to be very pleased with his new acquisitions, and gave the caretaker to understand that they were of extraordinary rarity and value.

"Now, this cupboard has been cleared out. Not a vestige is left in it but the wrappings of the parcels, so, although nothing else has been touched, it is pretty clear that goods to the value of four thousand pounds have been taken; but when we consider what an excellent buyer my brother is, it becomes highly probable that the actual value of those things is two or three times that amount, or even more. It is a dreadful, dreadful business, and Isaac will hold me responsible for it all."

"Is there no further clue?" asked Thorndyke. "What about the cab, for instance?"

"Oh, the cab," groaned Löwe – "that clue failed. The police must have mistaken the number. They telephoned immediately to all the police stations, and a watch was set, with the result that number 72,863 was stopped as it was going home for the night. But it then turned out that the cab had not been off the rank since eleven o'clock, and the driver had been in the shelter all the time with several other men. But there *is* a clue; I have it here."

Mr Löwe's face brightened for once as he reached out for the bandbox.

"The houses in Howard Street," he explained, as he untied the fastening, "have small balconies to the first-floor windows at the back. Now, the thief entered by one of these windows, having climbed up a rain-water pipe to the balcony. It was a gusty night, as you will remember, and this morning, as I was leaving the house, the butler next door called to me and gave me this; he had found it lying in the balcony of his house."

He opened the bandbox with a flourish, and brought forth a rather shabby billycock hat.

"I understand," said he, "that by examining a hat it is possible to deduce from it, not only the bodily characteristics of the wearer, but also his mental and moral qualities, his state of health, his pecuniary position, his past history, and even his domestic relations and the peculiarities of his place of abode. Am I right in this supposition?"

The ghost of a smile flitted across Thorndyke's face as he laid the hat upon the remains of the newspaper. "We must not expect too much," he observed. "Hats, as you know, have a way of changing owners. Your own hat, for instance" (a very spruce, hard felt), "is a new one, I think."

"Got it last week," said Mr Löwe.

"Exactly. It is an expensive hat, by Lincoln and Bennett, and I see you have judiciously written your name in indelible marking-ink on the lining. Now, a new hat suggests a discarded predecessor. What do you do with your old hats?"

"My man has them, but they don't fit him. I suppose he sells them or gives them away."

"Very well. Now, a good hat like yours has a long life, and remains serviceable long after it has become shabby; and the probability is that many of your hats pass from owner to owner; from you to the shabby-genteel, and from them to the shabby un-genteel. And it is a fair assumption that there are, at this moment, an appreciable number of tramps and casuals wearing hats by Lincoln and Bennett, marked in indelible ink with the name S Löwe; and anyone who should examine those hats, as you suggest, might draw some very misleading deductions as to the personal habits of S Löwe."

Mr Marchmont chuckled audibly, and then, remembering the gravity of the occasion, suddenly became portentously solemn.

"So you think that the hat is of no use, after all?" said Mr Löwe, in a tone of deep disappointment.

"I won't say that," replied Thorndyke. "We may learn something from it. Leave it with me, at any rate; but you must let the police know that I have it. They will want to see it, of course."

"And you will try to get those things, won't you?" pleaded Löwe.

"I will think over the case. But you understand, or Mr Marchmont does, that this is hardly in my province. I am a medical jurist, and this is not a medico-legal case."

"Just what I told him," said Marchmont. "But you will do me a great kindness if you will look into the matter. Make it a medico-legal case," he added persuasively.

Thorndyke repeated his promise, and the two men took their departure.

For some time after they had left, my colleague remained silent, regarding the hat with a quizzical smile. "It is like a game of forfeits," he remarked at length, "and we have to find the owner of 'this very pretty thing'." He lifted it with a pair of forceps into a better light, and began to look at it more closely.

"Perhaps," said he, "we have done Mr Löwe an injustice, after all. This is certainly a very remarkable hat."

"It is as round as a basin," I exclaimed. "Why, the fellow's head must have been turned in a lathe!"

Thorndyke laughed. "The point," said he, "is this. This is a hard hat, and so must have fitted fairly, or it could not have been worn; and it was a cheap hat, and so was not made to measure. But a man with a head that shape has got to come to a clear understanding with his hat. No ordinary hat would go on at all.

"Now, you see what he has done – no doubt on the advice of some friendly hatter. He has bought a hat of a suitable size, and he has made it hot – probably steamed it. Then he has jammed it, while still hot and soft, on to his head, and allowed it to cool and set before removing it. That is evident from the distortion of the brim. The important corollary is, that this hat fits his head exactly – is, in fact, a perfect mould of it; and this fact, together with the cheap quality of the hat, furnishes the further corollary that it has probably only had a single owner.

"And now let us turn it over and look at the outside. You notice at once the absence of old dust. Allowing for the circumstance that it had been out all night, it is decidedly clean. Its owner has been in the habit of brushing it, and is therefore presumably a decent, orderly man. But if you look at it in a good light, you see a kind of bloom on the felt, and through this lens you can make out particles of a fine white powder which has worked into the surface."

He handed me his lens, through which I could distinctly see the particles to which he referred.

"Then," he continued, "under the curl of the brim and in the folds of the hatband, where the brush has not been able to reach it, the powder has collected quite thickly, and we can see that it is a very fine powder, and very white, like flour. What do you make of that?"

"I should say that it is connected with some industry. He may be engaged in some factory or works, or, at any rate, may live near a factory, and have to pass it frequently."

"Yes; and I think we can distinguish between the two possibilities. For, if he only passes the factory, the dust will be on the outside of the hat only; the inside will be protected by his head.

But if he is engaged in the works, the dust will be inside, too, as the hat will hang on a peg in the dust-laden atmosphere, and his head will also be powdered, and so convey the dust to the inside."

He turned the hat over once more, and as I brought the powerful lens to bear upon the dark lining, I could clearly distinguish a number of white particles in the interstices of the fabric.

"The powder is on the inside, too," I said.

He took the lens from me, and, having verified my statement, proceeded with the examination. "You notice," he said, "that the leather head-lining is stained with grease, and this staining is more pronounced at the sides and back. His hair, therefore, is naturally greasy, or he greases it artificially; for if the staining were caused by perspiration, it would be most marked opposite the forehead."

He peered anxiously into the interior of the hat, and eventually turned down the head-lining; and immediately there broke out upon his face a gleam of satisfaction.

"Ha!" he exclaimed. "This is a stroke of luck. I was afraid our neat and orderly friend had defeated us with his brush. Pass me the small dissecting forceps, Jervis."

I handed him the instrument, and he proceeded to pick out daintily from the space behind the head-lining some half a dozen short pieces of hair, which he laid, with infinite tenderness, on a sheet of white paper.

"There are several more on the other side," I said, pointing them out to him.

"Yes, but we must leave some for the police," he answered, with a smile. "They must have the same chance as ourselves, you know."

"But surely," I said, as I bent down over the paper, "these are pieces of horsehair!"

"I think not," he replied; "but the microscope will show. At any rate, this is the kind of hair I should expect to find with a head of that shape."

"Well, it is extraordinarily coarse," said I, "and two of the hairs are nearly white."

"Yes; black hairs beginning to turn grey. And now, as our preliminary survey has given such encouraging results, we will proceed to more exact methods; and we must waste no time, for we shall have the police here presently to rob us of our treasure."

He folded up carefully the paper containing the hairs, and taking the hat in both hands, as though it were some sacred vessel, ascended with me to the laboratory on the next floor.

"Now, Polton," he said to his laboratory assistant, "we have here a specimen for examination, and time is precious. First of all, we want your patent dust-extractor."

The little man bustled to a cupboard and brought forth a singular appliance, of his own manufacture, somewhat like a miniature vacuum cleaner. It had been made from a bicycle foot-pump, by reversing the piston-valve, and was fitted with a glass nozzle and a small detachable glass receiver for collecting the dust, at the end of a flexible metal tube.

"We will sample the dust from the outside first," said Thorndyke, laying the hat upon the work-bench. "Are you ready, Polton?"

The assistant slipped his foot into the stirrup of the pump and worked the handle vigorously, while Thorndyke drew the glass nozzle slowly along the hat-brim under the curled edge. And as the nozzle passed along, the white coating vanished as if by magic, leaving the felt absolutely clean and black, and simultaneously the glass receiver became clouded over with a white deposit.

"We will leave the other side for the police," said Thorndyke, and as Polton ceased pumping he detached the receiver, and laid it on a sheet of paper, on which he wrote in pencil, "Outside," and covered it with a small bell-glass. A fresh receiver having been fitted on, the nozzle was now drawn over the silk lining of the hat, and then through the space behind the leather head-lining on one side; and now the dust that collected in the receiver was much of the usual grey colour and fluffy texture, and included two more hairs.

"And now," said Thorndyke, when the second receiver had been detached and set aside, "we want a mould of the inside of the hat, and we must make it by the quickest method; there is no time to make a paper mould. It is a most astonishing head," he added, reaching down from a nail a pair of large callipers, which he applied to the inside of the hat; "six inches and nine-tenths long by six and six-tenths broad, which gives us" – he made a rapid calculation on a scrap of paper – "the extraordinarily high cephalic index of 95.6."

Polton now took possession of the hat, and, having stuck a band of wet tissue-paper round the inside, mixed a small bowl of plaster-of-Paris, and very dexterously ran a stream of the thick liquid on to the tissue-paper, where it quickly solidified. A second and third application resulted in a broad ring of solid plaster an inch thick, forming a perfect mould of the inside of the hat, and in a few minutes the slight contraction of the plaster in setting rendered the mould sufficiently loose to allow of its being slipped out on to a board to dry.

We were none too soon, for even as Polton was removing the mould, the electric bell, which I had switched on to the laboratory, announced a visitor, and when I went down I found a police-sergeant waiting with a note from Superintendent Miller, requesting the immediate transfer of the hat.

"The next thing to be done," said Thorndyke, when the sergeant had departed with the bandbox, "is to measure the thickness of the hairs, and make a transverse section of one, and examine the dust. The section we will leave to Polton – as time is an object, Polton, you had better imbed the hair in thick gum and freeze it hard on the microtome, and be very careful to cut the section at right angles to the length of the hair – meanwhile, we will get to work with the microscope."

The hairs proved on measurement to have the surprisingly large diameter of $1/135$ of an inch – fully double that of ordinary hairs, although they were unquestionably human. As to the white dust, it presented a problem that even Thorndyke was unable to solve.

The application of reagents showed it to be carbonate of lime, but its source for a time remained a mystery.

"The larger particles," said Thorndyke, with his eye applied to the microscope, "appear to be transparent, crystalline, and distinctly laminated in structure. It is not chalk, it is not whiting, it is not any kind of cement. What can it be?"

"Could it be any kind of shell?" I suggested. "For instance – "

"Of course!" he exclaimed, starting up; "you have hit it, Jervis, as you always do. It must be mother-of-pearl. Polton, give me a pearl shirt-button out of your oddments box."

The button was duly produced by the thrifty Polton, dropped into an agate mortar, and speedily reduced to powder, a tiny pinch of which Thorndyke placed under the microscope.

"This powder," said he, "is, naturally, much coarser than our specimen, but the identity of character is unmistakable. Jervis, you are a treasure. Just look at it."

I glanced down the microscope, and then pulled out my watch. "Yes," I said, "there is no doubt about it, I think; but I must be off. Anstey urged me to be in court by 11.30 at the latest."

With infinite reluctance I collected my notes and papers and departed, leaving Thorndyke diligently copying addresses out of the Post Office Directory.

My business at the court detained me the whole of the day, and it was near upon dinner-time when I reached our chambers. Thorndyke had not yet come in, but he arrived half an hour later, tired and hungry, and not very communicative.

"What have I done?" he repeated, in answer to my inquiries. "I have walked miles of dirty pavement, and I have visited every pearl-shell cutter's in London, with one exception, and I have not found what I was looking for. The one mother-of-pearl factory that remains, however, is the most likely, and I propose to look in there tomorrow morning. Meanwhile, we have completed our data, with Polton's assistance. Here is a tracing of our friend's skull taken from the mould; you see it is an extreme type of brachycephalic skull, and markedly unsymmetrical. Here is a transverse section of his hair, which is quite circular – unlike yours or mine, which would be oval. We have the mother-of-pearl dust from the outside of the hat, and from the inside similar dust mixed with various fibres and a few granules of rice starch. Those are our data."

"Supposing the hat should not be that of the burglar after all?" I suggested.

"That would be annoying. But I think it is his, and I think I can guess at the nature of the art treasures that were stolen."

"And you don't intend to enlighten me?"

"My dear fellow," he replied, "you have all the data. Enlighten yourself by the exercise of your own brilliant faculties. Don't give way to mental indolence."

I endeavoured, from the facts in my possession, to construct the personality of the mysterious burglar, and failed utterly; nor was I more successful in my endeavour to guess at the nature of the stolen property; and it was not until the following morning, when we had set out on our quest and were approaching Limehouse, that Thorndyke would revert to the subject.

"We are now," he said, "going to the factory of Badcomb and Martin, shell importers and cutters, in the West India Dock Road. If I don't find my man there, I shall hand the facts over to the police, and waste no more time over the case."

"What is your man like?" I asked.

"I am looking for an elderly Japanese, wearing a new hat or, more probably, a cap, and having a bruise on his right cheek or temple. I am also looking for a cab-yard; but here we are at the works, and as it is now close on the dinner-hour, we will wait and see the hands come out before making any inquiries."

We walked slowly past the tall, blank-faced building, and were just turning to re-pass it when a steam whistle sounded, a wicket opened in the main gate, and a stream of workmen – each powdered with white, like a miller – emerged into the street. We halted to watch the men as they came out, one by one, through the wicket, and turned to the right or left towards their homes or some adjacent coffee-shop; but none of them answered to the description that my friend had given.

The outcoming stream grew thinner, and at length ceased; the wicket was shut with a bang, and once more Thorndyke's quest appeared to have failed.

"Is that all of them, I wonder?" he said, with a shade of disappointment in his tone; but even as he spoke the wicket opened again, and a leg protruded. The leg was followed by a back and a curious globular head, covered with iron-grey hair, and surmounted by a cloth cap, the whole appertaining to a short, very thick-set man, who remained thus, evidently talking to someone inside.

Suddenly he turned his head to look across the street; and immediately I recognized, by the pallid yellow complexion and narrow eye-slits, the physiognomy of a typical Japanese. The man remained talking for nearly another minute; then, drawing out his other leg, he turned towards us; and now I perceived that the right side of his face, over the prominent cheekbone, was discoloured as though by a severe bruise.

"Ha!" said Thorndyke, turning round sharply as the man approached, "either this is our man or it is an incredible coincidence." He walked away at a moderate pace, allowing the Japanese to overtake us slowly, and when the man had at length passed us, he increased his speed somewhat, so as to maintain the distance.

Our friend stepped along briskly, and presently turned up a side street, whither we followed at a respectful distance, Thorndyke holding open his pocket-book, and appearing to engage me in an earnest discussion, but keeping a sharp eye on his quarry.

"There he goes!" said my colleague, as the man suddenly disappeared – "the house with the green window-sashes. That will be number thirteen."

It was; and, having verified the fact, we passed on, and took the next turning that would lead us back to the main road.

Some twenty minutes later, as we were strolling past the door of a coffee-shop, a man came out, and began to fill his pipe with an air of leisurely satisfaction. His hat and clothes were powdered with white like those of the workmen whom we had seen come out of the factory. Thorndyke accosted him.

"Is that a flour-mill up the road there?"

"No, sir; pearl-shell. I work there myself."

"Pearl-shell, eh?" said Thorndyke. "I suppose that will be an industry that will tend to attract the aliens. Do you find it so?"

"No, sir; not at all. The work's too hard. We've only got one foreigner in the place, and he ain't an alien – he's a Jap."

"A Jap!" exclaimed Thorndyke. "Really. Now, I wonder if that would chance to be our old friend Kotei – you remember Kotei?" he added, turning to me.

"No, sir; this man's name is Futashima. There was another Jap in the works, a chap named Itu, a pal of Futashima's, but he's left."

"Ah! I don't know either of them. By the way, usen't there to be a cab-yard just about here?"

"There's a yard up Rankin Street where they keep vans and one or two cabs. That chap Itu works there now. Taken to horseflesh. Drives a van sometimes. Queer start for a Jap."

"Very." Thorndyke thanked the man for his information, and we sauntered on towards Rankin Street. The yard was at this time nearly deserted, being occupied only by an ancient and crazy four-wheeler and a very shabby hansom.

"Curious old houses, these that back on to the yard," said Thorndyke, strolling into the enclosure. "That timber gable, now," pointing to a house, from a window of which a man was watching us suspiciously, "is quite an interesting survival."

"What's your business, mister?" demanded the man in a gruff tone.

"We are just having a look at these quaint old houses," replied Thorndyke, edging towards the back of the hansom, and opening his pocket-book, as though to make a sketch.

"Well, you can see 'em from outside," said the man.

"So we can," said Thorndyke suavely, "but not so well, you know."

At this moment the pocket-book slipped from his hand and fell, scattering a number of loose papers about the ground under the hansom, and our friend at the window laughed joyously.

"No hurry," murmured Thorndyke, as I stooped to help him to gather up the papers – which he did in the most surprisingly slow and clumsy manner. "It is fortunate that the ground is dry." He stood up with the rescued papers in his hand, and, having scribbled down a brief note, slipped the book in his pocket.

"Now you'd better mizzle," observed the man at the window.

"Thank you," replied Thorndyke, "I think we had;" and, with a pleasant nod at the custodian, he proceeded to adopt the hospitable suggestion.

"Mr Marchmont has been here, sir, with Inspector Badger and another gentleman," said Polton, as we entered our chambers. "They said they would call again about five."

"Then," replied Thorndyke, "as it is now a quarter to five, there is just time for us to have a wash while you get the tea ready. The particles that float in the atmosphere of Limehouse are not all mother-of-pearl."

Our visitors arrived punctually, the third gentleman being, as we had supposed, Mr Solomon Löwe. Inspector Badger I had not seen before, and he now impressed me as showing a tendency to invert the significance of his own name by endeavouring to "draw" Thorndyke; in which, however, he was not brilliantly successful.

"I hope you are not going to disappoint Mr Löwe, sir," he commenced facetiously. "You have had a good look at that hat – we saw your marks on it – and he expects that you will be able to point us out the man, name and address all complete." He grinned patronizingly at our unfortunate client, who was looking even more haggard and worn than he had been on the previous morning.

"Have you – have you made any – discovery?" Mr Löwe asked with pathetic eagerness.

"We examined the hat very carefully, and I think we have established a few facts of some interest."

"Did your examination of the hat furnish any information as to the nature of the stolen property, sir?" inquired the humorous inspector.

Thorndyke turned to the officer with a face as expressionless as a wooden mask.

"We thought it possible," said he, "that it might consist of works of Japanese art, such as netsukes, paintings, and such like."

Mr Löwe uttered an exclamation of delighted astonishment, and the facetiousness faded rather suddenly from the inspector's countenance.

"I don't know how you can have found out," said he. "We have only known it half an hour ourselves, and the wire came direct from Florence to Scotland Yard."

"Perhaps you can describe the thief to us," said Mr Löwe, in the same eager tone.

"I dare say the inspector can do that," replied Thorndyke.

"Yes, I think so," replied the officer. "He is a short strong man with a dark complexion and hair turning grey. He has a very round head, and he is probably a workman engaged at some whiting or cement works. That is all we know; if you can tell us any more, sir, we shall be very glad to hear it."

"I can only offer a few suggestions," said Thorndyke, "but perhaps you may find them useful. For instance, at 13, Birket Street, Limehouse, there is living a Japanese gentleman named Futashima, who works at Badcomb and Martin's mother-of-pearl factory. I think that if you were to call on him, and let him try on the hat that you have, it would probably fit him."

The inspector scribbled ravenously in his notebook, and Mr Marchmont – an old admirer of Thorndyke's – leaned back in his chair, chuckling softly and rubbing his hands.

"Then," continued my colleague, "there is in Rankin Street, Limehouse, a cab-yard, where another Japanese gentleman named Itu is employed. You might find out where Itu was the night before last; and if you should chance to see a hansom cab there – number 22,481 – have a good look at it. In the frame of the number-plate you will find six small holes. Those holes may have held brads, and the brads may have held a false number card. At any rate, you might ascertain where that cab was at 11.30 the night before last. That is all I have to suggest."

Mr Löwe leaped from his chair. "Let us go – now – at once – there is no time to be lost. A thousand thanks to you, doctor – a thousand million thanks. Come!"

He seized the inspector by the arm and forcibly dragged him towards the door, and a few moments later we heard the footsteps of our visitors clattering down the stairs.

"It was not worth while to enter into explanations with them," said Thorndyke, as the footsteps died away – "nor perhaps with you?"

"On the contrary," I replied, "I am waiting to be fully enlightened."

"Well, then, my inferences in this case were perfectly simple ones, drawn from well-known anthropological facts. The human race, as you know, is roughly divided into three groups – the black, the white, and the yellow races. But apart from the variable quality of colour, these races have certain fixed characteristics associated especially with the shape of the skull, of the eye-sockets, and the hair.

"Thus in the black races the skull is long and narrow, the eye-sockets are long and narrow, and the hair is flat and ribbon-like, and usually coiled up like a watch-spring. In the white races the skull is oval, the eye-sockets are oval, and the hair is slightly flattened or oval in section, and tends to be wavy; while in the yellow or Mongol races, the skull is short and round, the eye-sockets are short and round, and the hair is straight and circular in section. So that we have, in the black races, long skull, long orbits, flat hair; in the white races, oval skull, oval orbits, oval hair; and in the yellow races, round skull, round orbits, round hair.

"Now, in this case we had to deal with a very short round skull. But you cannot argue from races to individuals; there are many short-skulled Englishmen. But when I found, associated with that skull, hairs which were circular in section, it became practically certain that the individual was a Mongol of some kind. The mother-of-pearl dust and the granules of rice starch from the inside of the hat favoured this view, for the pearl-shell industry is specially connected with China and Japan, while starch granules from the hat of an Englishman would probably be wheat starch.

"Then as to the hair: it was, as I mentioned to you, circular in section, and of very large diameter. Now, I have examined many thousands of hairs, and the thickest that I have ever seen came from the heads of Japanese; but the hairs from this hat were as thick as any of them. But the hypothesis that the burglar was a Japanese received confirmation in various ways. Thus, he was short, though strong and active, and the Japanese are the shortest of the Mongol races, and very strong and active.

"Then his remarkable skill in handling the powerful caretaker – a retired police-sergeant – suggested the Japanese art of ju-jitsu, while the nature of the robbery was consistent with the value set by the Japanese on works of art. Finally, the fact that only a particular collection was taken, suggested a special, and probably national, character in the things stolen, while their portability – you will remember that goods of the value of from eight to twelve thousand pounds were taken away in two hand-packages – was much more consistent with Japanese than Chinese works, of which the latter tend rather to be bulky and ponderous. Still, it was nothing but a bare hypothesis until we had seen Futashima – and, indeed, is no more now. I may, after all, be entirely mistaken."

He was not, however; and at this moment there reposes in my drawing-room an ancient netsuke, which came as a thank-offering from Mr Isaac Löwe on the recovery of the booty from a back room in No. 13, Birket Street, Limehouse. The treasure, of course, was given in the first place to Thorndyke, but transferred by him to my wife on the pretence that but for my suggestion of shell-dust the robber would never have been traced. Which is, on the face of it, preposterous.

FOUR

The Blue Sequin

Thorndyke stood looking up and down the platform with anxiety that increased as the time drew near for the departure of the train.

"This is very unfortunate," he said, reluctantly stepping into an empty smoking compartment as the guard executed a flourish with his green flag. "I am afraid we have missed our friend." He closed the door, and, as the train began to move, thrust his head out of the window.

"Now I wonder if that will be he," he continued. "If so, he has caught the train by the skin of his teeth, and is now in one of the rear compartments."

The subject of Thorndyke's speculations was Mr Edward Stopford, of the firm of Stopford and Myers, of Portugal Street, solicitors, and his connection with us at present arose out of a telegram that had reached our chambers on the preceding evening. It was reply-paid, and ran thus:

"Can you come here tomorrow to direct defence? Important case. All costs undertaken by us. – Stopford and Myers."

Thorndyke's reply had been in the affirmative, and early on this present morning a further telegram – evidently posted overnight – had been delivered:

"Shall leave for Woldhurst by 8.25 from Charing Cross. Will call for you if possible. – Edward Stopford."

He had not called, however, and, since he was unknown personally to us both, we could not judge whether or not he had been among the passengers on the platform.

"It is most unfortunate," Thorndyke repeated, "for it deprives us of that preliminary consideration of the case which is so invaluable." He filled his pipe thoughtfully, and, having made a fruitless inspection of the platform at London Bridge, took up the paper that he had bought at the bookstall, and began to turn over the leaves, running his eye quickly down the columns, unmindful of the journalistic baits in paragraph or article.

"It is a great disadvantage," he observed, while still glancing through the paper, "to come plump into an inquiry without preparation – to be confronted with the details before one has a chance of considering the case in general terms. For instance – "

He paused, leaving the sentence unfinished, and as I looked up inquiringly I saw that he had turned over another page, and was now reading attentively.

"This looks like our case, Jervis," he said presently, handing me the paper and indicating a paragraph at the top of the page. It was quite brief, and was headed "Terrible Murder in Kent", the account being as follows:

"A shocking crime was discovered yesterday morning at the little town of Woldhurst, which lies on the branch line from Halbury Junction. The discovery was made by a porter who was inspecting the carriages of the train which had just come in. On opening the door of a first-class compartment, he was horrified to find the body of a fashionably-dressed woman stretched upon the floor. Medical aid was immediately summoned, and on the arrival of the divisional surgeon, Dr Morton, it was ascertained that the woman had not been dead more than a few minutes.

"The state of the corpse leaves no doubt that a murder of a most brutal kind has been perpetrated, the cause of death being a penetrating wound of the head, inflicted with some pointed implement, which must have been used with terrible violence, since it has perforated the skull and entered the brain. That robbery was not the motive of the crime is made clear by the fact that an expensively fitted dressing-bag was found on the rack, and that the dead woman's jewellery, including several valuable diamond rings, was untouched. It is rumoured that an arrest has been made by the local police."

"A gruesome affair," I remarked, as I handed back the paper, "but the report does not give us much information."

"It does not," Thorndyke agreed, "and yet it gives us something to consider. Here is a perforating wound of the skull, inflicted with some pointed implement – that is, assuming that it is not a bullet wound. Now, what kind of implement would be capable of inflicting such an injury? How would such an implement be used in the confined space of a railway carriage, and what sort of person would be in possession of such an implement? These are preliminary questions that are worth considering, and I commend them to you, together with the further problems of the possible motive – excluding robbery – and any circumstances other than murder which might account for the injury."

"The choice of suitable implements is not very great," I observed.

"It is very limited, and most of them, such as a plasterer's pick or a geological hammer, are associated with certain definite occupations. You have a notebook?"

I had, and, accepting the hint, I produced it and pursued my further reflections in silence, while my companion, with his notebook also on his knee, gazed steadily out of the window. And thus he remained, wrapped in thought, jotting down an entry now and again in his book, until the train slowed down at Halbury Junction, where we had to change on to a branch line.

As we stepped out, I noticed a well-dressed man hurrying up the platform from the rear and eagerly scanning the faces of the few passengers who had alighted. Soon he espied us, and, approaching quickly, asked, as he looked from one of us to the other: "Dr Thorndyke?"

"Yes," replied my colleague, adding: "And you, I presume, are Mr Edward Stopford?"

The solicitor bowed. "This is a dreadful affair," he said, in an agitated manner. "I see you have the paper. A most shocking affair. I am immensely relieved to find you here. Nearly missed the train, and feared I should miss you."

"There appears to have been an arrest," Thorndyke began.

"Yes − my brother. Terrible business. Let us walk up the platform; our train won't start for a quarter of an hour yet."

We deposited our joint Gladstone and Thorndyke's travelling-case in an empty first-class compartment, and then, with the solicitor between us, strolled up to the unfrequented end of the platform.

"My brother's position," said Mr Stopford, "fills me with dismay − but let me give you the facts in order, and you shall judge for yourself. This poor creature who has been murdered so brutally was a Miss Edith Grant. She was formerly an artist's model, and as such was a good deal employed by my brother, who is a painter − Harold Stopford, you know, ARA now − "

"I know his work very well, and charming work it is."

"I think so, too. Well, in those days he was quite a youngster − about twenty − and he became very intimate with Miss Grant, in quite an innocent way, though not very discreet; but she was a nice respectable girl, as most English models are, and no one thought any harm. However, a good many letters passed between them, and some little presents, amongst which was a beaded chain carrying a locket, and in this he was fool enough to put his portrait and the inscription, 'Edith, from Harold'.

"Later on Miss Grant, who had a rather good voice, went on the stage, in the comic opera line, and, in consequence, her habits and associates changed somewhat; and, as Harold had meanwhile become engaged, he was naturally anxious to get his letters back, and especially to exchange the locket for some less compromising gift. The letters she eventually sent him, but refused absolutely to part with the locket.

"Now, for the last month Harold has been staying at Halbury, making sketching excursions into the surrounding country, and yesterday morning he took the train to Shinglehurst, the third station from here, and the one before Woldhurst.

"On the platform here he met Miss Grant, who had come down from London, and was going on to Worthing. They entered the branch train together, having a first-class compartment to themselves. It seems she was wearing his locket at the time, and he made another appeal to her to make an exchange, which she refused, as before. The discussion appears to have become rather heated and angry on both sides, for the guard and a porter at Munsden both noticed that they seemed to be quarrelling; but the upshot of the affair was that the lady snapped the chain, and tossed it together with the locket to my brother, and they parted quite amiably at Shinglehurst, where Harold got out. He was then carrying his full sketching kit, including a large holland umbrella, the lower joint of which is an ash staff fitted with a powerful steel spike for driving into the ground.

"It was about half-past ten when he got out at Shinglehurst; by eleven he had reached his pitch and got to work, and he painted steadily for three hours. Then he packed up his traps, and was just starting on his way back to the station, when he was met by the police and arrested.

"And now, observe the accumulation of circumstantial evidence against him. He was the last person seen in company with the murdered woman – for no one seems to have seen her after they left Munsden; he appeared to be quarrelling with her when she was last seen alive, he had a reason for possibly wishing for her death, he was provided with an implement – a spiked staff – capable of inflicting the injury which caused her death, and, when he was searched, there was found in his possession the locket and broken chain, apparently removed from her person with violence.

"Against all this is, of course, his known character – he is the gentlest and most amiable of men – and his subsequent conduct – imbecile to the last degree if he had been guilty; but, as a lawyer, I can't help seeing that appearances are almost hopelessly against him."

"We won't say 'hopelessly'," replied Thorndyke, as we took our places in the carriage, "though I expect the police are pretty cocksure. When does the inquest open?"

"Today at four. I have obtained an order from the coroner for you to examine the body and be present at the *post-mortem*."

"Do you happen to know the exact position of the wound?"

"Yes; it is a little above and behind the left ear – a horrible round hole, with a ragged cut or tear running from it to the side of the forehead."

"And how was the body lying?"

"Right along the floor, with the feet close to the offside door."

"Was the wound on the head the only one?"

"No; there was a long cut or bruise on the right cheek – a contused wound the police-surgeon called it, which he believes to have been inflicted with a heavy and rather blunt weapon. I have not heard of any other wounds or bruises."

"Did anyone enter the train yesterday at Shinglehurst?" Thorndyke asked.

"No one entered the train after it left Halbury."

Thorndyke considered these statements in silence, and presently fell into a brown study, from which he roused only as the train moved out of Shinglehurst station.

"It would be about here that the murder was committed," said Mr Stopford; "at least, between here and Woldhurst."

Thorndyke nodded rather abstractedly, being engaged at the moment in observing with great attention the objects that were visible from the windows.

"I notice," he remarked presently, "a number of chips scattered about between the rails, and some of the chair-wedges look new. Have there been any platelayers at work lately?"

"Yes," answered Stopford, "they are on the line now, I believe – at least, I saw a gang working near Woldhurst yesterday, and they are said to have set a rick on fire; I saw it smoking when I came down."

"Indeed; and this middle line of rails is, I suppose, a sort of siding?"

"Yes; they shunt the goods trains and empty trucks on to it. There are the remains of the rick – still smouldering, you see."

Thorndyke gazed absently at the blackened heap until an empty cattle-truck on the middle track hid it from view. This was succeeded by a line of goods-wagons, and these by a passenger coach, one compartment of which – a first-class – was closed up and sealed. The train now began to slow down rather suddenly, and a couple of minutes later we brought up in Woldhurst station.

It was evident that rumours of Thorndyke's advent had preceded us, for the entire staff – two porters, an inspector, and the station-master – were waiting expectantly on the platform, and the latter came forward, regardless of his dignity, to help us with our luggage.

"Do you think I could see the carriage?" Thorndyke asked the solicitor.

"Not the inside, sir," said the station-master, on being appealed to. "The police have sealed it up. You would have to ask the inspector."

"Well, I can have a look at the outside, I suppose?" said Thorndyke, and to this the station-master readily agreed, and offered to accompany us.

"What other first-class passengers were there?" Thorndyke asked.

"None, sir. There was only one first-class coach, and the deceased was the only person in it. It has given us all a dreadful turn, this affair has," he continued, as we set off up the line. "I was on the platform when the train came in. We were watching a rick that was burning up the line, and a rare blaze it made, too; and I was just saying that we should have to move the cattle-truck that was on the mid-track, because, you see, sir, the smoke and sparks were blowing across, and I thought it would frighten the poor beasts. And Mr Felton he don't like his beasts handled roughly. He says it spoils the meat."

"No doubt he is right," said Thorndyke. "But now, tell me, do you think it is possible for any person to board or leave the train on the offside unobserved? Could a man, for instance, enter a compartment on the offside at one station and drop off as the train was slowing down at the next, without being seen?"

"I doubt it," replied the station-master. "Still, I wouldn't say it is impossible."

"Thank you. Oh, and there's another question. You have a gang of men at work on the line, I see. Now, do those men belong to the district?"

"No, sir; they are strangers, every one, and pretty rough diamonds some of 'em are. But I shouldn't say there was any real harm in 'em. If you was suspecting any of 'em of being mixed up in this – "

"I am not," interrupted Thorndyke rather shortly. "I suspect nobody; but I wish to get all the facts of the case at the outset."

"Naturally, sir," replied the abashed official; and we pursued our way in silence.

"Do you remember, by the way," said Thorndyke, as we approached the empty coach, "whether the offside door of the compartment was closed and locked when the body was discovered?"

"It was closed, sir, but not locked. Why, sir, did you think – ?"

"Nothing, nothing. The sealed compartment is the one, of course?"

Without waiting for a reply, he commenced his survey of the coach, while I gently restrained our two companions from shadowing him, as they were disposed to do. The offside footboard occupied his attention specially, and when he had scrutinized minutely the part opposite the fatal compartment, he walked slowly from end to end with his eyes but a few inches from its surface, as though he was searching for something.

Near what had been the rear end he stopped, and drew from his pocket a piece of paper; then, with a moistened finger-tip he picked up from the footboard some evidently minute object, which he carefully transferred to the paper, folding the latter and placing it in his pocket-book.

He next mounted the footboard, and, having peered in through the window of the sealed compartment, produced from his pocket a small insufflator or powder-blower, with which he blew a stream of impalpable smoke-like powder on to the edges of the middle window, bestowing the closest attention on the irregular dusty patches in which it settled, and even measuring one on the jamb of the window with a pocket-rule. At length he stepped down, and, having carefully looked over the near-side footboard, announced that he had finished for the present.

As we were returning down the line, we passed a working man, who seemed to be viewing the chairs and sleepers with more than casual interest.

"That, I suppose, is one of the platelayers?" Thorndyke suggested to the station-master.

"Yes, the foreman of the gang," was the reply.

"I'll just step back and have a word with him, if you will walk on slowly." And my colleague turned back briskly and overtook the man, with whom he remained in conversation for some minutes.

"I think I see the police-inspector on the platform," remarked Thorndyke, as we approached the station.

"Yes, there he is," said our guide. "Come down to see what you are after, sir, I expect." Which was doubtless the case, although the officer professed to be there by the merest chance.

"You would like to see the weapon, sir, I suppose?" he remarked, when he had introduced himself.

"The umbrella-spike," Thorndyke corrected. "Yes, if I may. We are going to the mortuary now."

"Then you'll pass the station on the way; so, if you care to look in, I will walk up with you."

This proposition being agreed to, we all proceeded to the police-station, including the station-master, who was on the very tiptoe of curiosity.

"There you are, sir," said the inspector, unlocking his office, and ushering us in. "Don't say we haven't given every facility to the defence. There are all the effects of the accused, including the very weapon the deed was done with."

"Come, come," protested Thorndyke; "we mustn't be premature." He took the stout ash staff from the officer, and, having examined the formidable spike through a lens, drew from his pocket a steel calliper-gauge, with which he carefully measured the diameter of the spike, and the staff to which it was fixed. "And now," he said, when he had made a note of the measurements in his book, "we will look at the colour-box and the sketch. Ha! a very orderly man, your brother, Mr Stopford. Tubes all in their places, palette-knives wiped clean, palette cleaned off and rubbed bright, brushes wiped – they ought to be washed before they stiffen – all this is very significant." He unstrapped the sketch from the blank canvas to which it was pinned, and, standing it on a chair in a good light, stepped back to look at it.

"And you tell me that that is only three hours' work!" he exclaimed, looking at the lawyer. "It is really a marvellous achievement."

"My brother is a very rapid worker," replied Stopford dejectedly.

"Yes, but this is not only amazingly rapid; it is in his very happiest vein – full of spirit and feeling. But we mustn't stay to look at it longer." He replaced the canvas on its pins, and having glanced at the locket and some other articles that lay in a drawer, thanked the inspector for his courtesy and withdrew.

"That sketch and the colour-box appear very suggestive to me," he remarked, as we walked up the street.

"To me also," said Stopford gloomily, "for they are under lock and key, like their owner, poor old fellow."

He sighed heavily, and we walked on in silence.

The mortuary-keeper had evidently heard of our arrival, for he was waiting at the door with the key in his hand, and, on being shown the coroner's order, unlocked the door, and we entered together; but, after a momentary glance at the ghostly, shrouded figure lying upon the slate table, Stopford turned pale and retreated, saying that he would wait for us outside with the mortuary-keeper.

As soon as the door was closed and locked on the inside, Thorndyke glanced curiously round the bare, whitewashed building. A stream of sunlight poured in through the skylight, and fell upon the silent form that lay so still under its covering-sheet, and one stray beam glanced into a corner by the door, where, on a row of pegs and a deal table, the dead woman's clothing was displayed.

"There is something unspeakably sad in these poor relics, Jervis," said Thorndyke, as we stood before them. "To me they are more tragic, more full of pathetic suggestion, than the corpse itself. See the smart, jaunty hat, and the costly skirts hanging there, so desolate and forlorn; the dainty *lingerie* on the table, neatly folded – by the mortuary-man's wife, I hope – the little French shoes and open-work silk stockings. How pathetically eloquent they are of harmless, womanly vanity, and the gay, careless life, snapped short in the twinkling of an eye. But we must not give way to sentiment. There is another life threatened, and it is in our keeping."

He lifted the hat from its peg, and turned it over in his hand. It was, I think, what is called a "picture-hat" – a huge, flat, shapeless mass of gauze and ribbon and feather, spangled over freely with dark-blue sequins. In one part of the brim was a ragged hole, and from this the glittering sequins dropped off in little showers when the hat was moved.

"This will have been worn tilted over on the left side," said Thorndyke, "judging by the general shape and the position of the hole."

"Yes," I agreed. "Like that of the Duchess of Devonshire in Gainsborough's portrait."

"Exactly."

He shook a few of the sequins into the palm of his hand, and, replacing the hat on its peg, dropped the little discs into an envelope, on which he wrote, "From the hat," and slipped it into his pocket. Then, stepping over to the table, he drew back the sheet reverently and even tenderly from the dead woman's face, and looked down at it with grave pity. It was a comely face, white as marble, serene and peaceful in expression, with half-closed eyes, and framed with a mass of brassy, yellow hair; but its beauty was marred by a long linear wound, half cut, half bruise, running down the right cheek from the eye to the chin.

"A handsome girl," Thorndyke commented – "a dark-haired blonde. What a sin to have disfigured herself so with that horrible peroxide." He smoothed the hair back from her forehead, and added: "She seems to have applied the stuff last about ten days ago. There is about a quarter of an inch of dark hair at the roots. What do you make of that wound on the cheek?"

"It looks as if she had struck some sharp angle in falling, though, as the seats are padded in first-class carriages, I don't see what she could have struck."

"No. And now let us look at the other wound. Will you note down the description?" He handed me his notebook, and I wrote down as he dictated: "A clean-punched circular hole in skull, an inch behind and above margin of left ear – diameter, an inch and seven-sixteenths; starred fracture of parietal bone; membranes perforated, and brain entered deeply; ragged scalp-wound, extending forward to margin of left orbit; fragments of gauze and sequins in edges of wound. That will do for the present. Dr Morton will give us further details if we want them."

He pocketed his callipers and rule, drew from the bruised scalp one or two loose hairs, which he placed in the envelope with the sequins, and, having looked over the body for other wounds or bruises (of which there were none), replaced the sheet, and prepared to depart.

As we walked away from the mortuary, Thorndyke was silent and deeply thoughtful, and I gathered that he was piecing together the facts that he had acquired. At length Mr Stopford, who had several times looked at him curiously, said: "The *post-mortem* will take place at three, and it is now only half-past eleven. What would you like to do next?"

Thorndyke, who, in spite of his mental preoccupation, had been looking about him in his usual keen, attentive way, halted suddenly.

"Your reference to the *post-mortem*," said he, "reminds me that I forgot to put the ox-gall into my case."

"Ox-gall!" I exclaimed, endeavouring vainly to connect this substance with the technique of the pathologist. "What were you going to do with – "

But here I broke off, remembering my friend's dislike of any discussion of his methods before strangers.

"I suppose," he continued, "there would hardly be an artist's colourman in a place of this size?"

"I should think not," said Stopford. "But couldn't you get the stuff from a butcher? There's a shop just across the road."

"So there is," agreed Thorndyke, who had already observed the shop. "The gall ought, of course, to be prepared, but we can filter it ourselves – that is, if the butcher has any. We will try him, at any rate."

He crossed the road towards the shop, over which the name "Felton" appeared in gilt lettering, and, addressing himself to the proprietor, who stood at the door, introduced himself and explained his wants.

"Ox-gall?" said the butcher. "No, sir, I haven't any just now; but I am having a beast killed this afternoon, and I can let you have some then. In fact," he added, after a pause, "as the matter is of importance, I can have one killed at once if you wish it."

"That is very kind of you," said Thorndyke, "and it would greatly oblige me. Is the beast perfectly healthy?"

"They're in splendid condition, sir. I picked them out of the herd myself. But you shall see them – ay, and choose the one that you'd like killed."

"You are really very good," said Thorndyke warmly. "I will just run into the chemist's next door, and get a suitable bottle, and then I will avail myself of your exceedingly kind offer."

He hurried into the chemist's shop, from which he presently emerged, carrying a white paper parcel; and we then followed the butcher down a narrow lane by the side of his shop. It led to an enclosure containing a small pen, in which were confined three handsome steers, whose glossy, black coats contrasted in a very striking manner with their long, greyish-white, nearly straight horns.

"These are certainly very fine beasts, Mr Felton," said Thorndyke, as we drew up beside the pen, "and in excellent condition, too."

He leaned over the pen and examined the beasts critically, especially as to their eyes and horns; then, approaching the nearest one, he raised his stick and bestowed a smart tap on the under-side of the right horn, following it by a similar tap on the left one, a proceeding that the beast viewed with stolid surprise.

"The state of the horns," explained Thorndyke, as he moved on to the next steer, "enables one to judge, to some extent, of the beast's health."

"Lord bless you, sir," laughed Mr Felton, "they haven't got no feeling in their horns, else what good 'ud their horns be to 'em?"

Apparently he was right, for the second steer was as indifferent to a sounding rap on either horn as the first. Nevertheless, when Thorndyke approached the third steer, I unconsciously drew nearer to watch; and I noticed that, as the stick struck the horn, the beast drew back in evident alarm, and that when the blow was repeated, it became manifestly uneasy.

"He don't seem to like that," said the butcher. "Seems as if – Hullo, that's queer!"

Thorndyke had just brought his stick up against the left horn, and immediately the beast had winced and started back, shaking his head and moaning. There was not, however, room for him to back out of reach, and Thorndyke, by leaning into the pen, was able to inspect the sensitive horn, which he did with the closest attention, while the butcher looked on with obvious perturbation.

"You don't think there's anything wrong with this beast, sir, I hope," said he.

"I can't say without a further examination," replied Thorndyke. "It may be the horn only that is affected. If you will have it sawn off close to the head, and sent up to me at the hotel, I will look at it and tell you. And, by way of preventing any mistakes, I will mark it and cover it up, to protect it from injury in the slaughter-house."

He opened his parcel and produced from it a wide-mouthed bottle labelled "Ox-gall", a sheet of gutta-percha tissue, a roller bandage, and a stick of sealing-wax. Handing the bottle to Mr Felton, he encased the distal half of the horn in a covering by means of the tissue and the bandage, which he fixed securely with the sealing-wax.

"I'll saw the horn off and bring it up to the hotel myself, with the ox-gall," said Mr Felton. "You shall have them in half an hour."

He was as good as his word, for in half an hour Thorndyke was seated at a small table by the window of our private sitting-room in the Black Bull Hotel. The table was covered with newspaper, and on it lay the long grey horn and Thorndyke's travelling-case, now open and displaying a small microscope and its accessories. The butcher was seated solidly in an armchair waiting, with a half-suspicious eye on Thorndyke, for the report; and I was endeavouring by cheerful talk to keep Mr Stopford from sinking into utter despondency, though I, too, kept a furtive watch on my colleague's rather mysterious proceedings.

I saw him unwind the bandage and apply the horn to his ear, bending it slightly to and fro. I watched him, as he scanned the surface closely through a lens, and observed him as he scraped some substance from the pointed end on to a glass slide, and, having applied a drop of some reagent, began to tease out the scraping with a pair of mounted needles. Presently he placed the slide under the microscope, and, having observed it attentively for a minute or two, turned round sharply.

"Come and look at this, Jervis," said he.

I wanted no second bidding, being on tenterhooks of curiosity, but came over and applied my eye to the instrument.

"Well, what is it?" he asked.

"A multipolar nerve corpuscle – very shrivelled, but unmistakable."

"And this?"

He moved the slide to a fresh spot.

"Two pyramidal nerve corpuscles and some portions of fibres."

"And what do you say the tissue is?"

"Cortical brain substance, I should say, without a doubt."

"I entirely agree with you. And that being so," he added, turning to Mr Stopford, "we may say that the case for the defence is practically complete."

"What, in Heaven's name, do you mean?" exclaimed Stopford, starting up.

"I mean that we can now prove when and where and how Miss Grant met her death. Come and sit down here, and I will explain. No, you needn't go away, Mr Felton. We shall have to subpœna you. Perhaps," he continued, "we had better go over the facts and see what they suggest. And first we note the position of the body, lying with the feet close to the offside door, showing that, when she fell, the deceased was sitting, or more probably standing, close to that door. Next there is this." He drew from his pocket a folded paper, which he opened, displaying a tiny blue disc. "It is one of the sequins with which her hat was trimmed, and I have in this envelope several more which I took from the hat itself.

"This single sequin I picked up on the rear end of the offside footboard, and its presence there makes it nearly certain that at some time Miss Grant had put her head out of the window on that side.

"The next item of evidence I obtained by dusting the margins of the offside window with a light powder, which made visible a greasy impression three and a quarter inches long on the sharp corner of the right-hand jamb (right-hand from the inside, I mean).

"And now as to the evidence furnished by the body. The wound in the skull is behind and above the left ear, is roughly circular, and measures one inch and seven-sixteenths at most, and a ragged scalp-wound runs from it towards the left eye. On the right cheek is a linear contused wound three and a quarter inches long. There are no other injuries.

"Our next facts are furnished by this." He took up the horn and tapped it with his finger, while the solicitor and Mr Felton stared at him in speechless wonder. "You notice it is a left horn, and you remember that it was highly sensitive. If you put your ear to it while I strain it, you will hear the grating of a fracture in the bony core. Now look at the pointed end, and you will see several deep scratches running lengthwise, and where those scratches end the diameter of the horn is, as you see by this calliper-gauge, one inch and seven-sixteenths. Covering the scratches is a dry blood-stain, and at the extreme tip is a small mass of a dried substance which Dr Jervis and I have examined with the microscope and are satisfied is brain tissue."

"Good God!" exclaimed Stopford eagerly. "Do you mean to say – "

"Let us finish with the facts, Mr Stopford," Thorndyke interrupted. "Now, if you look closely at that blood-stain, you will see a short piece of hair stuck to the horn, and through this lens you can make out the root-bulb. It is a golden hair, you notice, but near the root it is black, and our calliper-gauge shows us that the black portion is fourteen sixty-fourths of an inch long. Now, in this envelope are some hairs that I removed from the dead woman's head. They also are golden hairs, black at the roots, and when I measure the black portion I find it to be fourteen sixty-fourths of an inch long. Then, finally, there is this."

He turned the horn over, and pointed to a small patch of dried blood. Embedded in it was a blue sequin.

Mr Stopford and the butcher both gazed at the horn in silent amazement; then the former drew a deep breath and looked up at Thorndyke.

"No doubt," said he, "you can explain this mystery, but for my part I am utterly bewildered, though you are filling me with hope."

"And yet the matter is quite simple," returned Thorndyke, "even with these few facts before us, which are only a selection from the body of evidence in our possession. But I will state my theory, and you shall judge." He rapidly sketched a rough plan on a sheet of paper, and continued: "These were the conditions when the train was approaching Woldhurst: Here was the passenger-coach, here was the burning rick, and here was a cattle-truck. This steer was in that truck. Now my hypothesis is that at that time Miss Grant was standing with her head out of the offside window, watching the burning rick. Her wide hat, worn on the left side, hid from her view the cattle-truck which she was approaching, and then this is what happened." He sketched another plan to a larger scale. "One of the steers – this one – had thrust its long horn out through the bars. The point of that horn struck the deceased's head, driving her face violently against the corner of the window, and then, in disengaging, ploughed its way through the scalp, and suffered a fracture of its core from the violence of the wrench. This hypothesis is inherently probable, it fits all the facts, and those facts admit of no other explanation."

The solicitor sat for a moment as though dazed, then he rose impulsively and seized Thorndyke's hands.

"I don't know what to say to you," he exclaimed huskily, "except that you have saved my brother's life, and for that may God reward you!"

The butcher rose from his chair with a slow grin.

"It seems to me," said he, "as if that ox-gall was what you might call a blind, eh, sir?"

And Thorndyke smiled an inscrutable smile.

When we returned to town on the following day we were a party of four, which included Mr Harold Stopford. The verdict of "Death by misadventure", promptly returned by the coroner's jury, had been shortly followed by his release from custody, and he now sat with his brother and me, listening with rapt attention to Thorndyke's analysis of the case.

"So, you see," the latter concluded, "I had six possible theories of the cause of death worked out before I reached Halbury, and it only remained to select the one that fitted the facts. And when I had seen the cattle-truck, had picked up that sequin, had heard the description of the steers, and had seen the hat and the wounds, there was nothing left to do but the filling in of details."

"And you never doubted my innocence?" asked Harold Stopford.

Thorndyke smiled at his quondam client.

"Not after I had seen your colour-box and your sketch," said he, "to say nothing of the spike."

FIVE

The Moabite Cipher

A large and motley crowd lined the pavements of Oxford Street as Thorndyke and I made our way leisurely eastward. Floral decorations and drooping bunting announced one of those functions inaugurated from time to time by a benevolent Government for the entertainment of fashionable loungers and the relief of distressed pickpockets. For a Russian Grand Duke, who had torn himself away, amidst valedictory explosions, from a loving if too demonstrative people, was to pass anon on his way to the Guildhall; and a British Prince, heroically indiscreet, was expected to occupy a seat in the ducal carriage.

Near Rathbone Place Thorndyke halted and drew my attention to a smart-looking man who stood lounging in a doorway, cigarette in hand.

"Our old friend Inspector Badger," said Thorndyke. "He seems mightily interested in that gentleman in the light overcoat. How d'ye do, Badger?" for at this moment the detective caught his eye and bowed. "Who is your friend?"

"That's what I want to know, sir," replied the inspector. "I've been shadowing him for the last half-hour, but I can't make him out, though I believe I've seen him somewhere. He don't look like a foreigner but he has got something bulky in his pocket, so I must keep him in sight until the Duke is safely past. I wish," he added gloomily, "these beastly Russians would stop at home. They give us no end of trouble."

"Are you expecting any – occurrences, then?" asked Thorndyke.

"Bless you, sir," exclaimed Badger, "the whole route is lined with plain-clothes men. You see, it is known that several desperate characters followed the Duke to England, and there are a good many exiles living here who would like to have a rap at him. Hallo! What's he up to now?"

The man in the light overcoat had suddenly caught the inspector's too inquiring eye, and forthwith dived into the crowd at the edge of the pavement. In his haste he trod heavily on the foot of a big, rough-looking man, by whom he was in a moment hustled out into the road with such violence that he fell sprawling face downwards. It was an unlucky moment. A mounted constable was just then backing in upon the crowd, and before he could gather the meaning of the shout that arose from the bystanders, his horse had set down one hind-hoof firmly on the prostrate man's back.

The inspector signalled to a constable, who forthwith made a way for us through the crowd; but even as we approached the injured man, he rose stiffly and looked round with a pale, vacant face.

"Are you hurt?" Thorndyke asked gently, with an earnest look into the frightened, wondering eyes.

"No, sir," was the reply; "only I feel queer – sinking – just here."

He laid a trembling hand on his chest, and Thorndyke, still eyeing him anxiously, said in a low voice to the inspector: "Cab or ambulance, as quickly as you can."

A cab was led round from Newman Street, and the injured man put into it. Thorndyke, Badger, and I entered, and we drove off up Rathbone Place. As we proceeded, our patient's face grew more and more ashen, drawn, and anxious; his breathing was shallow and uneven, and his teeth chattered slightly. The cab swung round into

Goodge Street, and then – suddenly, in the twinkling of an eye – there came a change. The eyelids and jaw relaxed, the eyes became filmy, and the whole form subsided into the corner in a shrunken heap, with the strange gelatinous limpness of a body that is dead as a whole, while its tissues are still alive.

"God save us! The man's dead!" exclaimed the inspector in a shocked voice – for even policemen have their feelings. He sat staring at the corpse, as it nodded gently with the jolting of the cab, until we drew up inside the courtyard of the Middlesex Hospital, when he got out briskly, with suddenly renewed cheerfulness, to help the porter to place the body on the wheeled couch.

"We shall know who he is now, at any rate," said he, as we followed the couch to the casualty-room. Thorndyke nodded unsympathetically. The medical instinct in him was for the moment stronger than the legal.

The house-surgeon leaned over the couch, and made a rapid examination as he listened to our account of the accident. Then he straightened himself up and looked at Thorndyke.

"Internal hæmorrhage, I expect," said he. "At any rate, he's dead, poor beggar! – as dead as Nebuchadnezzar. Ah! here comes a bobby; it's his affair now."

A sergeant came into the room, breathing quickly, and looked in surprise from the corpse to the inspector. But the latter, without loss of time, proceeded to turn out the dead man's pockets, commencing with the bulky object that had first attracted his attention; which proved to be a brown-paper parcel tied up with red tape.

"Pork-pie, begad!" he exclaimed with a crestfallen air as he cut the tape and opened the package. "You had better go through his other pockets, sergeant."

The small heap of odds and ends that resulted from this process tended, with a single exception, to throw little light on the man's identity; the exception being a letter, sealed, but not stamped, addressed in an exceedingly illiterate hand to Mr Adolf Schönberg, 213, Greek Street, Soho.

"He was going to leave it by hand, I expect," observed the inspector, with a wistful glance at the sealed envelope. "I think I'll take it round myself, and you had better come with me, sergeant."

He slipped the letter into his pocket, and, leaving the sergeant to take possession of the other effects, made his way out of the building.

"I suppose, Doctor," said he, as we crossed into Berners Street, "you are not coming our way? Don't want to see Mr Schönberg, h'm?"

Thorndyke reflected for a moment. "Well, it isn't very far, and we may as well see the end of the incident. Yes; let us go together."

No. 213, Greek Street, was one of those houses that irresistibly suggest to the observer the idea of a church organ, either jamb of the doorway being adorned with a row of brass bell-handles corresponding to the stop-knobs.

These the sergeant examined with the air of an expert musician, and having, as it were, gauged the capacity of the instrument, selected the middle knob on the right-hand side and pulled it briskly; whereupon a first-floor window was thrown up and a head protruded. But it afforded us a momentary glimpse only, for, having caught the sergeant's upturned eye, it retired with surprising precipitancy, and before we had time to speculate on the apparition, the street-door was opened and a man emerged. He was about to close the door after him when the inspector interposed.

"Does Mr Adolf Schönberg live here?"

The newcomer, a very typical Jew of the red-haired type, surveyed us thoughtfully through his gold-rimmed spectacles as he repeated the name.

"Schönberg—Schönberg? Ah, yes! I know. He lives on the third-floor. I saw him go up a short time ago. Third-floor back;" and indicating the open door with a wave of the hand, he raised his hat and passed into the street.

"I suppose we had better go up," said the inspector, with a dubious glance at the row of bell-pulls. He accordingly started up the stairs, and we all followed in his wake.

There were two doors at the back on the third-floor, but as the one was open, displaying an unoccupied bedroom, the inspector rapped smartly on the other. It flew open almost immediately, and a fierce-looking little man confronted us with a hostile stare.

"Well?" said he.

"Mr Adolf Schönberg?" inquired the inspector,

"Well? What about him?" snapped our new acquaintance.

"I wished to have a few words with him," said Badger.

"Then what the deuce do you come banging at *my* door for?" demanded the other.

"Why, doesn't he live here?"

"No. First-floor front," replied our friend, preparing to close the door.

"Pardon me," said Thorndyke, "but what is Mr Schönberg like? I mean – "

"Like?" interrupted the resident. "He's like a blooming Sheeny, with a carroty beard and gold gig-lamps!" and, having presented this impressionist sketch, he brought the interview to a definite close by slamming the door and turning the key.

With a wrathful exclamation, the inspector turned towards the stairs, down which the sergeant was already clattering in hot haste, and made his way back to the ground-floor, followed, as before, by Thorndyke and me. On the doorstep we found the sergeant breathlessly interrogating a smartly-dressed youth, whom I had seen alight from a hansom as we entered the house, and who now stood with a notebook tucked under his arm, sharpening a pencil with deliberate care.

"Mr James saw him come out, sir," said the sergeant. "He turned up towards the Square."

"Did he seem to hurry?" asked the inspector.

"Rather," replied the reporter. "As soon as you were inside, he went off like a lamplighter. You won't catch him now."

"We don't want to catch him," the detective rejoined gruffly; then, backing out of earshot of the eager pressman, he said in a lower tone: "That was Mr Schönberg, beyond a doubt, and it is clear that he has some reason for making himself scarce; so I shall consider myself justified in opening that note."

He suited the action to the word, and, having cut the envelope open with official neatness, drew out the enclosure.

"My hat!" he exclaimed, as his eye fell upon the contents. "What in creation is this? It isn't shorthand, but what the deuce is it?"

He handed the document to Thorndyke, who, having held it up to the light and felt the paper critically, proceeded to examine it with keen interest. It consisted of a single half-sheet of thin notepaper, both sides of which were covered with strange, crabbed characters, written with a brownish-black ink in continuous lines, without any spaces to indicate the divisions into words; and, but for the modern material which bore the writing, it might have been a portion of some ancient manuscript or forgotten codex.

"What do you make of it, Doctor?" inquired the inspector anxiously, after a pause, during which Thorndyke had scrutinized the strange writing with knitted brows.

"Not a great deal," replied Thorndyke. "The character is the Moabite or Phœnician – primitive Semitic, in fact – and reads from right to left. The language I take to be Hebrew. At any rate, I can find no Greek words, and I see here a group of letters which *may* form one of the few Hebrew words that I know – the word *badim*, 'lies'. But you had better get it deciphered by an expert."

"If it is Hebrew," said Badger, "we can manage it all right. There are plenty of Jews at our disposal."

"You had much better take the paper to the British Museum," said Thorndyke, "and submit it to the keeper of the Phœnician antiquities for decipherment."

Inspector Badger smiled a foxy smile as he deposited the paper in his pocket-book. "We'll see what we can make of it ourselves first," he said; "but many thanks for your advice, all the same, Doctor. No, Mr James, I can't give you any information just at present; you had better apply at the hospital."

"I suspect," said Thorndyke, as we took our way homewards, "that Mr James has collected enough material for his purpose already. He must have followed us from the hospital, and I have no doubt that he has his report, with 'full details', mentally arranged at this moment. And I am not sure that he didn't get a peep at the mysterious paper, in spite of the inspector's precautions."

"By the way," I said, "what do you make of the document?"

"A cipher, most probably," he replied. "It is written in the primitive Semitic alphabet, which, as you know, is practically identical with primitive Greek. It is written from right to left, like the Phœnician, Hebrew, and Moabite, as well as the earliest Greek, inscriptions. The paper is common cream-laid notepaper, and the ink is ordinary indelible Chinese ink, such as is used by draughtsmen. Those are the facts, and without further study of the document itself, they don't carry us very far."

"Why do you think it is a cipher rather than a document in straightforward Hebrew?"

"Because it is obviously a secret message of some kind. Now, every educated Jew knows more or less Hebrew, and, although he is able to read and write only the modern square Hebrew character, it is so easy to transpose one alphabet into another that the mere language would afford no security. Therefore, I expect that, when the experts translate this document, the translation or transliteration will be a mere farrago of unintelligible nonsense. But we shall see, and meanwhile the facts that we have offer several interesting suggestions which are well worth consideration."

"As, for instance – ?"

"Now, my dear Jervis," said Thorndyke, shaking an admonitory forefinger at me, "don't, I pray you, give way to mental indolence. You have these few facts that I have mentioned. Consider them separately and collectively, and in their relation to the circumstances. Don't attempt to suck my brain when you have an excellent brain of your own to suck."

On the following morning the papers fully justified my colleague's opinion of Mr James. All the events which had occurred, as well as a number that had not, were given in the fullest and most vivid detail, a lengthy reference being made to the paper "found on the person of the dead anarchist," and "written in a private shorthand or cryptogram."

The report concluded with the gratifying – though untrue – statement that "in this intricate and important case, the police have wisely secured the assistance of Dr John Thorndyke, to whose acute intellect and vast experience the portentous cryptogram will doubtless soon deliver up its secret."

"Very flattering," laughed Thorndyke, to whom I read the extract on his return from the hospital, "but a little awkward if it should induce our friends to deposit a few trifling mementoes in the form of nitro-compounds on our main staircase or in the cellars. By the way, I met Superintendent Miller on London Bridge. The 'cryptogram', as Mr James calls it, has set Scotland Yard in a mighty ferment."

"Naturally. What have they done in the matter?"

"They adopted my suggestion, after all, finding that they could make nothing of it themselves, and took it to the British Museum. The Museum people referred them to Professor Poppelbaum, the great palæographer, to whom they accordingly submitted it."

"Did he express any opinion about it?"

"Yes, provisionally. After a brief examination, he found it to consist of a number of Hebrew words sandwiched between apparently meaningless groups of letters. He furnished the Superintendent off-hand with a translation of the words, and Miller forthwith struck off a number of hectograph copies of it, which he has distributed among the senior officials of his department; so that at present" – here Thorndyke gave vent to a soft chuckle – "Scotland Yard is engaged in a sort of missing word – or, rather, missing sense – competition. Miller invited me to join in the sport, and to that end presented me with one of the hectograph copies on which to exercise my wits, together with a photograph of the document."

"And shall you?" I asked.

"Not I," he replied, laughing. "In the first place, I have not been formally consulted, and consequently am a passive, though interested, spectator. In the second place, I have a theory of my own which I shall test if the occasion arises. But if you would like to take part in the competition, I am authorized to show you the photograph and the translation. I will pass them on to you, and I

THE CIPHER

wish you joy of them."

127

He handed me the photograph and a sheet of paper that he had just taken from his pocket-book, and watched me with grim amusement as I read out the first few lines.

"Woe, city, lies, robbery, prey, noise, whip, rattling, wheel, horse, chariot, day, darkness, gloominess, clouds, darkness, morning, mountain, people, strong, fire, them, flame."

"It doesn't look very promising at first sight," I remarked. "What is the Professor's theory?"

"His theory – provisionally, of course – is that the words form the message, and the groups of letters represent more filled-up spaces between the words."

"But surely," I protested, "that would be a very transparent device."

Thorndyke laughed. "There is a childlike simplicity about it," said he, "that is highly attractive – but discouraging. It is much more probable that the words are dummies, and that the letters contain the message. Or, again, the solution may lie in an entirely different direction. But listen! Is that cab coming here?"

It was. It drew up opposite our chambers, and a few moments later a brisk step ascending the stairs heralded a smart rat-tat at our door. Flinging open the latter, I found myself confronted by a well-dressed stranger, who, after a quick glance at me, peered inquisitively over my shoulder into the room.

"I am relieved, Dr Jervis," said he, "to find you and Dr Thorndyke at home, as I have come on somewhat urgent professional business. My name," he continued, entering in response to my invitation, "is Barton, but you don't know me, though I know you both by sight. I have come to ask you if one of you – or, better still, both – could come tonight and see my brother."

"That," said Thorndyke, "depends on the circumstances and on the whereabouts of your brother."

"The circumstances," said Mr Barton, "are, in my opinion, highly suspicious, and I will place them before you – of course, in strict confidence."

Thorndyke nodded and indicated a chair.

"My brother," continued Mr Barton, taking the proferred seat, "has recently married for the second time. His age is fifty-five, and that of his wife twenty-six, and I may say that the marriage has been – well, by no means a success. Now, within the last fortnight, my brother has been attacked by a mysterious and extremely painful affection of the stomach, to which his doctor seems unable to give a name. It has resisted all treatment hitherto. Day by day the pain and distress increase, and I feel that, unless something decisive is done, the end cannot be far off."

"Is the pain worse after taking food?" inquired Thorndyke.

"That's just it!" exclaimed our visitor. "I see what is in your mind, and it has been in mine, too; so much so that I have tried repeatedly to obtain samples of the food that he is taking. And this morning I succeeded." Here he took from his pocket a wide-mouthed bottle, which, disengaging from its paper wrappings, he laid on the table. "When I called, he was taking his breakfast of arrowroot, which he complained had a gritty taste, supposed by his wife to be due to the sugar. Now I had provided myself with this bottle, and, during the absence of his wife, I managed unobserved to convey a portion of the arrowroot that he had left into it, and I should be greatly obliged if you would examine it and tell me if this arrowroot contains anything that it should not."

He pushed the bottle across to Thorndyke, who carried it to the window, and, extracting a small quantity of the contents with a glass rod, examined the pasty mass with the aid of a lens; then, lifting the bell-glass cover from the microscope, which stood on its table by the window, he smeared a small quantity of the suspected matter on to a glass slip, and placed it on the stage of the instrument.

"I observe a number of crystalline particles in this," he said, after a brief inspection, "which have the appearance of arsenious acid."

"Ah!" ejaculated Mr Barton, "just what I feared. But are you certain?"

"No," replied Thorndyke; "but the matter is easily tested."

He pressed the button of the bell that communicated with the laboratory, a summons that brought the laboratory assistant from his lair with characteristic promptitude.

"Will you please prepare a Marsh's apparatus, Polton," said Thorndyke.

"I have a couple ready, sir," replied Polton.

"Then pour the acid into one and bring it to me, with a tile."

As his familiar vanished silently, Thorndyke turned to Mr Barton.

"Supposing we find arsenic in this arrowroot, as we probably shall, what do you want us to do?"

"I want you to come and see my brother," replied our client.

"Why not take a note from me to his doctor?"

"No, no; I want you to come – I should like you both to come – and put a stop at once to this dreadful business. Consider! It's a matter of life and death. You won't refuse! I beg you not to refuse me your help in these terrible circumstances."

"Well," said Thorndyke, as his assistant reappeared, "let us first see what the test has to tell us."

Polton advanced to the table, on which he deposited a small flask, the contents of which were in a state of brisk effervescence, a bottle labelled "calcium hypochlorite", and a white porcelain tile. The flask was fitted with a safety-funnel and a glass tube drawn out to a fine jet, to which Polton cautiously applied a lighted match. Instantly there sprang from the jet a tiny, pale violet flame. Thorndyke now took the tile, and held it in the flame for a few seconds, when the appearance of the surface remained unchanged save for a small circle of condensed moisture. His next proceeding was to thin the arrowroot with distilled water until it was quite fluid, and then pour a small quantity into the funnel. It ran slowly down the tube into the flask, with the bubbling contents of which it became speedily mixed. Almost immediately a change began to appear in the character of the flame, which from a pale violet turned gradually to a sickly blue, while above it hung a faint cloud of white smoke. Once more Thorndyke held the tile above the jet, but this time, no sooner had the pallid flame touched the cold surface of the porcelain, than there appeared on the latter a glistening black stain. "That is pretty conclusive," observed Thorndyke, lifting the stopper out of the reagent bottle, "but we will apply the final test." He dropped a few drops of the hypochlorite solution on to the tile, and immediately the black stain faded away and vanished. "We can now answer your question, Mr Barton," said he, replacing the stopper as he turned to our client. "The specimen that you brought us certainly contains arsenic, and in very considerable quantities."

"Then," exclaimed Mr Barton, starting from his chair, "you will come and help me to rescue my brother from this dreadful peril. Don't refuse me, Dr Thorndyke, for mercy's sake, don't refuse."

Thorndyke reflected for a moment.

"Before we decide," said he, "we must see what engagements we have."

With a quick, significant glance at me, he walked into the office, whither I followed in some bewilderment, for I knew that we had no engagements for the evening.

"Now, Jervis," said Thorndyke, as he closed the office door, "what are we to do?"

"We must go, I suppose," I replied. "It seems a pretty urgent case."

"It does," he agreed. "Of course, the man may be telling the truth, after all."

"You don't think he is, then?"

"No. It is a plausible tale, but there is too much arsenic in that arrowroot. Still, I think I ought to go. It is an ordinary professional risk. But there is no reason why you should put your head into the noose."

"Thank you," said I, somewhat huffily. "I don't see what risk there is, but if any exists I claim the right to share it."

"Very well," he answered with a smile, "we will both go. I think we can take care of ourselves."

He re-entered the sitting-room, and announced his decision to Mr Barton, whose relief and gratitude were quite pathetic.

"But," said Thorndyke, "you have not yet told us where your brother lives."

"Rexford," was the reply – "Rexford, in Essex. It is an out-of-the-way place, but if we catch the seven-fifteen train from Liverpool Street, we shall be there in an hour and a half."

"And as to the return? You know the trains, I suppose?"

"Oh yes," replied our client; "I will see that you don't miss your train back."

"Then I will be with you in a minute," said Thorndyke; and, taking the still-bubbling flask, he retired to the laboratory, whence he returned in a few minutes carrying his hat and overcoat.

The cab which had brought our client was still waiting, and we were soon rattling through the streets towards the station, where we arrived in time to furnish ourselves with dinner-baskets and select our compartment at leisure.

During the early part of the journey our companion was in excellent spirits. He despatched the cold fowl from the basket and quaffed the rather indifferent claret with as much relish as if he had not had a single relation in the world, and after dinner he became genial to the verge of hilarity. But, as time went on, there crept into his manner a certain anxious restlessness. He became silent and preoccupied, and several times furtively consulted his watch.

"The train is confoundedly late!" he exclaimed irritably. "Seven minutes behind time already!"

"A few minutes more or less are not of much consequence," said Thorndyke.

"No, of course not; but still – Ah, thank Heaven, here we are!"

He thrust his head out of the offside window, and gazed eagerly down the line; then, leaping to his feet, he bustled out on to the platform while the train was still moving.

Even as we alighted a warning bell rang furiously on the up-platform, and as Mr Barton hurried us through the empty booking-office to the outside of the station, the rumble of the approaching train could be heard above the noise made by our own train moving off.

"My carriage doesn't seem to have arrived yet," exclaimed Mr Barton, looking anxiously up the station approach. "If you will wait here a moment, I will go and make inquiries."

He darted back into the booking-office and through it on to the platform, just as the up-train roared into the station. Thorndyke followed him with quick but stealthy steps, and, peering out of the booking-office door, watched his proceedings; then he turned and beckoned to me.

"There he goes," said he, pointing to an iron footbridge that spanned the line; and, as I looked, I saw, clearly defined against the dim night sky, a flying figure racing towards the "up" side.

It was hardly two-thirds across when the guard's whistle sang out its shrill warning.

"Quick, Jervis," exclaimed Thorndyke; "she's off!"

He leaped down on to the line, whither I followed instantly, and, crossing the rails, we clambered up together on to the foot-board opposite an empty first-class compartment. Thorndyke's magazine knife, containing, among other implements, a railway-key, was already in his hand. The door was speedily unlocked, and, as we entered, Thorndyke ran through and looked out on to the platform.

"Just in time!" he exclaimed. "He is in one of the forward compartments."

He relocked the door, and, seating himself, proceeded to fill his pipe.

"And now," said I, as the train moved out of the station, "perhaps you will explain this little comedy."

"With pleasure," he replied, "if it needs any explanation. But you can hardly have forgotten Mr James' flattering remarks in his report of the Greek Street incident, clearly giving the impression that the mysterious document was in my possession. When I read that, I knew I must look out for some attempt to recover it, though I hardly expected such promptness. Still, when Mr Barton called without credentials or appointment, I viewed him with some suspicion. That suspicion deepened when he wanted us both to come. It deepened further when I found an impossible quantity of arsenic in his sample, and it gave place to certainty when, having allowed him to select the trains by which we were to travel, I went up to the laboratory and examined the time-table; for I then found that the last train for London left Rexford ten minutes after we were due to arrive. Obviously this was a plan to get us both safely out of the way while he and some of his friends ransacked our chambers for the missing document."

"I see; and that accounts for his extraordinary anxiety at the lateness of the train. But why did you come, if you knew it was a 'plant'?"

"My dear fellow," said Thorndyke, "I never miss an interesting experience if I can help it. There are possibilities in this, too, don't you see?"

"But supposing his friends have broken into our chambers already?"

"That contingency has been provided for; but I think they will wait for Mr Barton – and us."

Our train, being the last one up, stopped at every station, and crawled slothfully in the intervals, so that it was past eleven o'clock when we reached Liverpool Street. Here we got out cautiously, and, mingling with the crowd, followed the unconscious Barton up the platform, through the barrier, and out into the street. He seemed in no special hurry, for, after pausing to light a cigar, he set off at an easy pace up New Broad Street.

Thorndyke hailed a hansom, and, motioning me to enter, directed the cabman to drive to Clifford's Inn Passage.

"Sit well back," said he, as we rattled away up New Broad Street. "We shall be passing our gay deceiver presently – in fact, there he is, a living, walking illustration of the folly of underrating the intelligence of one's adversary."

At Clifford's Inn Passage we dismissed the cab, and, retiring into the shadow of the dark, narrow alley, kept an eye on the gate of

Inner Temple Lane. In about twenty minutes we observed our friend approaching on the south side of Fleet Street. He halted at the gate, plied the knocker, and after a brief parley with the night-porter vanished through the wicket. We waited yet five minutes more, and then, having given him time to get clear of the entrance, we crossed the road.

The porter looked at us with some surprise.

"There's a gentleman just gone down to your chambers, sir," said he. "He told me you were expecting him."

"Quite right," said Thorndyke, with a dry smile, "I was. Good night."

We slunk down the lane, past the church, and through the gloomy cloisters, giving a wide berth to all lamps and lighted entries, until, emerging into Paper Buildings, we crossed at the darkest part to King's Bench Walk, where Thorndyke made straight for the chambers of our friend Anstey, which were two doors above our own.

"Why are we coming here?" I asked, as we ascended the stairs.

But the question needed no answer when we reached the landing, for through the open door of our friend's chambers I could see in the darkened room Anstey himself with two uniformed constables and a couple of plain-clothes men.

"There has been no signal yet, sir," said one of the latter, whom I recognized as a detective-sergeant of our division.

"No," said Thorndyke, "but the MC has arrived. He came in five minutes before us."

"Then," exclaimed Anstey, "the ball will open shortly, ladies and gents. The boards are waxed, the fiddlers are tuning up, and – "

"Not quite so loud, if you please, sir," said the sergeant. "I think there is somebody coming up Crown Office Row."

The ball had, in fact, opened. As we peered cautiously out of the open window, keeping well back in the darkened room, a stealthy figure crept out of the shadow, crossed the road, and stole noiselessly into the entry of Thorndyke's chambers. It was quickly followed by a second figure, and then by a third, in which I recognized our elusive client.

"Now listen for the signal," said Thorndyke. "They won't waste time. Confound that clock!"

The soft-voiced bell of the Inner Temple clock, mingling with the harsher tones of St Dunstan's and the Law Courts, slowly told out the hour of midnight; and as the last reverberations were dying away, some metallic object, apparently a coin, dropped with a sharp clink on to the pavement under our window.

At the sound the watchers simultaneously sprang to their feet.

"You two go first," said the sergeant, addressing the uniformed men, who thereupon stole noiselessly, in their rubber-soled boots, down the stone stairs and along the pavement. The rest of us followed, with less attention to silence, and as we ran up to Thorndyke's chambers, we were aware of quick but stealthy footsteps on the stairs above.

"They've been at work, you see," whispered one of the constables, flashing his lantern on to the iron-bound outer door of our sitting-room, on which the marks of a large jemmy were plainly visible.

The sergeant nodded grimly, and, bidding the constables to remain on the landing, led the way upwards.

As we ascended, faint rustlings continued to be audible from above, and on the second-floor landing we met a man descending briskly, but without hurry, from the third. It was Mr Barton, and I could not but admire the composure with which he passed the two detectives. But suddenly his glance fell on Thorndyke, and his composure vanished. With a wild stare of incredulous horror, he halted as if petrified; then he broke away and raced furiously down the stairs, and a moment later a muffled shout and the sound of a scuffle told us that he had received a check. On the next flight we met two more men, who, more hurried and less self-possessed, endeavoured to push past; but the sergeant barred the way.

"Why, bless me!" exclaimed the latter, "it's Moakey; and isn't that Tom Harris?"

"It's all right, sergeant," said Moakey plaintively, striving to escape from the officer's grip. "We've come to the wrong house, that's all."

The sergeant smiled indulgently. "I know," he replied. "But you're always coming to the wrong house, Moakey; and now you're just coming along with me to the right house."

He slipped his hand inside his captive's coat, and adroitly fished out a large, folding jemmy; whereupon the discomforted burglar abandoned all further protest.

On our return to the first-floor, we found Mr Barton sulkily awaiting us, handcuffed to one of the constables, and watched by Polton with pensive disapproval.

"I needn't trouble you tonight, Doctor," said the sergeant, as he marshalled his little troop of captors and captives. "You'll hear from us in the morning. Good night, sir."

The melancholy procession moved off down the stairs, and we retired into our chambers with Anstey to smoke a last pipe.

"A capable man, that Barton," observed Thorndyke — "ready, plausible, and ingenious, but spoilt by prolonged contact with fools. I wonder if the police will perceive the significance of this little affair."

"They will be more acute than I am if they do," said I.

"Naturally," interposed Anstey, who loved to "cheek" his revered senior, "because there isn't any. It's only Thorndyke's bounce. He is really in a deuce of a fog himself."

However this may have been, the police were a good deal puzzled by the incident, for, on the following morning, we received a visit from no less a person than Superintendent Miller, of Scotland Yard.

"This is a queer business," said he, coming to the point at once — "this burglary, I mean. Why should they want to crack your place, right here in the Temple, too? You've got nothing of value here, have you? No 'hard stuff', as they call it, for instance?"

"Not so much as a silver teaspoon," replied Thorndyke, who had a conscientious objection to plate of all kinds.

"It's odd," said the superintendent, "deuced odd. When we got your note, we thought these anarchist idiots had mixed you up with the case – you saw the papers, I suppose – and wanted to go through your rooms for some reason. We thought we had our hands on the gang, instead of which we find a party of common crooks that we're sick of the sight of. I tell you, sir, it's annoying when you think you've hooked a salmon, to bring up a blooming eel."

"It must be a great disappointment," Thorndyke agreed, suppressing a smile.

"It is," said the detective. "Not but what we're glad enough to get these beggars, especially Halkett, or Barton, as he calls himself – a mighty slippery customer is Halkett, and mischievous, too – but we're not wanting any disappointments just now. There was that big jewel job in Piccadilly, Taplin and Horne's; I don't mind telling you that we've not got the ghost of a clue. Then there's this anarchist affair. We're all in the dark there, too."

"But what about the cipher?" asked Thorndyke.

"Oh, hang the cipher!" exclaimed the detective irritably. "This Professor Poppelbaum may be a very learned man, but he doesn't help *us* much. He says the document is in Hebrew, and he has translated it into Double Dutch. Just listen to this!" He dragged out of his pocket a bundle of papers, and, dabbing down a photograph of the document before Thorndyke, commenced to read the Professor's report. " 'The document is written in the characters of the well-known inscription of Mesha, King of Moab' (who the devil's he? Never heard of him. Well known, indeed!) 'The language is Hebrew, and the words are separated by groups of letters, which are meaningless, and obviously introduced to mislead and confuse the reader. The words themselves are not strictly consecutive, but, by the interpellation of certain other words, a series of intelligible sentences is obtained, the meaning of which is not very clear, but is no doubt allegorical. The method of decipherment is shown in the accompanying tables, and the full rendering suggested on the enclosed sheet. It is to be noted that the writer of this document was apparently quite unacquainted with the Hebrew language, as appears from the absence of any grammatical construction.' That's the Professor's report, Doctor, and here are the tables showing how he worked it out. It makes my head spin to look at 'em."

He handed to Thorndyke a bundle of ruled sheets, which my colleague examined attentively for a while, and then passed on to me.

"This is very systematic and thorough," said he. "But now let us see the final result at which he arrives."

"It may be all very systematic," growled the superintendent, sorting out his papers, "but I tell you, sir, it's all BOSH!" The latter word he jerked out viciously, as he slapped down on the table the final product of the Professor's labours. "There," he continued, "that's what he calls the 'full rendering', and I reckon it'll make your hair curl. It might be a message from Bedlam."

Thorndyke took up the first sheet, and as he compared the constructed renderings with the literal translation, the ghost of a smile stole across his usually immovable countenance.

"The meaning is certainly a little obscure," he observed, "though the reconstruction is highly ingenious; and, moreover, I think the Professor is probably right. That is to say, the words which he has supplied are probably the omitted parts of the passages from which the words of the cryptogram were taken. What do you think, Jervis?"

He handed me the two papers, of which one gave the actual words of the cryptogram, and the other a suggested reconstruction, with omitted words supplied. The first read:

"Woe   city   lies   robbery   prey   noise
whip rattling   wheel   horse   chariot   day
darkness   gloominess   cloud   darkness   morning
mountain   people   strong   fire   them
flame."

Analysis of the cipher with transliteration into modern square Hebrew characters and translation into English. N.B. The cipher reads from right to left.

	Space	Word	Space	Word	Space	Word
Moabite	Y꒐	꒐꒐Ꝺ	꒐꒐	4ꝶ0	꒐4	꒐Y4
Hebrew		בְּדָּמִים		עִיר		אוֹי
Translation		LIES		CITY		WOE
Moabite	꒐ ꒐	6Y꒐	6 ꒐꒐	74x	H꒐	6꒐꒐
Hebrew		קֹל		טֶרֶף		גֹל
Translation		NOISE		PREY		ROBBERY
Moabite	w 4	꒐7Y꒐	ꝿ ꒐	w o4	7o ꒐	xYw
Hebrew		אוֹפַן		רַעַשׁ		שׁוֹט
Translation		WHEEL		RATTLING		WHIP
Moabite	Y꒐	꒐Y꒐	꒐ ꒐	39 ꒐Y꒐꒐	4꒐x	꒐Y꒐
Hebrew		יוֹם		מֶרְכָּבָה		סוּס
Translation		DAY		CHARIOT		HORSE

THE PROFESSOR'S ANALYSIS

Turning to the second paper, I read out the suggested rendering:

" 'Woe *to the bloody* city! *It is full of* lies *and* robbery; *the* prey *departeth not. The* noise *of a* whip, *and the noise of the* rattling *of the* wheels, *and of the prancing* horses, *and of the jumping* chariots.

" '*A* day *of* darkness *and of* gloominess, *a* day *of* clouds, *and of thick* darkness, *as* the morning *spread upon the* mountains, *a great* people *and a* strong.

" '*A* fire *devoureth before* them, *and behind them a* flame *burneth*'"

Here the first sheet ended, and, as I laid it down, Thorndyke looked at me inquiringly.

"There is a good deal of reconstruction in proportion to the original matter," I objected. "The Professor has 'supplied' more than three-quarters of the final rendering."

"Exactly," burst in the superintendent; "it's all Professor and no cryptogram."

"Still, I think the reading is correct," said Thorndyke. "As far as it goes, that is."

"Good Lord!" exclaimed the dismayed detective. "Do you mean to tell me, sir, that that balderdash is the real meaning of the thing?"

"I don't say that," replied Thorndyke. "I say it is correct as far as it goes; but I doubt its being the solution of the cryptogram."

"Have you been studying that photograph that I gave you?" demanded Miller, with sudden eagerness.

"I have looked at it," said Thorndyke evasively, "but I should like to examine the original if you have it with you."

"I have," said the detective. "Professor Poppelbaum sent it back with the solution. You can have a look at it, though I can't leave it with you without special authority."

He drew the document from his pocket-book and handed it to Thorndyke, who took it over to the window and scrutinized it closely. From the window he drifted into the adjacent office, closing the door after him; and presently the sound of a faint explosion told me that he had lighted the gas-fire.

"Of course," said Miller, taking up the translation again, "this gibberish is the sort of stuff you might expect from a parcel of crack-brained anarchists; but it doesn't seem to mean anything."

"Not to us," I agreed; "but the phrases may have some pre-arranged significance. And then there are the letters between the words. It is possible that they may really form a cipher."

"I suggested that to the Professor," said Miller, "but he wouldn't hear of it. He is sure they are only dummies."

"I think he is probably mistaken, and so, I fancy, does my colleague. But we shall hear what he has to say presently."

"Oh, I know what he will say," growled Miller. "He will put the thing under the microscope, and tell us who made the paper, and what the ink is composed of, and then we shall be just where we were." The superintendent was evidently deeply depressed.

We sat for some time pondering in silence on the vague sentences of the Professor's translation, until, at length, Thorndyke reappeared, holding the document in his hand. He laid it quietly on the table by the officer, and then inquired: "Is this an official consultation?"

"Certainly," replied Miller. "I was authorized to consult you respecting the translation, but nothing was said about the original. Still, if you want it for further study, I will get it for you."

"No, thank you," said Thorndyke. "I have finished with it. My theory turned out to be correct."

"Your theory!" exclaimed the superintendent, eagerly. "Do you mean to say – ?"

"And, as you are consulting me officially, I may as well give you this."

He held out a sheet of paper, which the detective took from him and began to read.

"What is this?" he asked, looking up at Thorndyke with a puzzled frown. "Where did it come from?"

"It is the solution of the cryptogram," replied Thorndyke.

The detective reread the contents of the paper, and, with the frown of perplexity deepening, once more gazed at my colleague.

"This is a joke, sir; you are fooling me," he said sulkily.

"Nothing of the kind," answered Thorndyke. "That is the genuine solution."

"But it's impossible!" exclaimed Miller. "Just look at it, Dr Jervis."

I took the paper from his hand, and, as I glanced at it, I had no difficulty in understanding his surprise. It bore a short inscription in printed Roman capitals, thus:

"THE PICKERDILLEY STUF IS UP THE CHIMBLY 416 WARDOUR ST 2ND FLOUR BACK IT WAS HID BECOS OF OLD MOAKEYS JOOD MOAKEY IS A BLITER."

"Then that fellow wasn't an anarchist at all!" I exclaimed."

"No," said Miller. "He was one of Moakey's gang. We suspected Moakey of being mixed up with that job, but we couldn't fix it on him. By Jove!" he added, slapping his thigh, "if this is right, and I can lay my hands on the loot! Can you lend me a bag, doctor? I'm off to Wardour Street this very moment."

We furnished him with an empty suitcase, and, from the window, watched him making for Mitre Court at a smart double. "I wonder if he will find the booty," said Thorndyke. "It just depends on whether the hiding-place was known to more than one of the gang. Well, it has been a quaint case, and instructive, too. I suspect our friend Barton and the evasive Schönberg were the collaborators who produced that curiosity of literature."

"May I ask how you deciphered the thing?" I said. "It didn't appear to take long."

"It didn't. It was merely a matter of testing a hypothesis; and you ought not to have to ask that question," he added, with mock severity, "seeing that you had what turn out to have been all the necessary facts, two days ago. But I will prepare a document and demonstrate to you tomorrow morning."

"So Miller was successful in his quest," said Thorndyke, as we smoked our morning pipes after breakfast. "The 'entire swag', as he calls it, was 'up the chimbly', undisturbed."

He handed me a note which had been left, with the empty suit-case, by a messenger, shortly before, and I was about to read it when an agitated knock was heard at our door. The visitor, whom I admitted, was a rather haggard and dishevelled elderly gentleman, who, as he entered, peered inquisitively through his concave spectacles from one of us to the other.

"Allow me to introduce myself, gentlemen," said he. "I am Professor Poppelbaum."

Thorndyke bowed and offered a chair.

"I called yesterday afternoon," our visitor continued, "at Scotland Yard, where I heard of your remarkable decipherment and of the convincing proof of its correctness. Thereupon I borrowed the cryptogram, and have spent the entire night in studying it, but I cannot connect your solution with any of the characters. I wonder if you would do me the great favour of enlightening me as to your method of decipherment, and so save me further sleepless nights? You may rely on my discretion."

"Have you the document with you?" asked Thorndyke.

The Professor produced it from his pocket-book, and passed it to my colleague.

"You observe, Professor," said the latter, "that this is a laid paper, and has no water-mark?"

"Yes, I noticed that."

"And that the writing is in indelible Chinese ink?"

"Yes, yes," said the savant impatiently; "but it is the inscription that interests me, not the paper and ink."

"Precisely," said Thorndyke. "Now, it was the ink that interested me when I caught a glimpse of the document three days ago. 'Why,' I asked myself, 'should anyone use this troublesome medium' – for this appears to be stick ink – 'when good writing ink is to be had?' What advantages has Chinese ink over writing ink? It has several advantages as a drawing ink, but for writing purposes it has only one: it is quite unaffected by wet. The obvious inference, then, was that this document was, for some reason, likely to be exposed to wet. But this inference instantly suggested another, which I was yesterday able to put to the test – thus."

He filled a tumbler with water, and, rolling up the document, dropped it in. Immediately there began to appear on it a new set of characters of a curious grey colour. In a few seconds Thorndyke lifted out the wet paper, and held it up to the light, and now there was plainly visible an inscription in transparent lettering, like a very distinct water-mark. It was in printed Roman capitals, written across the other writing, and read:

"THE PICKERDILLEY STUF IS UP THE CHIMBLY 416 WARDOUR ST 2ND FLOUR BACK IT WAS HID BECOS OF OLD MOAKEYS JOOD MOAKEY IS A BLITER."

The Professor regarded the inscription with profound disfavour.

"How do you suppose this was done?" he asked gloomily.

"I will show you," said Thorndyke. "I have prepared a piece of paper to demonstrate the process to Dr Jervis. It is exceedingly simple."

He fetched from the office a small plate of glass, and a photographic dish in which a piece of thin notepaper was soaking in water.

"This paper," said Thorndyke, lifting it out and laying it on the glass, "has been soaking all night, and is now quite pulpy."

He spread a dry sheet of paper over the wet one, and on the former wrote heavily with a hard pencil, "Moakey is a bliter." On lifting the upper sheet, the writing was seen to be transferred in a deep grey to the wet paper, and when the latter was held up to the light the inscription stood out clear and transparent as if written with oil.

"When this dries," said Thorndyke, "the writing will completely disappear, but it will reappear whenever the paper is again wetted."

The Professor nodded.

"Very ingenious," said he – "a sort of artificial palimpsest, in fact. But I do not understand how that illiterate man could have written in the difficult Moabite script."

"He did not," said Thorndyke. "The 'cryptogram' was probably written by one of the leaders of the gang, who, no doubt, supplied copies to the other members to use instead of blank paper for secret communications. The object of the Moabite writing was evidently to divert attention from the paper itself, in case the communication fell into the wrong hands, and I must say it seems to have answered its purpose very well."

The Professor started, stung by the sudden recollection of his labours.

"Yes," he snorted; "but I am a scholar, sir, not a policeman. Every man to his trade."

He snatched up his hat, and with a curt "Good morning," flung out of the room in dudgeon.

Thorndyke laughed softly.

"Poor Professor!" he murmured. "Our playful friend Barton has much to answer for."

Six

The Mandarin's Pearl

Mr Brodribb stretched out his toes on the kerb before the blazing fire with the air of a man who is by no means insensible to physical comfort.

"You are really an extraordinarily polite fellow, Thorndyke," said he.

He was an elderly man, rosy-gilled, portly, and convivial, to whom a mass of bushy, white hair, an expansive double chin, and a certain prim sumptuousness of dress imparted an air of old-world distinction. Indeed, as he dipped an amethystine nose into his wine-glass, and gazed thoughtfully at the glowing end of his cigar, he looked the very type of the well-to-do lawyer of an older generation.

"You are really an extraordinarily polite fellow, Thorndyke," said Mr Brodribb.

"I know," replied Thorndyke. "But why this reference to an admitted fact?"

"The truth has just dawned on me," said the solicitor. "Here am I, dropping in on you, uninvited and unannounced, sitting in your own armchair before your fire, smoking your cigars, drinking your Burgundy – and deuced good Burgundy, too, let me add – and you have not dropped a single hint of curiosity as to what has brought me here."

"I take the gifts of the gods, you see, and ask no questions," said Thorndyke.

"Devilish handsome of you, Thorndyke – unsociable beggar like you, too," rejoined Mr Brodribb, a fan of wrinkles spreading out genially from the corners of his eyes; "but the fact is I have come, in a sense, on business – always glad of a pretext to look you up, as you know – but I want to take your opinion on a rather queer case. It is about young Calverley. You remember Horace Calverley? Well, this is his son. Horace and I were schoolmates, you know, and after his death the boy, Fred, hung on to me rather. We're near neighbours down at Weybridge, and very good friends. I like Fred. He's a good fellow, though cranky, like all his people."

"What has happened to Fred Calverley?" Thorndyke asked, as the solicitor paused.

"Why, the fact is," said Mr Brodribb, "just lately he seems to be going a bit queer – not mad, mind you – at least, I think not – but undoubtedly queer. Now, there is a good deal of property, and a good many highly interested relatives, and, as a natural consequence, there is some talk of getting him certified. They're afraid he may do something involving the estate or develop homicidal tendencies, and they talk of possible suicide – you remember his father's death – but I say that's all bunkum. The fellow is just a bit cranky, and nothing more."

"What are his symptoms?" asked Thorndyke.

"Oh, he thinks he is being followed about and watched, and he has delusions; sees himself in the glass with the wrong face, and that sort of thing, you know."

"You are not highly circumstantial," Thorndyke remarked.

Mr Brodribb looked at me with a genial smile.

"What a glutton for facts this fellow is, Jervis. But you're right, Thorndyke; I'm vague. However, Fred will be here presently. We travel down together, and I took the liberty of asking him to call for me. We'll get him to tell you about his delusions, if you don't mind. He's not shy about them. And meanwhile I'll give you a few preliminary facts. The trouble began about a year ago. He was in a railway accident, and that knocked him all to pieces. Then he went for a voyage to recruit, and the ship broke her propeller-shaft in a storm and became helpless. That didn't improve the state of his nerves. Then he went down the Mediterranean, and after a month or two, back he came, no better than when he started. But here he is, I expect."

He went over to the door and admitted a tall, frail young man whom Thorndyke welcomed with quiet geniality, and settled in a chair by the fire. I looked curiously at our visitor. He was a typical neurotic – slender, fragile, eager. Wide-open blue eyes with broad pupils, in which I could plainly see the characteristic "hippus" – that incessant change of size that marks the unstable nervous equilibrium – parted lips, and wandering taper fingers, were as the stigmata of his disorder. He was of the stuff out of which prophets and devotees, martyrs, reformers, and third-rate poets are made.

"I have been telling Dr Thorndyke about these nervous troubles of yours," said Mr Brodribb presently. "I hope you don't mind. He is an old friend, you know, and he is very much interested."

"It is very good of him," said Calverley. Then he flushed deeply, and added: "But they are not really nervous, you know. They can't be merely subjective."

"You think they can't be?" said Thorndyke.

"No, I am sure they are not." He flushed again like a girl, and looked earnestly at Thorndyke with his big, dreamy eyes. "But you doctors," he said, "are so dreadfully sceptical of all spiritual phenomena. You are such materialists."

"Yes," said Mr Brodribb; "the doctors are not hot on the supernatural, and that's the fact."

"Supposing you tell us about your experiences," said Thorndyke persuasively. "Give us a chance to believe, if we can't explain away."

Calverley reflected for a few moments; then, looking earnestly at Thorndyke, he said: "Very well; if it won't bore you, I will. It is a curious story."

"I have told Dr Thorndyke about your voyage and your trip down the Mediterranean," said Mr Brodribb.

"Then," said Calverley, " I will begin with the events that are actually connected with these strange visitations. The first of these occurred in Marseilles. I was in a curio-shop there, looking over some Algerian and Moorish things, when my attention was attracted by a sort of charm or pendant that hung in a glass case. It was not particularly beautiful, but its appearance was quaint and curious, and took my fancy. It consisted of an oblong block of ebony in which was set a single pear-shaped pearl more than three-quarters of an inch long. The sides of the ebony block were lacquered − probably to conceal a joint − and bore a number of Chinese characters, and at the top was a little gold image with a hole through it, presumably for a string to suspend it by. Excepting for the pearl, the whole thing was uncommonly like one of those ornamental tablets of Chinese ink.

"Now, I had taken a fancy to the thing, and I can afford to indulge my fancies in moderation. The man wanted five pounds for it; he assured me that the pearl was a genuine one of fine quality, and obviously did not believe it himself. To me, however, it looked like a real pearl, and I determined to take the risk; so I paid the money, and he bowed me out with a smile − I may almost say a grin − of satisfaction. He would not have been so well pleased if he had followed me to a jeweller's to whom I took it for an expert opinion; for the jeweller pronounced the pearl to be undoubtedly genuine, and worth anything up to a thousand pounds.

"A day or two later, I happened to show my new purchase to some men whom I knew, who had dropped in at Marseilles in their yacht. They were highly amused at my having bought the thing, and when I told them what I had paid for it, they positively howled with derision.

" 'Why, you silly guffin,' said one of them, a man named Halliwell, 'I could have had it ten days ago for half a sovereign, or probably five shillings. I wish now I had bought it; then I could have sold it to you.'

"It seemed that a sailor had been hawking the pendant round the harbour, and had been on board the yacht with it.

" 'Deuced anxious the beggar was to get rid of it, too,' said Halliwell, grinning at the recollection. 'Swore it was a genuine pearl of priceless value, and was willing to deprive himself of it for the trifling sum of half a jimmy. But we'd heard that sort of thing before. However, the curio-man seems to have speculated on the chance of meeting with a greenhorn, and he seems to have pulled it off. Lucky curio-man!'

"I listened patiently to their gibes, and when they had talked themselves out I told them about the jeweller. They were most frightfully sick; and when we had taken the pendant to a dealer in gems who happened to be staying in the town, and he had offered me five hundred pounds for it, their language wasn't fit for a divinity students' debating club. Naturally the story got noised abroad, and when I left, it was the talk of the place. The general opinion was that the sailor, who was traced to a tea-ship that had put into the harbour, had stolen it from some Chinese passenger; and no less than seventeen different Chinamen came forward to claim it as their stolen property.

"Soon after this I returned to England, and, as my nerves were still in a very shaky state, I came to live with my cousin Alfred, who has a large house at Weybridge. At this time he had a friend staying with him, a certain Captain Raggerton, and the two men appeared to be on very intimate terms. I did not take to Raggerton at all. He was a good-looking man, pleasant in his manners, and remarkably plausible. But the fact is — I am speaking in strict confidence, of course — he was a bad egg. He had been in the Guards, and I don't quite know why he left; but I do know that he played bridge and baccarat pretty heavily at several clubs, and that he had a reputation for being a rather uncomfortably lucky player. He did a good deal at the race-meetings, too, and was in general such an obvious undesirable that I could never understand my cousin's intimacy with him, though I must say that Alfred's habits had changed somewhat for the worse since I had left England.

"The fame of my purchase seems to have preceded me, for when, one day, I produced the pendant to show them, I found that they knew all about it. Raggerton had heard the story from a naval man, and I gathered vaguely that he had heard something that I had not, and that he did not care to tell me; for when my cousin and he talked about the pearl, which they did pretty often, certain significant looks passed between them, and certain veiled references were made which I could not fail to notice.

"One day I happened to be telling them of a curious incident that occurred on my way home. I had travelled to England on one of Holt's big China boats, not liking the crowd and bustle of the regular passenger-lines. Now, one afternoon, when we had been at sea a couple of days, I took a book down to my berth, intending to have a quiet read till tea-time. Soon, however, I dropped off into a doze, and must have remained asleep for over an hour. I awoke suddenly, and as I opened my eyes, I perceived that the door of the state-room was half-open, and a well-dressed Chinaman, in native costume, was looking in at me. He closed the door immediately, and I remained for a few moments paralysed by the start that he had given me. Then I leaped from my bunk, opened the door, and looked out. But the alley-way was empty. The Chinaman had vanished as if by magic.

"This little occurrence made me quite nervous for a day or two, which was very foolish of me; but my nerves were all on edge – and I am afraid they are still."

"Yes," said Thorndyke. "There was nothing mysterious about the affair. These boats carry a Chinese crew, and the man you saw was probably a Serang, or whatever they call the gang-captains on these vessels. Or he may have been a native passenger who had strayed into the wrong part of the ship."

"Exactly," agreed our client. "But to return to Raggerton. He listened with quite extraordinary interest as I was telling this story, and when I had finished he looked very queerly at my cousin.

" 'A deuced odd thing, this, Calverley,' said he. 'Of course, it may be only a coincidence, but it really does look as if there was something, after all, in that – '

" 'Shut up, Raggerton,' said my cousin. 'We don't want any of that rot.'

" 'What is he talking about?' I asked.

" 'Oh, it's only a rotten, silly yarn that he has picked up somewhere. You're not to tell him, Raggerton.'

" 'I don't see why I am not to be told,' I said, rather sulkily. 'I'm not a baby.'

" 'No,' said Alfred, 'but you're an invalid. You don't want any horrors.'

"In effect, he refused to go into the matter any further, and I was left on tenterhooks of curiosity.

"However, the very next day I got Raggerton alone in the smoking-room, and had a little talk with him. He had just dropped a hundred pounds on a double event that hadn't come off, and I expected to find him pliable. Nor was I disappointed, for, when we had negotiated a little loan, he was entirely at my service, and willing to tell me everything, on my promising not to give him away to Alfred.

" 'Now, you understand,' he said, 'that this yarn about your pearl is nothing but a damn silly fable that's been going the round in Marseilles. I don't know where it came from, or what sort of demented rotter invented it; I had it from a Johnnie in the Mediterranean Squadron, and you can have a copy of his letter if you want it.'

"I said that I did want it. Accordingly, that same evening he handed me a copy of the narrative extracted from his friend's letter, the substance of which was this:

"About four months ago there was lying in Canton Harbour a large English barque. Her name is not mentioned, but that is not material to the story. She had got her cargo stowed and her crew signed on, and was only waiting for certain official formalities to be completed before putting to sea on her homeward voyage. Just ahead of her, at the same quay, was a Danish ship that had been in collision outside, and was now laid up pending the decision of the Admiralty Court. She had been unloaded, and her crew paid off, with the exception of one elderly man, who remained on board as ship-keeper. Now, a considerable part of the cargo of the English barque was the property of a certain wealthy mandarin, and this person had been about the vessel a good deal while she was taking in her lading.

"One day, when the mandarin was on board the barque, it happened that three of the seamen were sitting in the galley smoking and chatting with the cook – an elderly Chinaman named Wo-li – and the latter, pointing out the mandarin to the sailors, expatiated on his enormous wealth, assuring them that he was commonly believed to carry on his person articles of sufficient value to buy up the entire lading of a ship.

"Now, unfortunately for the mandarin, it chanced that these three sailors were about the greatest rascals on board; which is saying a good deal when one considers the ordinary moral standard that prevails in the forecastle of a sailing-ship. Nor was Wo-li himself an angel; in fact, he was a consummate villain, and seems to have been the actual originator of the plot which was presently devised to rob the mandarin.

"This plot was as remarkable for its simplicity as for its cold-blooded barbarity. On the evening before the barque sailed, the three seamen, Nilsson, Foucault, and Parratt, proceeded to the Danish ship with a supply of whisky, made the ship-keeper royally drunk, and locked him up in an empty berth. Meanwhile Wo-li made a secret communication to the mandarin to the effect that certain stolen property, believed to be his, had been secreted in the hold of the empty ship. Thereupon the mandarin came down hot-foot to the quay-side, and was received on board by the three seamen, who had got the covers off the after-hatch in readiness. Parratt now ran down the iron ladder to show the way, and the mandarin followed; but when they reached the lower deck, and looked down the hatch into the black darkness of the lower hold, he seems to have taken fright, and begun to climb up again. Meanwhile Nilsson had made a running bowline in the end of a loose halyard that was rove through a block aloft, and had been used for hoisting out the cargo. As the mandarin came up, he leaned over the coaming of the hatch, dropped the noose over the Chinaman's head, jerked it tight, and then he and Foucault hove on the fall of the rope. The unfortunate Chinaman was dragged from the ladder, and, as he swung clear, the two rascals let go the rope, allowing him to drop through the hatches into the lower hold. Then they belayed the rope, and went down below. Parratt had already lighted a slush-lamp, by the glimmer of which they could see the mandarin swinging to and fro like a pendulum within a few feet of the ballast, and still quivering and twitching in his death-throes. They were now joined by Wo-li, who had watched the proceedings from the quay, and the four villains proceeded, without loss of time, to rifle the body as it hung. To their surprise and disgust, they found nothing of value excepting an ebony pendant set with a single large pearl; but Wo-li, though evidently disappointed at the nature of the booty, assured his comrades that this alone was well worth the hazard, pointing out the great size and exceptional beauty of the pearl. As to this, the seamen knew nothing about pearls, but the thing was done, and had to be made the best of; so they made the rope fast to the lower deck-beams, cut off the remainder and unrove it from the block, and went back to their ship.

"It was twenty-four hours before the ship-keeper was sufficiently sober to break out of the berth in which he had been locked, by which time the barque was well out to sea; and it was another three days before the body of the mandarin was found. An active search was then made for the murderers, but as they were strangers to the ship-keeper, no clues to their whereabouts could be discovered.

"Meanwhile, the four murderers were a good deal exercised as to the disposal of the booty. Since it could not be divided, it was evident that it must be entrusted to the keeping of one of them.

The choice in the first place fell upon Wo-li, in whose chest the pendant was deposited as soon as the party came on board, it being arranged that the Chinaman should produce the jewel for inspection by his confederates whenever called upon.

"For six weeks nothing out of the common occurred; but then a very singular event befell. The four conspirators were sitting outside the galley one evening, when suddenly the cook uttered a cry of amazement and horror. The other three turned to see what it was that had so disturbed their comrade, and then they, too, were struck dumb with consternation; for, standing at the door of the companion-hatch – the barque was a flush-decked vessel – was the mandarin whom they had left for dead. He stood quietly regarding them for fully a minute, while they stared at him transfixed with terror. Then he beckoned to them, and went below.

"So petrified were they with astonishment and mortal fear that they remained for a long time motionless and dumb. At last they plucked up courage, and began to make furtive inquiries among the crew; but no one – not even the steward – knew anything of any passengers, or, indeed, of any Chinaman, on board the ship, excepting Wo-li.

"At day-break the next morning, when the cook's mate went to the galley to fill the coppers, he found Wo-li hanging from a hook in the ceiling. The cook's body was stiff and cold, and had evidently been hanging several hours. The report of the tragedy quickly spread through the ship, and the three conspirators hurried off to remove the pearl from the dead man's chest before the officers should come to examine it. The cheap lock was easily picked with a bent wire, and the jewel abstracted; but now the question arose as to who should take charge of it. The eagerness to be the actual custodian of the precious bauble, which had been at first displayed, now gave place to equally strong reluctance. But someone had to take charge of it, and after a long and angry discussion Nilsson was prevailed upon to stow it in his chest.

"A fortnight passed. The three conspirators went about their duties soberly, like men burdened with some secret anxiety, and in their leisure moments they would sit and talk with bated breath of the apparition at the companion-hatch, and the mysterious death of their late comrade.

"At last the blow fell.

"It was at the end of the second dog-watch that the hands were gathered on the forecastle, preparing to make sail after a spell of bad weather. Suddenly Nilsson gave a husky shout, and rushed at Parratt, holding out the key of his chest.

" 'Here you, Parratt,' he exclaimed, 'go below and take that accursed thing out of my chest.'

" 'What for?' demanded Parratt; and then he and Foucault, who was standing close by, looked aft to see what Nilsson was staring at.

"Instantly they both turned white as ghosts, and fell trembling so that they could hardly stand; for there was the mandarin, standing calmly by the companion, returning with a steady, impassive gaze their looks of horror. And even as they looked he beckoned and went below.

" 'D'ye hear, Parratt?' gasped Nilsson; 'take my key and do what I say, or else – '

"But at this moment the order was given to go aloft and set all plain sail; the three men went off to their respective posts, Nilsson going up the fore-topmast rigging, and the other two to the main-top. Having finished their work aloft, Foucault and Parratt, who were both in the port watch, came down on deck, and then, it being their watch below, they went and turned in.

"When they turned out with their watch at midnight, they looked about for Nilsson, who was in the starboard watch, but he was nowhere to be seen. Thinking he might have slipped below unobserved, they made no remark, though they were very uneasy about him; but when the starboard watch came on deck at four o'clock, and Nilsson did not appear with his mates, the two men became alarmed, and made inquiries about him. It was now discovered that no one had seen him since eight o'clock on the previous evening, and, this being reported to the officer of the watch, the latter ordered all hands to be called. But still Nilsson did not appear. A thorough search was now instituted, both below and aloft, and as there was still no sign of the missing man, it was concluded that he had fallen overboard.

"But at eight o'clock two men were sent aloft to shake out the fore-royal. They reached the yard almost simultaneously, and were just stepping on to the foot-ropes when one of them gave a shout; then the pair came sliding down a backstay, with faces as white as tallow. As soon as they reached the deck, they took the officer of the watch forward, and, standing on the heel of the bowsprit, pointed aloft. Several of the hands, including Foucault and Parratt, had followed, and all looked up; and there they saw the body of Nilsson, hanging on the front of the fore-top gallant sail. He was dangling at the end of a gasket, and bouncing up and down on the taut belly of the sail as the ship rose and fell to the send of the sea.

"The two survivors were now in some doubt about having anything further to do with the pearl. But the great value of the jewel, and the consideration that it was now to be divided between two instead of four, tempted them. They abstracted it from Nilsson's chest, and then, as they could not come to an agreement in any other way, they decided to settle who should take charge of it by tossing a coin. The coin was accordingly spun, and the pearl went to Foucault's chest.

"From this moment Foucault lived in a state of continual apprehension. When on deck, his eyes were for ever wandering towards the companion hatch, and during his watch below, when not asleep, he would sit moodily on his chest, lost in gloomy reflection. But a fortnight passed, then three weeks, and still nothing happened. Land was sighted, the Straits of Gibraltar passed, and the end of the voyage was but a matter of days. And still the dreaded mandarin made no sign.

"At length the ship was within twenty-four hours of Marseilles, to which port a large part of the cargo was consigned. Active preparations were being made for entering the port, and among other things the shore tackle was being overhauled. A share in this latter work fell to Foucault and Parratt, and about the middle of the second dog-watch – seven o'clock in the evening – they were sitting on the deck working an eye-splice in the end of a large rope. Suddenly Foucault, who was facing forward, saw his companion turn pale and stare aft with an expression of terror. He immediately turned and looked over his shoulder to see what Parratt was staring at. It was the mandarin, standing by the companion, gravely watching them; and as Foucault turned and met his gaze, the Chinaman beckoned and went below.

"For the rest of that day Parratt kept close to his terrified comrade, and during their watch below he endeavoured to remain awake, that he might keep his friend in view. Nothing happened through the night, and the following morning, when they came on deck for the forenoon watch, their port was well in sight. The two men now separated for the first time, Parratt going aft to take his trick at the wheel, and Foucault being set to help in getting ready the ground tackle.

"Half an hour later Parratt saw the mate stand on the rail and lean outboard, holding on to the mizzen-shrouds while he stared along the ship's side. Then he jumped on to the deck and shouted angrily: 'Forward, there! What the deuce is that man up to under the starboard cat-head?'

"The men on the forecastle rushed to the side and looked over; two of them leaned over the rail with the bight of a rope between them, and a third came running aft to the mate. 'It's Foucault, sir,' Parratt heard him say. 'He's hanged hisself from the cat-head.'

"As soon as he was off duty, Parratt made his way to his dead comrade's chest, and, opening it with his pick-lock, took out the pearl. It was now his sole property, and, as the ship was within an hour or two of her destination, he thought he had little to fear from its murdered owner. As soon as the vessel was alongside the wharf, he would slip ashore and get rid of the jewel, even if he sold it at a comparatively low price. The thing looked perfectly simple.

"In actual practice, however, it turned out quite otherwise. He began by accosting a well-dressed stranger and offering the pendant for fifty pounds; but the only reply that he got was a knowing smile and a shake of the head. When this experience had been repeated a dozen times or more, and he had been followed up and down the streets for nearly an hour by a suspicious gendarme, he began to grow anxious. He visited quite a number of ships and yachts in the harbour, and at each refusal the price of his treasure came down, until he was eager to sell it for a few francs. But still no one would have it. Everyone took it for granted that the pearl was a sham, and most of the persons whom he accosted assumed that it had been stolen. The position was getting desperate. Evening was approaching – the time of the dreaded dog-watches – and still the pearl was in his possession. Gladly would he now have given it away for nothing, but he dared not try, for this would lay him open to the strongest suspicion.

"At last, in a by-street, he came upon the shop of a curio-dealer. Putting on a careless and cheerful manner, he entered and offered the pendant for ten francs. The dealer looked at it, shook his head, and handed it back.

" 'What will you give me for it?' demanded Parratt, breaking out into a cold sweat at the prospect of a final refusal.

"The dealer felt in his pocket, drew out a couple of francs, and held them out.

" 'Very well,' said Parratt. He took the money as calmly as he could, and marched out of the shop, with a gasp of relief, leaving the pendant in the dealer's hand.

"The jewel was hung up in a glass case, and nothing more was thought about it until some ten days later, when an English tourist, who came into the shop, noticed it and took a liking to it. Thereupon the dealer offered it to him for five pounds, assuring him that it was a genuine pearl, a statement that, to his amazement, the stranger evidently believed. He was then deeply afflicted at not having asked a higher price, but the bargain had been struck, and the Englishman went off with his purchase.

"This was the story told by Captain Raggerton's friend, and I have given it to you in full detail, having read the manuscript over many times since it was given to me. No doubt you will regard it as a mere traveller's tale, and consider me a superstitious idiot for giving any credence to it."

"It certainly seems more remarkable for picturesqueness than for credibility," Thorndyke agreed. "May I ask," he continued, "whether Captain Raggerton's friend gave any explanation as to how this singular story came to his knowledge, or to that of anybody else?"

"Oh yes," replied Calverley; "I forgot to mention that the seaman, Parratt, very shortly after he had sold the pearl, fell down the hatch into the hold as the ship was unloading, and was very badly injured. He was taken to the hospital, where he died on the following day; and it was while he was lying there in a dying condition that he confessed to the murder, and gave this circumstantial account of it."

"I see," said Thorndyke; "and I understand that you accept the story as literally true?"

"Undoubtedly." Calverley flushed defiantly as he returned Thorndyke's look, and continued: "You see, I am not a man of science: therefore my beliefs are not limited to things that can be weighed and measured. There are things, Dr Thorndyke, which are outside the range of our puny intellects; things that science, with its arrogant materialism, puts aside and ignores with close-shut eyes. I prefer to believe in things which obviously exist, even though I cannot explain them. It is the humbler and, I think, the wiser attitude."

"But, my dear Fred," protested Mr Brodribb, "this is a rank fairy-tale."

Calverley turned upon the solicitor. "If you had seen what I have seen, you would not only believe: you would *know.*"

"Tell us what you have seen, then," said Mr Brodribb.

"I will, if you wish to hear it," said Calverley. "I will continue the strange history of the Mandarin's Pearl."

He lit a fresh cigarette and continued: "The night I came to Beech-hurst – that is my cousin's house, you know – a rather absurd thing happened, which I mention on account of its connection with what has followed. I had gone to my room early, and sat for some time writing letters before getting ready for bed. When I had finished my letters, I started on a tour of inspection of my room, I was then, you must remember, in a very nervous state, and it had become my habit to examine the room in which I was to sleep before undressing, looking under the bed, and in any cupboards and closets that there happened to be. Now, on looking round my new room, I perceived that there was a second door, and I at once proceeded to open it to see where it led to. As soon as I opened the door, I got a terrible start. I found myself looking into a narrow closet or passage, lined with pegs, on which the servant had hung some of my clothes; at the farther end was another door, and, as I stood looking into the closet, I observed, with startled amazement, a man standing holding the door half-open, and silently regarding me. I stood for a moment staring at him, with my heart thumping and my limbs all of a tremble; then I slammed the door and ran off to look for my cousin.

"He was in the billiard-room with Raggerton, and the pair looked up sharply as I entered.

" 'Alfred,' I said, 'where does that passage lead to out of my room?'

" 'Lead to?' said he. 'Why, it doesn't lead anywhere. It used to open into a cross corridor, but when the house was altered, the corridor was done away with, and this passage closed up. It is only a cupboard now.'

" 'Well, there's a man in it – or there was just now.'

" 'Nonsense!' he exclaimed; 'impossible! Let us go and look at the place.'

"He and Raggerton rose, and we went together to my room. As we flung open the door of the closet and looked in, we all three burst into a laugh. There were three men now looking at us from the open door at the other end, and the mystery was solved. A large mirror had been placed at the end of the closet to cover the partition which cut it off from the cross corridor.

"This incident naturally exposed me to a good deal of chaff from my cousin and Captain Raggerton; but I often wished that the mirror had not been placed there, for it happened over and over again that, going to the cupboard hurriedly, and not thinking of the mirror, I got quite a bad shock on being confronted by a figure apparently coming straight at me through an open door. In fact, it annoyed me so much, in my nervous state, that I even thought of asking my cousin to give me a different room; but, happening to refer to the matter when talking to Raggerton, I found the Captain so scornful of my cowardice that my pride was touched, and I let the affair drop.

"And now I come to a very strange occurrence, which I shall relate quite frankly, although I know beforehand that you will set me down as a liar or a lunatic. I had been away from home for a fortnight, and as I returned rather late at night, I went straight to my room. Having partly undressed, I took my clothes in one hand and a candle in the other, and opened the cupboard door. I stood for a moment looking nervously at my double, standing, candle in hand, looking at me through the open door at the other end of the passage; then I entered, and, setting the candle on a shelf, proceeded to hang up my clothes. I had hung them up, and had just reached up for the candle, when my eye was caught by something strange in the mirror. It no longer reflected the candle in my hand, but, instead of it, a large coloured paper lantern. I stood petrified with astonishment, and gazed into the mirror; and then I saw that my own reflection was changed, too; that, in place of my own figure, was that of an elderly Chinaman, who stood regarding me with stony calm.

"I must have stood for near upon a minute, unable to move and scarce able to breathe, face to face with that awful figure. At length I turned to escape, and, as I turned, he turned also, and I could see him, over my shoulder, hurrying away. As I reached the door, I halted for a moment, looking back with the door in my hand, holding the candle above my head; and even so *he* halted, looking back at me, with his hand upon the door and his lantern held above his head.

"I was so much upset that I could not go to bed for some hours, but continued to pace the room, in spite of my fatigue. Now and again I was impelled, irresistibly, to peer into the cupboard, but nothing was to be seen in the mirror save my own figure, candle in hand, peeping in at me through the half-open door. And each time that I looked into my own white, horror-stricken face, I shut the door hastily and turned away with a shudder; for the pegs, with the clothes hanging on them, seemed to call to me. I went to bed at last, and before I fell asleep I formed the resolution that, if I was spared until the next day, I would write to the British Consul at Canton, and offer to restore the pearl to the relatives of the murdered mandarin.

"On the following day I wrote and despatched the letter, after which I felt more composed, though I was haunted continually by the recollection of that stony, impassive figure; and from time to time I felt an irresistible impulse to go and look in at the door of the closet, at the mirror and the pegs with the clothes hanging from them. I told my cousin of the visitation that I had received, but he merely laughed, and was frankly incredulous; while the Captain bluntly advised me not to be a superstitious donkey.

"For some days after this I was left in peace, and began to hope that my letter had appeased the spirit of the murdered man; but on the fifth day, about six o'clock in the evening, happening to want some papers that I had left in the pocket of a coat which was hanging in the closet, I went in to get them. I took in no candle, as it was not yet dark, but left the door wide open to light me. The coat that I wanted was near the end of the closet, not more than four paces from the mirror, and as I went towards it I watched my reflection rather nervously as it advanced to meet me. I found my coat, and as I felt for the papers, I still kept a suspicious eye on my double. And, even as I looked, a most strange phenomenon appeared: the mirror seemed for an instant to darken or cloud over, and then, as it cleared again, I saw, standing dark against the light of the open door behind him, the figure of the mandarin. After a single glance, I ran out of the closet, shaking with agitation; but as I turned to shut the door, I noticed that it was my own figure that was reflected in the glass. The Chinaman had vanished in an instant.

"It now became evident that my letter had not served its purpose, and I was plunged in despair; the more so since, on this day, I felt again the dreadful impulse to go and look at the pegs on the walls of the closet. There was no mistaking the meaning of that impulse, and each time that I went, I dragged myself away reluctantly, though shivering with horror. One circumstance, indeed, encouraged me a little; the mandarin had not, on either occasion, beckoned to me as he had done to the sailors, so that perhaps some way of escape yet lay open to me.

"During the next few days I considered very earnestly what measures I could take to avert the doom that seemed to be hanging over me. The simplest plan, that of passing the pearl on to some other person, was out of the question; it would be nothing short of murder. On the other hand, I could not wait for an answer to my letter; for even if I remained alive, I felt that my reason would have given way long before the reply reached me. But while I was debating what I should do, the mandarin appeared to me again; and then, after an interval of only two days, he came to me once more. That was last night. I remained gazing at him, fascinated, with my flesh creeping, as he stood, lantern in hand, looking steadily in my face. At last he held out his hand to me, as if asking me to give him the pearl; then the mirror darkened, and he vanished in a flash; and in the place where he had stood there was my own reflection looking at me out of the glass.

"That last visitation decided me. When I left home this morning the pearl was in my pocket, and as I came over Waterloo Bridge, I leaned over the parapet and flung the thing into the water. After that I felt quite relieved for a time; I had shaken the accursed thing off without involving anyone in the curse that it carried. But presently I began to feel fresh misgivings, and the conviction has been growing upon me all day that I have done the wrong thing. I have only placed it for ever beyond the reach of its owner, whereas I ought to have burnt it, after the Chinese fashion, so that its non-material essence could have joined the spiritual body of him to whom it had belonged when both were clothed with material substance.

"But it can't be altered now. For good or for evil, the thing is done, and God alone knows what the end of it will be."

As he concluded, Calverley uttered a deep sigh, and covered his face with his slender, delicate hands. For a space we were all silent and, I think, deeply moved; for, grotesquely unreal as the whole thing was, there was a pathos, and even a tragedy, in it that we all felt to be very real indeed.

Suddenly Mr Brodribb started and looked at his watch.

"Good gracious, Calverley, we shall lose our train."

The young man pulled himself together and stood up. "We shall just do it if we go at once," said he. "Goodbye," he added, shaking Thorndyke's hand and mine. "You have been very patient, and I have been rather prosy, I am afraid. Come along, Mr Brodribb."

Thorndyke and I followed them out on to the landing, and I heard my colleague say to the solicitor in a low tone, but very earnestly: "Get him away from that house, Brodribb, and don't let him out of your sight for a moment."

I did not catch the solicitor's reply, if he made any, but when we were back in our room I noticed that Thorndyke was more agitated than I had ever seen him.

"I ought not to have let them go," he exclaimed. "Confound me! If I had had a grain of wit, I should have made them lose their train."

He lit his pipe and fell to pacing the room with long strides, his eyes bent on the floor with an expression sternly reflective. At last, finding him hopelessly taciturn, I knocked out my pipe and went to bed.

As I was dressing on the following morning, Thorndyke entered my room. His face was grave even to sternness, and he held a telegram in his hand.

"I am going to Weybridge this morning," he said shortly, holding the "flimsy" out to me. "Shall you come?"

I took the paper from him, and read:

"Come, for God's sake! FC is dead. You will understand.
                                          – Brodribb."

I handed him back the telegram, too much shocked for a moment to speak. The whole dreadful tragedy summed up in that curt message rose before me in an instant, and a wave of deep pity swept over me at this miserable end to the sad, empty life.

"What an awful thing, Thorndyke!" I exclaimed at length. "To be killed by a mere grotesque delusion."

"Do you think so?" he asked dryly. "Well, we shall see; but you will come?"

"Yes," I replied; and as he retired, I proceeded hurriedly to finish dressing.

Half an hour later, as we rose from a rapid breakfast, Polton came into the room, carrying a small roll-up case of tools and a bunch of skeleton keys.

"Will you have them in a bag, sir?" he asked.

"No," replied Thorndyke; "in my overcoat pocket. Oh, and here is a note, Polton, which I want you to take round to Scotland Yard. It is to the Assistant Commissioner, and you are to make sure that it is in the right hands before you leave. And here is a telegram to Mr Brodribb."

He dropped the keys and the tool-case into his pocket, and we went down together to the waiting hansom.

At Weybridge Station we found Mr Brodribb pacing the platform in a state of extreme dejection. He brightened up somewhat when he saw us, and wrung our hands with emotional heartiness.

"It was very good of you both to come at a moment's notice," he said warmly, "and I feel your kindness very much. You understood, of course, Thorndyke?"

"Yes," Thorndyke replied. "I suppose the mandarin beckoned to him."

Mr Brodribb turned with a look of surprise. "How did you guess that?" he asked; and then, without waiting for a reply, he took from his pocket a note, which he handed to my colleague. "The poor old fellow left this for me," he said. "The servant found it on his dressing-table."

Thorndyke glanced through the note and passed it to me. It consisted of but a few words, hurriedly written in a tremulous hand.

"He has beckoned to me, and I must go. Goodbye, dear old friend."

"How does his cousin take the matter?" asked Thorndyke.

"He doesn't know of it yet," replied the lawyer. "Alfred and Raggerton went out after an early breakfast, to cycle over to Guildford on some business or other, and they have not returned yet. The catastrophe was discovered soon after they left. The maid went to his room with a cup of tea, and was astonished to find that his bed had not been slept in. She ran down in alarm and reported to the butler, who went up at once and searched the room; but he could find no trace of the missing one, except my note, until it occurred to him to look in the cupboard. As he opened the door he got rather a start from his own reflection in the mirror; and then he saw poor Fred hanging from one of the pegs near the end of the closet, close to the glass. It's a melancholy affair – but here is the house, and here is the butler waiting for us. Mr Alfred is not back yet, then, Stevens?"

"No, sir." The white-faced, frightened-looking man had evidently been waiting at the gate from distaste of the house, and he now walked back with manifest relief at our arrival. When we entered the house, he ushered us without remark up on to the first-floor, and, preceding us along a corridor, halted near the end. "That's the room, sir," said he; and without another word he turned and went down the stairs.

We entered the room, and Mr Brodribb followed on tiptoe, looking about him fearfully, and casting awe-struck glances at the shrouded form on the bed. To the latter Thorndyke advanced, and gently drew back the sheet.

"You'd better not look, Brodribb," said he, as he bent over the corpse. He felt the limbs and examined the cord, which still remained round the neck, its raggedly-severed end testifying to the terror of the servants who had cut down the body. Then he replaced the sheet and looked at his watch. "It happened at about three o'clock in the morning," said he. "He must have struggled with the impulse for some time, poor fellow! Now let us look at the cupboard."

We went together to a door in the corner of the room, and, as we opened it, we were confronted by three figures, apparently looking in at us through an open door at the other end.

"It is really rather startling," said the lawyer, in a subdued voice, looking almost apprehensively at the three figures that advanced to meet us. "The poor lad ought never to have been here."

It was certainly an eerie place, and I could not but feel, as we walked down the dark, narrow passage, with those other three dimly-seen figures silently coming towards us, and mimicking our every gesture, that it was no place for a nervous, superstitious man like poor Fred Calverley. Close to the end of the long row of pegs was one from which hung an end of stout box-cord, and to this Mr Brodribb pointed with an awe-struck gesture. But Thorndyke gave it only a brief glance, and then walked up to the mirror, which he proceeded to examine minutely. It was a very large glass, nearly seven feet high, extending the full width of the closet, and reaching to within a foot of the floor; and it seemed to have been let into the partition from behind, for, both above and below, the woodwork was in front of it. While I was making these observations, I watched Thorndyke with no little curiosity. First he rapped his knuckles on the glass; then he lighted a wax match, and, holding it close to the mirror, carefully watched the reflection of the flame. Finally, laying his cheek on the glass, he held the match at arm's length, still close to the mirror, and looked at the reflection along the surface. Then he blew out the match and walked back into the room, shutting the cupboard door as we emerged.

"I think," said he, "that as we shall all undoubtedly be supœnaed by the coroner, it would be well to put together a few notes of the facts. I see there is a writing-table by the window, and I would propose that you, Brodribb, just jot down a *précis* of the statement that you heard last night, while Jervis notes down the exact condition of the body. While you are doing this, I will take a look round."

"We might find a more cheerful place to write in," grumbled Mr Brodribb; "however – "

Without finishing the sentence, he sat down at the table, and, having found some sermon paper, dipped a pen in the ink by way of encouraging his thoughts. At this moment Thorndyke quietly slipped out of the room, and I proceeded to make a detailed examination of the body; in which occupation I was interrupted at intervals by requests from the lawyer that I should refresh his memory.

We had been occupied thus for about a quarter of an hour, when a quick step was heard outside, the door was opened abruptly, and a man burst into the room. Brodribb rose and held out his hand.

"This is a sad home-coming for you, Alfred," said he.

"Yes, my God!" the newcomer exclaimed. "It's awful."

He looked askance at the corpse on the bed, and wiped his forehead with his handkerchief. Alfred Calverley was not extremely prepossessing. Like his cousin, he was obviously neurotic, but there were signs of dissipation in his face, which, just now, was pale and ghastly, and wore an expression of abject fear. Moreover, his entrance was accompanied by that of a perceptible odour of brandy.

He had walked over, without noticing me, to the writing-table, and as he stood there, talking in subdued tones with the lawyer, I suddenly found Thorndyke at my side. He had stolen in noiselessly through the door that Calverley had left open.

"Show him Brodribb's note," he whispered, "and then make him go in and look at the peg."

With this mysterious request, he slipped out of the room as silently as he had come, unperceived either by Calverley or the lawyer.

"Has Captain Raggerton returned with you?" Brodribb was inquiring.

"No, he has gone into the town," was the reply; "but he won't be long. This will be a frightful shock to him."

At this point I stepped forward. "Have you shown Mr Calverley the extraordinary letter that the deceased left for you?" I asked.

"What letter was that?" demanded Calverley, with a start.

Mr Brodribb drew forth the note and handed it to him. As he read it through, Calverley turned white to the lips, and the paper trembled in his hand.

" 'He has beckoned to me, and I must go,'" he read. Then, with a furtive glance at the lawyer: "Who had beckoned? What did he mean?"

Mr Brodribb briefly explained the meaning of the allusion, adding: "I thought you knew all about it."

"Yes, yes," said Calverley, with some confusion; "I remember the matter now you mention it. But it's all so dreadful and bewildering."

At this point I again interposed. "There is a question," I said, "that may be of some importance. It refers to the cord with which the poor fellow hanged himself. Can you identify that cord, Mr Calverley?"

"I!" he exclaimed, staring at me, and wiping the sweat from his white face; "how should I? Where is the cord?"

"Part of it is still hanging from the peg in the closet. Would you mind looking at it?"

"If you would very kindly fetch it – you know I – er – naturally – have a – "

"It must not be disturbed before the inquest," said I; "but surely you are not afraid – "

"I didn't say I was afraid," he retorted angrily. "Why should I be?"

With a strange, tremulous swagger, he strode across to the closet, flung open the door, and plunged in.

A moment later we heard a shout of horror, and he rushed out, livid and gasping.

"What is it, Calverley?" exclaimed Mr Brodribb, starting up in alarm.

But Calverley was incapable of speech. Dropping limply into a chair, he gazed at us for a while in silent terror; then he fell back uttering a wild shriek of laughter.

Mr Brodribb looked at him in amazement. "What is it, Calverley?" he asked again.

As no answer was forthcoming, he stepped across to the open door of the closet and entered, peering curiously before him. Then he, too, uttered a startled exclamation, and backed out hurriedly, looking pale and flurried.

"Bless my soul!" he ejaculated. "Is the place bewitched?"

He sat down heavily and stared at Calverley, who was still shaking with hysteric laughter; while I, now consumed with curiosity, walked over to the closet to discover the cause of their singular behaviour. As I flung open the door, which the lawyer had closed, I must confess to being very considerably startled; for though the reflection of the open door was plain enough in the mirror, my own reflection was replaced by that of a Chinaman. After a momentary pause of astonishment, I entered the closet and walked towards the mirror; and simultaneously the figure of the

Chinaman entered and walked towards me. I had advanced more than halfway down the closet when suddenly the mirror darkened; there was a whirling flash, the Chinaman vanished in an instant, and, as I reached the glass, my own reflection faced me.

I turned back into the room pretty completely enlightened, and looked at Calverley with a new-born distaste. He still sat facing the bewildered lawyer, one moment sobbing convulsively, the next yelping with hysteric laughter. He was not an agreeable spectacle, and when, a few moments later, Thorndyke entered the room, and halted by the door with a stare of disgust, I was moved to join him. But at this juncture a man pushed past Thorndyke, and, striding up to Calverley, shook him roughly by the arm.

"Stop that row!" he exclaimed furiously. "Do you hear? Stop it!"

"I can't help it, Raggerton," gasped Calverley. "He gave me such a turn – the mandarin, you know."

"What!" ejaculated Raggerton.

He dashed across to the closet, looked in, and turned upon Calverley with a snarl. Then he walked out of the room.

"Brodribb," said Thorndyke, "I should like to have a word with you and Jervis outside." Then, as we followed him out on to the landing, he continued: "I have something rather interesting to show you. It is in here."

He softly opened an adjoining door, and we looked into a small unfurnished room. A projecting closet occupied one side of it, and at the door of the closet stood Captain Raggerton, with his hand upon the key. He turned upon us fiercely, though with a look of alarm, and demanded: "What is the meaning of this intrusion? and who the deuce are you? Do you know that this is my private room?"

"I suspected that it was," Thorndyke replied quietly. "Those will be your properties in the closet, then?"

Raggerton turned pale, but continued to bluster. "Do I understand that you have dared to break into my private closet?" he demanded.

"I have inspected it," replied Thorndyke, "and I may remark that it is useless to wrench at that key, because I have hampered the lock."

"The devil you have!" shouted Raggerton.

"Yes; you see, I am expecting a police-officer with a search warrant, so I wished to keep everything intact."

Raggerton turned livid with mingled fear and rage. He stalked up to Thorndyke with a threatening air, but, suddenly altering his mind, exclaimed, "I must see to this!" and flung out of the room.

Thorndyke took a key from his pocket, and, having locked the door, turned to the closet. Having taken out the key to unhamper the lock with a stout wire, he reinserted it and unlocked the door. As we entered, we found ourselves in a narrow closet, similar to the one in the other room, but darker, owing to the absence of a mirror. A few clothes hung from the pegs, and when Thorndyke had lit a candle that stood on a shelf, we could see more of the details.

"Here are some of the properties," said Thorndyke. He pointed to a peg from which hung a long, blue silk gown of Chinese make, a mandarin's cap, with a pigtail attached to it, and a beautifully-made papier-mâché mask. "Observe," said Thorndyke, taking the latter down and exhibiting a label on the inside, marked "Renouard à Paris", "no trouble has been spared."

He took off his coat, slipped on the gown, the mask, and the cap, and was, in a moment, in that dim light, transformed into the perfect semblance of a Chinaman.

"By taking a little more time," he remarked, pointing to a pair of Chinese shoes and a large paper lantern, "the make-up could be rendered more complete; but this seems to have answered for our friend Alfred."

"But," said Mr Brodribb, as Thorndyke shed the disguise, "still, I don't understand – "

"I will make it clear to you in a moment," said Thorndyke. He walked to the end of the closet, and, tapping the right-hand wall, said: "This is the back of the mirror. You see that it is hung on massive well-oiled hinges, and is supported on this large, rubber-tyred castor, which evidently has ball bearings. You observe three black cords running along the wall; and passing through those pulleys above. Now, when I pull this cord, notice what happens."

He pulled one cord firmly, and immediately the mirror swung noiselessly inwards on its great castor, until it stood diagonally across the closet, where it was stopped by a rubber buffer.

"Bless my soul!" exclaimed Mr Brodribb. "What an extraordinary thing!"

The effect was certainly very strange, for, the mirror being now exactly diagonal to the two closets they appeared to be a single, continuous passage, with a door at either end. On going up to the mirror, we found that the opening which it had occupied was filled by a sheet of plain glass, evidently placed there as a precaution to prevent any person from walking through from one closet into the other, and so discovering the trick.

"It's all very puzzling," said Mr Brodribb; "I don't clearly understand it now."

"Let us finish here," replied Thorndyke, "and then I will explain. Notice this black curtain. When I pull the second cord, it slides across the closet and cuts off the light. The mirror now reflects nothing into the other closet; it simply appears dark. And now I pull the third cord."

He did so, and the mirror swung noiselessly back into its place.

"There is only one other thing to observe before we go out," said Thorndyke, "and that is this other mirror standing with its face to the wall. This, of course, is the one that Fred Calverley originally saw at the end of the closet; it has since been removed, and the larger swinging glass put in its place. And now," he continued, when we came out into the room, "let me explain the mechanism in detail. It was obvious to me, when I heard poor Fred Calverley's story, that the mirror was 'faked', and I drew a diagram of the probable arrangement, which turns out to be correct. Here it is." He took a sheet of paper from his pocket and handed it to the lawyer. "There are two sketches. Sketch 1 shows the mirror in its ordinary position, closing the end of the closet. A person standing at A, of course, sees his reflection facing him at, apparently, A 1. Sketch 2 shows the mirror swung across. Now a person standing at A does not see his own reflection at all; but if some other person is standing in the other closet at B, A sees the reflection of B apparently at B 1 – that is, in the identical position that his own reflection occupied when the mirror was straight across."

"I see now," said Brodribb; "but who set up this apparatus, and why was it done?"

"Let me ask you a question," said Thorndyke. "Is Alfred Calverley the next-of-kin?"

"No; there is Fred's younger brother. But I may say that Fred has made a will quite recently very much in Alfred's favour."

"There is the explanation, then," said Thorndyke. "These two scoundrels have conspired to drive the poor fellow to suicide, and Raggerton was clearly the leading spirit. He was evidently concocting some story with which to work on poor Fred's superstitions when the mention of the Chinaman on the steamer gave him his cue. He then invented the very picturesque story of the murdered mandarin and the stolen pearl. You remember that these 'visitations' did not begin until after that story had been told, and Fred had been absent from the house on a visit. Evidently, during his absence, Raggerton took down the original mirror, and substituted this swinging arrangement; and at the same time procured the Chinaman's dress and mask from the theatrical property dealers. No doubt he reckoned on being able quietly to remove the swinging glass and other properties and replace the original mirror before the inquest."

"By God!" exclaimed Mr Brodribb, "it's the most infamous, cowardly plot I have ever heard of. They shall go to gaol for it, the villains, as sure as I am alive."

But in this Mr Brodribb was mistaken; for immediately on finding themselves detected, the two conspirators had left the house, and by nightfall were safely across the Channel; and the only satisfaction that the lawyer obtained was the setting aside of the will on facts disclosed at the inquest.

As to Thorndyke, he has never to this day forgiven himself for having allowed Fred Calverley to go home to his death.

SEVEN

The Aluminium Dagger

The "urgent call" – the instant, peremptory summons to professional duty – is an experience that appertains to the medical rather than the legal practitioner, and I had supposed, when I abandoned the clinical side of my profession in favour of the forensic, that henceforth I should know it no more; that the interrupted meal, the broken leisure, and the jangle of the night-bell, were things of the past; but in practice it was otherwise. The medical jurist is, so to speak, on the borderland of the two professions, and exposed to the vicissitudes of each calling, and so it happened from time to time that the professional services of my colleague or myself were demanded at a moment's notice. And thus it was in the case that I am about to relate.

The sacred rite of the "tub" had been duly performed, and the freshly-dried person of the present narrator was about to be insinuated into the first instalment of clothing, when a hurried step was heard upon the stair, and the voice of our laboratory assistant, Polton, arose at my colleague's door.

"There's a gentleman downstairs, sir, who says he must see you instantly on most urgent business. He seems to be in a rare twitter, sir – "

Polton was proceeding to descriptive particulars, when a second and more hurried step became audible, and a strange voice addressed Thorndyke.

"I have come to beg your immediate assistance, sir; a most dreadful thing has happened. A horrible murder has been committed. Can you come with me now?"

"I will be with you almost immediately," said Thorndyke. "Is the victim quite dead?"

"Quite. Cold and stiff. The police think – "

"Do the police know that you have come for me?" interrupted Thorndyke.

"Yes. Nothing is to be done until you arrive."

"Very well. I will be ready in a few minutes."

"And if you would wait downstairs, sir," Polton added persuasively, "I could help the doctor to get ready."

With this crafty appeal, he lured the intruder back to the sitting-room, and shortly after stole softly up the stairs with a small breakfast-tray, the contents of which he deposited firmly in our respective rooms, with a few timely words on the folly of "undertaking murders on an empty stomach". Thorndyke and I had meanwhile clothed ourselves with a celerity known only to medical practitioners and quick-change artists, and in a few minutes descended the stairs together, calling in at the laboratory for a few appliances that Thorndyke usually took with him on a visit of investigation.

As we entered the sitting-room, our visitor, who was feverishly pacing up and down, seized his hat with a gasp of relief. "You are ready to come?" he asked. "My carriage is at the door;" and, without waiting for an answer, he hurried out, and rapidly preceded us down the stairs.

The carriage was a roomy brougham, which fortunately accommodated the three of us, and as soon as we had entered and shut the door, the coachman whipped up his horse and drove off at a smart trot.

"I had better give you some account of the circumstances, as we go," said our agitated friend. "In the first place, my name is Curtis, Henry Curtis; here is my card. Ah! and here is another card, which I should have given you before. My solicitor, Mr Marchmont, was with me when I made this dreadful discovery, and he sent me to you. He remained in the rooms to see that nothing is disturbed until you arrive."

"That was wise of him," said Thorndyke. "But now tell us exactly what has occurred."

"I will," said Mr Curtis. "The murdered man was my brother-in-law, Alfred Hartridge, and I am sorry to say he was – well, he was a bad man. It grieves me to speak of him thus – *de mortuis*, you know – but, still, we must deal with the facts, even though they be painful."

"Undoubtedly," agreed Thorndyke.

"I have had a great deal of very unpleasant correspondence with him – Marchmont will tell you about that – and yesterday I left a note for him, asking for an interview, to settle the business, naming eight o'clock this morning as the hour, because I had to leave town before noon. He replied, in a very singular letter, that he would see me at that hour, and Mr Marchmont very kindly consented to accompany me. Accordingly, we went to his chambers together this morning, arriving punctually at eight o'clock. We rang the bell several times, and knocked loudly at the door, but as there was no response, we went down and spoke to the hall-porter. This man, it seems, had already noticed, from the courtyard, that the electric lights were full on in Mr Hartridge's sitting-room, as they had been all night, according to the statement of the night-porter; so now, suspecting that something was wrong, he came up with us, and rang the bell and battered at the door. Then, as there was still no sign of life within, he inserted his duplicate key and tried to open the door – unsuccessfully, however, as it proved to be bolted on the inside. Thereupon the porter fetched a constable, and, after a consultation, we decided that we were justified in breaking open the door; the porter produced a crowbar, and by our united efforts the door was eventually burst open. We entered, and – my God! Dr Thorndyke, what a terrible sight it was that met our eyes! My brother-in-law was lying dead on the floor of the sitting-room. He had been stabbed – stabbed to death; and the dagger had not even been withdrawn. It was still sticking out of his back."

He mopped his face with his handkerchief, and was about to continue his account of the catastrophe when the carriage entered a quiet side-street between Westminster and Victoria, and drew up before a block of tall, new, red-brick buildings. A flurried hall-porter ran out to open the door, and we alighted opposite the main entrance.

"My brother-in-law's chambers are on the second-floor," said Mr Curtis. "We can go up in the lift."

The porter had hurried before us, and already stood with his hand upon the rope. We entered the lift, and in a few seconds were discharged on to the second-floor, the porter, with furtive curiosity, following us down the corridor. At the end of the passage was a half-open door, considerably battered and bruised. Above the door, painted in white lettering, was the inscription, "Mr Hartridge"; and through the doorway protruded the rather foxy countenance of Inspector Badger.

"I am glad you have come, sir," said he, as he recognized my colleague. "Mr Marchmont is sitting inside like a watch-dog, and he growls if any of us even walks across the room."

The words formed a complaint, but there was a certain geniality in the speaker's manner which made me suspect that Inspector Badger was already navigating his craft on a lee shore.

We entered a small lobby or hall, and from thence passed into the sitting-room, where we found Mr Marchmont keeping his vigil, in company with a constable and a uniformed inspector. The three rose softly as we entered, and greeted us in a whisper; and then, with one accord, we all looked towards the other end of the room, and so remained for a time without speaking.

There was, in the entire aspect of the room, something very grim and dreadful. An atmosphere of tragic mystery enveloped the most commonplace objects; and sinister suggestions lurked in the most familiar appearances. Especially impressive was the air of suspense – of ordinary, every-day life suddenly arrested – cut short in the twinkling of an eye. The electric lamps, still burning dim and red, though the summer sunshine streamed in through the windows; the half-emptied tumbler and open book by the empty chair, had each its whispered message of swift and sudden disaster, as had the hushed voices and stealthy movements of the waiting men, and, above all, an awesome shape that was but a few hours since a living man, and that now sprawled, prone and motionless, on the floor.

"This is a mysterious affair," observed Inspector Badger, breaking the silence at length, "though it is clear enough up to a certain point. The body tells its own story."

We stepped across and looked down at the corpse. It was that of a somewhat elderly man, and lay, on an open space of floor before the fireplace, face downwards, with the arms extended. The slender hilt of a dagger projected from the back below the left shoulder, and, with the exception of a trace of blood upon the lips, this was the only indication of the mode of death. A little way from the body a clock-key lay on the carpet, and, glancing up at the clock on the mantelpiece, I perceived that the glass front was open.

"You see," pursued the inspector, noting my glance, "he was standing in front of the fireplace, winding the clock. Then the murderer stole up behind him – the noise of the turning key must have covered his movements – and stabbed him. And you see, from the position of the dagger on the left side of the back, that the murderer must have been left-handed. That is all clear enough. What is not clear is how he got in, and how he got out again."

"The body has not been moved, I suppose," said Thorndyke.

"No. We sent for Dr Egerton, the police-surgeon, and he certified that the man was dead. He will be back presently to see you and arrange about the *post-mortem.*"

"Then," said Thorndyke, "we will not disturb the body till he comes, except to take the temperature and dust the dagger-hilt."

He took from his bag a long, registering chemical thermometer and an insufflator or powder-blower. The former he introduced under the dead man's clothing against the abdomen, and with the latter blew a stream of fine yellow powder on to the black leather handle of the dagger. Inspector Badger stooped eagerly to examine the handle, as Thorndyke blew away the powder that had settled evenly on the surface.

"No finger-prints," said he, in a disappointed tone. "He must have worn gloves. But that inscription gives a pretty broad hint."

He pointed, as he spoke, to the metal guard of the dagger, on which was engraved, in clumsy lettering, the single word, "Traditore".

"That's the Italian for 'traitor'," continued the inspector, "and I got some information from the porter that fits in with that suggestion. We'll have him in presently, and you shall hear."

"Meanwhile," said Thorndyke, "as the position of the body may be of importance in the inquiry, I will take one or two photographs and make a rough plan to scale. Nothing has been moved, you say? Who opened the windows?"

"They were open when we came in," said Mr Marchmont. "Last night was very hot, you remember. Nothing whatever has been moved."

Thorndyke produced from his bag a small folding camera, a telescopic tripod, a surveyor's measuring-tape, a boxwood scale, and a sketch-block. He set up the camera in a corner, and exposed a plate, taking a general view of the room, and including the corpse. Then he moved to the door and made a second exposure.

"Will you stand in front of the clock, Jervis," he said, "and raise your hand as if winding it? Thanks; keep like that while I expose a plate."

I remained thus, in the position that the dead man was assumed to have occupied at the moment of the murder, while the plate was exposed, and then, before I moved, Thorndyke marked the position of my feet with a blackboard chalk. He next set up the tripod over the chalk marks, and took two photographs from that position, and finally photographed the body itself.

The photographic operations being concluded, he next proceeded, with remarkable skill and rapidity, to lay out on the sketch-block a ground-plan of the room, showing the exact position of the various objects, on a scale of a quarter of an inch to the foot – a process that the inspector was inclined to view with some impatience.

"You don't spare trouble, Doctor," he remarked; "nor time either," he added, with a significant glance at his watch.

"No," answered Thorndyke, as he detached the finished sketch from the block; "I try to collect all the facts that may bear on a case. They may prove worthless, or they may turn out of vital importance; one never knows beforehand, so I collect them all. But here, I think, is Dr Egerton."

The police-surgeon greeted Thorndyke with respectful cordiality, and we proceeded at once to the examination of the body. Drawing out the thermometer, my colleague noted the reading, and passed the instrument to Dr Egerton.

"Dead about ten hours," remarked the latter, after a glance at it. "This was a very determined and mysterious murder."

"Very," said Thorndyke. "Feel that dagger, Jervis."

I touched the hilt, and felt the characteristic grating of bone.

"It is through the edge of a rib!" I exclaimed.

"Yes; it must have been used with extraordinary force. And you notice that the clothing is screwed up slightly, as if the blade had been rotated as it was driven in. That is a very peculiar feature, especially when taken together with the violence of the blow."

"It is singular, certainly," said Dr Egerton, "though I don't know that it helps us much. Shall we withdraw the dagger before moving the body?"

"Certainly," replied Thorndyke, "or the movement may produce fresh injuries. But wait." He took a piece of string from his pocket, and, having drawn the dagger out a couple of inches, stretched the string in a line parallel to the flat of the blade. Then, giving me the ends to hold, he drew the weapon out completely. As the blade emerged, the twist in the clothing disappeared. "Observe," said he, "that the string gives the direction of the wound, and that the cut in the clothing no longer coincides with it. There is quite a considerable angle, which is the measure of the rotation of the blade."

"Yes, it is odd," said Dr Egerton, "though, as I said, I doubt that it helps us."

"At present," Thorndyke rejoined dryly, "we are noting the facts."

"Quite so," agreed the other, reddening slightly; "and perhaps we had better move the body to the bedroom, and make a preliminary inspection of the wound."

We carried the corpse into the bedroom, and, having examined the wound without eliciting anything new, covered the remains with a sheet, and returned to the sitting-room.

"Well, gentlemen," said the inspector, "you have examined the body and the wound, and you have measured the floor and the furniture, and taken photographs, and made a plan, but we don't seem much more forward. Here's a man murdered in his rooms. There is only one entrance to the flat, and that was bolted on the inside at the time of the murder. The windows are some forty feet from the ground; there is no rain-pipe near any of them; they are set flush in the wall, and there isn't a foothold for a fly on any part of that wall. The grates are modern, and there isn't room for a good-sized cat to crawl up any of the chimneys. Now, the question is, how did the murderer get in, and how did he get out again?"

"Still," said Mr Marchmont, "the fact is that he did get in, and that he is not here now; and therefore he must have got out; and therefore it must have been possible for him to get out. And, further, it must be possible to discover how he got out."

The inspector smiled sourly, but made no reply.

"The circumstances," said Thorndyke, "appear to have been these: The deceased seems to have been alone; there is no trace of a second occupant of the room, and only one half-emptied tumbler on the table. He was sitting reading when apparently he noticed that the clock had stopped – at ten minutes to twelve;

he laid his book, face downwards, on the table, and rose to wind the clock, and as he was winding it he met his death."

"By a stab dealt by a left-handed man, who crept up behind him on tiptoe," added the inspector.

Thorndyke nodded. "That would seem to be so," he said. "But now let us call in the porter, and hear what he has to tell us."

The custodian was not difficult to find, being, in fact, engaged at that moment in a survey of the premises through the slit of the letter-box.

"Do you know what persons visited these rooms last night?" Thorndyke asked him, when he entered, looking somewhat sheepish.

"A good many were in and out of the building," was the answer, "but I can't say if any of them came to this flat. I saw Miss Curtis pass in about nine."

"My daughter!" exclaimed Mr Curtis, with a start. "I didn't know that."

"She left about nine-thirty," the porter added.

"Do you know what she came about?" asked the inspector.

"I can guess," replied Mr Curtis.

"Then don't say," interrupted Mr Marchmont. "Answer no questions."

"You're very close, Mr Marchmont," said the inspector; "we are not suspecting the young lady. We don't ask, for instance, if she is left-handed."

He glanced craftily at Mr Curtis as he made this remark, and I noticed that our client suddenly turned deathly pale, whereupon the inspector looked away again quickly, as though he had not observed the change.

"Tell us about those Italians again," he said, addressing the porter. "When did the first of them come here?"

"About a week ago," was the reply. "He was a common-looking man – looked like an organ-grinder – and he brought a note to my lodge. It was in a dirty envelope, and was addressed 'Mr Hartridge, Esq., Brackenhurst Mansions', in a very bad handwriting.

The man gave me the note and asked me to give it to Mr Hartridge; then he went away, and I took the note up and dropped it into the letter-box."

"What happened next?"

"Why, the very next day an old hag of an Italian woman – one of them fortune-telling swines with a cage of birds on a stand – came and set up just by the main doorway. I soon sent her packing, but, bless you! she was back again in ten minutes, birds and all. I sent her off again – I kept on sending her off, and she kept on coming back, until I was reg'lar wore to a thread."

"You seem to have picked up a bit since then," remarked the inspector with a grin and a glance at the sufferer's very pronounced bow-window.

"Perhaps I have," the custodian replied haughtily. "Well, the next day there was a ice-cream man – a reg'lar waster, *he* was. Stuck outside as if he was froze to the pavement. Kept giving the errand-boys tasters, and when I tried to move him on, he told me not to obstruct his business. Business, indeed! Well, there them boys stuck, one after the other, wiping their tongues round the bottoms of them glasses, until I was fit to bust with aggravation. And *he* kept me going all day.

"Then, the day after that there was a barrel-organ, with a mangy-looking monkey on it. He was the worst of all. Profane, too, *he* was. Kept mixing up sacred tunes and comic songs: 'Rock of Ages', 'Bill Bailey', 'Cujus Animal', and 'Over the Garden Wall'. And when I tried to move him on, that little blighter of a monkey made a run at my leg; and then the man grinned and started playing, 'Wait till the Clouds roll by'. I tell you, it was fair sickening."

He wiped his brow at the recollection, and the inspector smiled appreciatively.

"And that was the last of them?" said the latter; and as the porter nodded sulkily, he asked: "Should you recognize the note that the Italian gave you?"

"I should," answered the porter with frosty dignity.

The inspector bustled out of the room, and returned a minute later with a letter-case in his hand.

"This was in his breast-pocket," said he, laying the bulging case on the table, and drawing up a chair. "Now, here are three letters tied together. Ah! this will be the one." He untied the tape, and held out a dirty envelope addressed in a sprawling, illiterate hand to "Mr Hartridge, Esq." "Is that the note the Italian gave you?"

The porter examined it critically. "Yes," said he; "that is the one."

The inspector drew the letter out of the envelope, and, as he opened it, his eyebrows went up.

"What do you make of that, Doctor?" he said, handing the sheet to Thorndyke.

Thorndyke regarded it for a while in silence, with deep attention. Then he carried it to the window, and, taking his lens from his pocket, examined the paper closely, first with the low power, and then with the highly magnifying Coddington attachment.

"I should have thought you could see that with the naked eye," said the inspector, with a sly grin at me. "It's a pretty bold design."

"Yes," replied Thorndyke; "a very interesting production. What do you say, Mr Marchmont?"

The solicitor took the note, and I looked over his shoulder. It was certainly a curious production. Written in red ink, on the commonest notepaper, and in the same sprawling hand as the address, was the following message: "You are given six days to do what is just. By the sign above, know what to expect if you fail." The sign referred to was a skull and crossbones, very neatly, but rather unskilfully, drawn at the top of the paper.

"This," said Mr Marchmont, handing the document to Mr Curtis, "explains the singular letter that he wrote yesterday. You have it with you, I think?"

"Yes," replied Mr Curtis; "here it is."

He produced a letter from his pocket, and read aloud:

" 'Yes: come if you like, though it is an ungodly hour. Your threatening letters have caused me great amusement. They are worthy of Sadler's Wells in its prime.

" 'Alfred Hartridge.' "

"Was Mr Hartridge ever in Italy?" asked Inspector Badger.

"Oh yes," replied Mr Curtis. "He stayed at Capri nearly the whole of last year."

"Why, then, that gives us our clue. Look here. Here are these two other letters; EC postmark – Saffron Hill is EC. And just look at that!"

He spread out the last of the mysterious letters, and we saw that, besides the *memento mori*, it contained only three words: "Beware! Remember Capri!"

"If you have finished, Doctor, I'll be off and have a look round Little Italy. Those four Italians oughtn't to be difficult to find, and we've got the porter here to identify them."

"Before you go," said Thorndyke, "there are two little matters that I should like to settle. One is the dagger: it is in your pocket, I think. May I have a look at it?"

The inspector rather reluctantly produced the dagger and handed it to my colleague.

"A very singular weapon, this," said Thorndyke, regarding the dagger thoughtfully, and turning it about to view its different parts. "Singular both in shape and material. I have never seen an aluminium hilt before, and bookbinder's morocco is a little unusual."

"The aluminium was for lightness," explained the inspector, "and it was made narrow to carry up the sleeve, I expect."

"Perhaps so," said Thorndyke.

He continued his examination, and presently, to the inspector's delight, brought forth his pocket lens.

"I never saw such a man!" exclaimed the jocose detective. "His motto ought to be, 'We magnify thee.' I suppose he'll measure it next."

The inspector was not mistaken. Having made a rough sketch of the weapon on his block, Thorndyke produced from his bag a folding rule and a delicate calliper-gauge. With these instruments he proceeded, with extraordinary care and precision, to take the dimensions of the various parts of the dagger, entering each measurement in its place on the sketch, with a few brief, descriptive details.

"The other matter," said he at length, handing the dagger back to the inspector, "refers to the houses opposite."

He walked to the window, and looked out at the backs of a row of tall buildings similar to the one we were in. They were about thirty yards distant, and were separated from us by a piece of ground, planted with shrubs and intersected by gravel paths.

"If any of those rooms were occupied last night," continued Thorndyke, "we might obtain an actual eyewitness of the crime. This room was brilliantly lighted, and all the blinds were up, so that an observer at any of those windows could see right into the room, and very distinctly, too. It might be worth inquiring into."

"Yes, that's true," said the inspector; "though I expect, if any of them have seen anything, they will come forward quick enough when they read the report in the papers. But I must be off now, and I shall have to lock you out of the rooms."

As we went down the stairs, Mr Marchmont announced his intention of calling on us in the evening, "unless," he added, "you want any information from me now."

"I do," said Thorndyke. "I want to know who is interested in this man's death."

"That," replied Marchmont, "is rather a queer story. Let us take a turn in that garden that we saw from the window. We shall be quite private there."

He beckoned to Mr Curtis, and, when the inspector had departed with the police-surgeon, we induced the porter to let us into the garden.

"The question that you asked," Mr Marchmont began, looking up curiously at the tall houses opposite, "is very simply answered. The only person immediately interested in the death of Alfred Hartridge is his executor and sole legatee, a man named Leonard Wolfe. He is no relation of the deceased, merely a friend, but he inherits the entire estate – about twenty thousand pounds. The circumstances are these: Alfred Hartridge was the elder of two brothers, of whom the younger, Charles, died before his father, leaving a widow and three children. Fifteen years ago the father died, leaving the whole of his property to Alfred, with the understanding that he should support his brother's family and make the children his heirs."

"Was there no will?" asked Thorndyke.

"Under great pressure from the friends of his son's widow, the old man made a will shortly before he died; but he was then very old and rather childish, so the will was contested by Alfred, on the grounds of undue influence, and was ultimately set aside. Since then Alfred Hartridge has not paid a penny towards the support of his brother's family. If it had not been for my client, Mr Curtis, they might have starved; the whole burden of the support of the widow and the education of the children has fallen upon him.

"Well, just lately the matter has assumed an acute form, for two reasons. The first is that Charles' eldest son, Edmund, has come of age. Mr Curtis had him articled to a solicitor, and, as he is now fully qualified, and a most advantageous proposal for a partnership has been made, we have been putting pressure on Alfred to supply the necessary capital in accordance with his father's wishes. This he had refused to do, and it was with reference to this matter that we were calling on him this morning. The second reason involves a curious and disgraceful story. There is a certain Leonard Wolfe, who has been an intimate friend of the deceased. He is, I may say, a man of bad character, and their association has been of a kind creditable to neither. There is also a certain woman named Hester Greene, who had certain claims upon the deceased, which we need not go into at present. Now, Leonard Wolfe and the deceased, Alfred Hartridge, entered into an agreement, the terms of which were these: (1) Wolfe was to marry Hester Greene, and in consideration of this service (2) Alfred Hartridge was to assign to Wolfe the whole of his property, absolutely, the actual transfer to take place on the death of Hartridge."

"And has this transaction been completed?" asked Thorndyke.

"Yes, it has, unfortunately. But we wished to see if anything could be done for the widow and the children during Hartridge's lifetime. No doubt, my client's daughter, Miss Curtis, called last night on a similar mission – very indiscreetly, since the matter was in our hands; but, you know, she is engaged to Edmund Hartridge – and I expect the interview was a pretty stormy one."

Thorndyke remained silent for a while, pacing slowly along the gravel path, with his eyes bent on the ground: not abstractedly, however, but with a searching, attentive glance that roved amongst the shrubs and bushes, as though he were looking for something.

"What sort of man," he asked presently, "is this Leonard Wolfe? Obviously he is a low scoundrel, but what is he like in other respects? Is he a fool, for instance?"

"Not at all, I should say," said Mr Curtis. "He was formerly an engineer, and, I believe, a very capable mechanician. Latterly he has lived on some property that came to him, and has spent both his time and his money in gambling and dissipation. Consequently, I expect he is pretty short of funds at present."

"And in appearance?"

"I only saw him once," replied Mr Curtis, "and all I can remember of him is that he is rather short, fair, thin, and clean-shaven, and that he has lost the middle finger of his left hand."

"And he lives at – ?"

"Eltham, in Kent. Morton Grange, Eltham," said Mr Marchmont. "And now, if you have all the information that you require, I must really be off, and so must Mr Curtis."

The two men shook our hands and hurried away, leaving Thorndyke gazing meditatively at the dingy flower-beds.

"A strange and interesting case, this, Jervis," said he, stooping to peer under a laurel-bush. "The inspector is on a hot scent – a most palpable red herring on a most obvious string; but that is his business. Ah, here comes the porter, intent, no doubt, on pumping us, whereas – " He smiled genially at the approaching custodian, and asked: "Where did you say those houses fronted?"

"Cotman Street, sir," answered the porter. "They are nearly all offices."

"And the numbers? That open second-floor window, for instance?"

"That is number six; but the house opposite Mr Hartridge's rooms is number eight."

"Thank you."

Thorndyke was moving away, but suddenly turned again to the porter.

"By the way," said he, "I dropped something out of the window just now – a small flat piece of metal, like this." He made on the back of his visiting card a neat sketch of a circular disc, with a hexagonal hole through it, and handed the card to the porter. "I can't say where it fell," he continued; "these flat things scale about so; but you might ask the gardener to look for it. I will give him a sovereign if he brings it to my chambers, for, although it is of no value to anyone else, it is of considerable value to me."

The porter touched his hat briskly, and as we turned out at the gate, I looked back and saw him already wading among the shrubs.

The object of the porter's quest gave me considerable mental occupation. I had not seen Thorndyke drop anything, and it was not his way to finger carelessly any object of value. I was about to question him on the subject, when, turning sharply round into Cotman Street, he drew up at the doorway of number six, and began attentively to read the names of the occupants.

" 'Third-floor'," he read out, " 'Mr Thomas Barlow, Commission Agent'. Hum! I think we will look in on Mr Barlow."

He stepped quickly up the stone stairs, and I followed, until we arrived, somewhat out of breath, on the third-floor. Outside the Commission Agent's door he paused for a moment, and we both listened curiously to an irregular sound of shuffling feet from within. Then he softly opened the door and looked into the room. After remaining thus for nearly a minute, he looked round at me with a broad smile, and noiselessly set the door wide open. Inside, a lanky youth of fourteen was practising, with no mean skill, the manipulation of an appliance known by the appropriate name of diabolo; and so absorbed was he in his occupation that we entered and shut the door without being observed. At length the shuttle missed the string and flew into a large waste-paper basket; the boy turned and confronted us, and was instantly covered with confusion.

"Allow me," said Thorndyke, rooting rather unnecessarily in the waste-paper basket, and handing the toy to its owner. "I need not ask if Mr Barlow is in," he added, "nor if he is likely to return shortly."

"He won't be back today," said the boy, perspiring with embarrassment; "he left before I came. I was rather late."

"I see," said Thorndyke. "The early bird catches the worm, but the late bird catches the diabolo. How did you know he would not be back?"

"He left a note. Here it is."

He exhibited the document, which was neatly written in red ink. Thorndyke examined it attentively, and then asked: "Did you break the inkstand yesterday?"

The boy stared at him in amazement. "Yes, I did," he answered. "How did you know?"

"I didn't, or I should not have asked. But I see that he has used his stylo to write this note."

The boy regarded Thorndyke distrustfully, as he continued: "I really called to see if your Mr Barlow was a gentleman whom

I used to know; but I expect you can tell me. My friend was tall and thin, dark, and clean-shaved."

"This ain't him, then," said the boy. "He's thin, but he ain't tall or dark. He's got a sandy beard, and he wears spectacles and a wig. I know a wig when I see one," he added cunningly, " 'cause my father wears one. He puts it on a peg to comb it, and he swears at me when I larf."

"My friend had injured his left hand," pursued Thorndyke.

"I dunno about that," said the youth. "Mr Barlow nearly always wears gloves; he always wears one on his left hand, anyhow."

"Ah well! I'll just write him a note on the chance, if you will give me a piece of notepaper. Have you any ink?"

"There's some in the bottle. I'll dip the pen in for you."

He produced, from the cupboard, an opened packet of cheap notepaper and a packet of similar envelopes, and, having dipped the pen to the bottom of the ink-bottle, handed it to Thorndyke, who sat down and hastily scribbled a short note. He had folded the paper, and was about to address the envelope, when he appeared suddenly to alter his mind.

"I don't think I will leave it, after all," he said, slipping the folded paper into his pocket. "No. Tell him I called – Mr Horace Budge – and say I will look in again in a day or two."

The youth watched our exit with an air of perplexity, and he even came out on to the landing, the better to observe us over the balusters; until, unexpectedly catching Thorndyke's eye, he withdrew his head with remarkable suddenness, and retired in disorder.

To tell the truth, I was now little less perplexed than the office-boy by Thorndyke's proceedings; in which I could discover no relevancy to the investigation that I presumed he was engaged upon: and the last straw was laid upon the burden of my curiosity when he stopped at a staircase window, drew the note out of his pocket, examined it with his lens, held it up to the light, and chuckled aloud.

"Luck," he observed, "though no substitute for care and intelligence, is a very pleasant addition. Really, my learned brother, we are doing uncommonly well."

When we reached the hall, Thorndyke stopped at the housekeeper's box, and looked in with a genial nod.

"I have just been up to see Mr Barlow," said he. "He seems to have left quite early."

"Yes, sir," the man replied. "He went away about half-past eight."

"That was very early; and presumably he came earlier still?"

"I suppose so," the man assented, with a grin; "but I had only just come on when he left."

"Had he any luggage with him?"

"Yes, sir. There was two cases, a square one and a long, narrow one, about five foot long. I helped him to carry them down to the cab."

"Which was a four-wheeler I suppose?"

"Yes, sir."

"Mr Barlow hasn't been here very long, has he?" Thorndyke inquired.

"No. He only came in last quarter-day — about six weeks ago."

"Ah well! I must call another day. Good morning;" and Thorndyke strode out of the building, and made directly for the cab-rank in the adjoining street. Here he stopped for a minute or two to parley with the driver of a four-wheeled cab, whom he finally commissioned to convey us to a shop in New Oxford Street. Having dismissed the cabman with his blessing and a half-sovereign, he vanished into the shop, leaving me to gaze at the lathes, drills, and bars of metal displayed in the window. Presently he emerged with a small parcel, and explained, in answer to my inquiring look: "A strip of tool steel and a block of metal for Polton."

His next purchase was rather more eccentric. We were proceeding along Holborn when his attention was suddenly arrested by the window of a furniture shop, in which was displayed a collection of obsolete French small-arms – relics of the tragedy of 1870 – which were being sold for decorative purposes. After a brief inspection, he entered the shop, and shortly reappeared carrying a long sword-bayonet and an old Chassepôt rifle.

"What may be the meaning of this martial display?" I asked, as we turned down Fetter Lane.

"House protection," he replied promptly. "You will agree that a discharge of musketry, followed by a bayonet charge, would disconcert the boldest of burglars."

I laughed at the absurd picture thus drawn of the strenuous house-protector, but nevertheless continued to speculate on the meaning of my friend's eccentric proceedings, which I felt sure were in some way related to the murder in Brackenhurst Chambers, though I could not trace the connection.

After a late lunch, I hurried out to transact such of my business as had been interrupted by the stirring events of the morning, leaving Thorndyke busy with a drawing-board, squares, scale, and

THE ALUMINIUM DAGGER

compasses, making accurate, scaled drawings from his rough sketches; while Polton, with the brown-paper parcel in his hand, looked on at him with an air of anxious expectation.

As I was returning homeward in the evening by way of Mitre Court, I overtook Mr Marchmont, who was also bound for our chambers, and we walked on together.

"I had a note from Thorndyke," he explained, "asking for a specimen of handwriting, so I thought I would bring it along myself, and hear if he has any news."

When we entered the chambers, we found Thorndyke in earnest consultation with Polton, and on the table before them I observed, to my great surprise, the dagger with which the murder had been committed.

"I have got you the specimen that you asked for," said Marchmont. "I didn't think I should be able to, but, by a lucky chance, Curtis kept the only letter he ever received from the party in question."

He drew the letter from his wallet, and handed it to Thorndyke, who looked at it attentively and with evident satisfaction.

"By the way," said Marchmont, taking up the dagger, "I thought the inspector took this away with him."

"He took the original," replied Thorndyke. "This is a duplicate, which Polton has made, for experimental purposes, from my drawings."

"Really!" exclaimed Marchmont, with a glance of respectful admiration at Polton; "it is a perfect replica – and you have made it so quickly, too."

"It was quite easy to make," said Polton, " to a man accustomed to work in metal."

"Which," added Thorndyke, "is a fact of some evidential value."

At this moment a hansom drew up outside. A moment later flying footsteps were heard on the stairs. There was a furious battering at the door, and, as Polton threw it open, Mr Curtis burst wildly into the room.

"Here is a frightful thing, Marchmont!" he gasped. "Edith – my daughter – arrested for the murder. Inspector Badger came to our house and took her. My God! I shall go mad!"

Thorndyke laid his hand on the excited man's shoulder. "Don't distress yourself, Mr Curtis," said he. "There is no occasion, I assure you. I suppose," he added, "your daughter is left-handed?"

"Yes, she is, by a most disastrous coincidence. But what are we to do? Good God! Dr Thorndyke, they have taken her to prison – to prison – think of it! My poor Edith!"

"We'll soon have her out," said Thorndyke. "But listen; there is someone at the door."

A brisk rat-tat confirmed his statement, and when I rose to open the door, I found myself confronted by Inspector Badger. There was a moment of extreme awkwardness, and then both the detective and Mr Curtis proposed to retire in favour of the other.

"Don't go, inspector," said Thorndyke; "I want to have a word with you. Perhaps Mr Curtis would look in again, say, in an hour. Will you? We shall have news for you by then, I hope."

Mr Curtis agreed hastily, and dashed out of the room with his characteristic impetuosity. When he had gone, Thorndyke turned to the detective, and remarked dryly: "You seem to have been busy, inspector?"

"Yes," replied Badger; "I haven't let the grass grow under my feet; and I've got a pretty strong case against Miss Curtis already. You see, she was the last person seen in the company of the deceased; she had a grievance against him; she is left-handed, and you remember that the murder was committed by a left-handed person."

"Anything else?"

"Yes. I have seen those Italians, and the whole thing was a put-up job. A woman, in a widow's dress and veil, paid them to go and play the fool outside the building, and she gave them the letter that was left with the porter. They haven't identified her yet, but she seems to agree in size with Miss Curtis."

"And how did she get out of the chambers, with the door bolted on the inside?"

"Ah, there you are! That's a mystery at present – unless you can give us an explanation." The inspector made this qualification with a faint grin, and added: "As there was no one in the place when we broke into it, the murderer must have got out somehow. You can't deny that."

"I do deny it, nevertheless," said Thorndyke. "You look surprised," he continued (which was undoubtedly true), "but yet the whole thing is exceedingly obvious. The explanation struck me directly I looked at the body. There was evidently no practicable exit from the flat, and there was certainly no one in it when you entered. Clearly, then, *the murderer had never been in the place at all.*"

"I don't follow you in the least," said the inspector.

"Well," said Thorndyke, "as I have finished with the case, and am handing it over to you, I will put the evidence before you *seriatim*. Now, I think we are agreed that, at the moment when the blow was struck, the deceased was standing before the fireplace, winding the clock. The dagger entered obliquely from the left, and, if you recall its position, you will remember that its hilt pointed directly towards an open window."

"Which was forty feet from the ground."

"Yes. And now we will consider the very peculiar character of the weapon with which the crime was committed."

He had placed his hand upon the knob of a drawer, when we were interrupted by a knock at the door. I sprang up, and, opening it, admitted no less a person than the porter of Brackenhurst Chambers. The man looked somewhat surprised on recognizing our visitors, but advanced to Thorndyke, drawing a folded paper from his pocket.

"I've found the article you were looking for, sir," said he, "and a rare hunt I had for it. It had stuck in the leaves of one of them shrubs."

Thorndyke opened the packet, and, having glanced inside, laid it on the table.

"Thank you," said he, pushing a sovereign across to the gratified official. "The inspector has your name, I think?"

"He have, sir," replied the porter; and, pocketing his fee, he departed, beaming.

"To return to the dagger," said Thorndyke, opening the drawer. "It was a very peculiar one, as I have said, and as you will see from this model, which is an exact duplicate." Here he exhibited Polton's production to the astonished detective. "You see that it is extraordinarily slender, and free from projections, and of unusual materials. You also see that it was obviously not made by an ordinary dagger-maker; that, in spite of the Italian word scrawled

199

on it, there is plainly written all over it 'British mechanic'. The blade is made from a strip of common three-quarter-inch tool steel; the hilt is turned from an aluminium rod; and there is not a line of engraving on it that could not be produced in a lathe by any engineer's apprentice. Even the boss at the top is mechanical, for it is just like an ordinary hexagon nut. Then, notice the dimensions, as shown on my drawing. The parts A and B, which just project beyond the blade, are exactly similar in diameter – and such exactness could hardly be accidental. They are each parts of a circle having a diameter of 10.9 millimetres – a dimension which happens, by a singular coincidence, to be exactly the calibre of the old Chassepôt rifle, specimens of which are now on sale at several shops in London. Here is one, for instance."

He fetched the rifle that he had bought, from the corner in which it was standing, and, lifting the dagger by its point, slipped the hilt into the muzzle. When he let go, the dagger slid quietly down the barrel, until its hilt appeared in the open breech.

"Good God!" exclaimed Marchmont. "You don't suggest that the dagger was shot from a gun?"

"I do, indeed; and you now see the reason for the aluminium hilt – to diminish the weight of the already heavy projectile – and also for this hexagonal boss on the end?"

"No, I do not," said the inspector; "but I say that you are suggesting an impossibility."

"Then," replied Thorndyke, "I must explain and demonstrate. To begin with, this projectile had to travel point foremost; therefore it had to be made to spin – and it certainly was spinning when it entered the body, as the clothing and the wound showed us. Now, to make it spin, it had to be fired from a rifled barrel; but as the hilt would not engage in the rifling, it had to be fitted with something that would. That something was evidently a soft metal washer, which fitted on to this hexagon, and which would be pressed into the grooves of the rifling, and so spin the dagger, but would drop off as soon as the weapon left the barrel. Here is such a washer, which Polton has made for us."

He laid on the table a metal disc, with a hexagonal hole through it.

"This is all very ingenious," said the inspector, "but I say it is impossible and fantastic."

"It certainly sounds rather improbable," Marchmont agreed.

"We will see," said Thorndyke. "Here is a makeshift cartridge of Polton's manufacture, containing an eighth charge of smokeless powder for a 20-bore gun."

He fitted the washer on to the boss of the dagger in the open breech of the rifle, pushed it into the barrel, inserted the cartridge, and closed the breech. Then, opening the office-door, he displayed a target of padded strawboard against the wall.

"The length of the two rooms," said he, "gives us a distance of thirty-two feet. Will you shut the windows, Jervis?"

I complied, and he then pointed the rifle at the target. There was a dull report – much less loud than I had expected – and when we looked at the target, we saw the dagger driven in up to its hilt at the margin of the bull's-eye.

"You see," said Thorndyke, laying down the rifle, "that the thing is practicable. Now for the evidence as to the actual occurrence. First, on the original dagger there are linear scratches which exactly correspond with the grooves of the rifling. Then there is the fact that the dagger was certainly spinning from left to right – in the direction of the rifling, that is – when it entered the body. And then there is this, which, as you heard, the porter found in the garden."

He opened the paper packet. In it lay a metal disc, perforated by a hexagonal hole. Stepping into the office, he picked up from the floor the washer that he had put on the dagger, and laid it on the paper beside the other. The two discs were identical in size, and the margin of each was indented with identical markings, corresponding to the rifling of the barrel.

The inspector gazed at the two discs in silence for a while; then, looking up at Thorndyke, he said: "I give in, Doctor. You're right, beyond all doubt; but how you came to think of it beats me into fits. The only question now is, who fired the gun, and why wasn't the report heard?"

"As to the latter," said Thorndyke, "it is probable that he used a compressed-air attachment, not only to diminish the noise, but also to prevent any traces of the explosive from being left on the dagger. As to the former, I think I can give you the murderer's name; but we had better take the evidence in order. You may remember," he continued, "that when Dr Jervis stood as if winding the clock, I chalked a mark on the floor where he stood. Now, standing on that marked spot, and looking out of the open window, I could see two of the windows of a house nearly opposite. They were the second- and third-floor windows of No. 6, Cotman Street. The second-floor is occupied by a firm of architects; the third-floor by a commission agent named Thomas Barlow. I called on Mr Barlow, but before describing my visit, I will refer to another matter. You haven't those threatening letters about you, I suppose?"

"Yes, I have," said the inspector; and he drew forth a wallet from his breast-pocket.

"Let us take the first one, then," said Thorndyke. "You see that the paper and envelope are of the very commonest, and the writing illiterate. But the ink does not agree with this. Illiterate people usually buy their ink in penny bottles. Now, this envelope is addressed with Draper's dichroic ink – a superior office ink, sold only in large bottles – and the red ink in which the note is written is an unfixed, scarlet ink, such as is used by draughtsmen, and has been used, as you can see, in a stylographic pen. But the most interesting thing about this letter is the design drawn at the top. In an artistic sense, the man could not draw, and the anatomical details of the skull are ridiculous. Yet the drawing is very neat. It has the clean, wiry line of a machine drawing, and is done with a steady, practised hand. It is also perfectly symmetrical; the skull, for instance, is exactly in the centre, and, when we examine it through a lens, we see why it is so, for we discover traces of a pencilled centre-line and ruled cross-lines. Moreover, the lens reveals a tiny particle of draughtsman's soft, red, rubber, with which the pencil lines were taken out; and all these facts, taken together, suggest that the drawing was made by someone accustomed to making accurate mechanical drawings. And now we will return to Mr Barlow. He was out when I called, but I took the liberty of glancing round the office, and this is what I saw. On the mantelshelf was a twelve-inch flat boxwood rule, such as engineers use, a piece of soft, red rubber, and a stone bottle of Draper's dichroic ink. I obtained, by a simple ruse, a specimen of the office notepaper and the ink. We will examine it presently. I found that Mr Barlow is a new tenant, that he is rather short, wears a wig and spectacles, and always wears a glove on his left hand. He left the office at 8.30 this morning, and no one saw him arrive. He had with him a square case, and a narrow, oblong one about five feet in length; and he took a cab to Victoria, and apparently caught the 8.51 train to Chatham."

"Ah!" exclaimed the inspector.

"But," continued Thorndyke, "now examine those three letters, and compare them with this note that I wrote in Mr Barlow's office. You see that the paper is of the same make, with the same water-mark, but that is of no great significance. What is of crucial importance is this: You see, in each of these letters, two tiny indentations near the bottom corner. Somebody has used compasses or drawing-pins over the packet of notepaper, and the points have made little indentations, which have marked several of the sheets. Now, notepaper is cut to its size after it is folded, and if you stick a pin into the top sheet of a section, the indentations on all the underlying sheets will be at exactly similar distances from the edges and corners of the sheet. But you see that these little dents are all at the same distance from the edges and the corner." He demonstrated the fact with a pair of compasses. "And now look at this sheet, which I obtained at Mr Barlow's office. There are two little indentations – rather faint, but quite visible – near the bottom corner, and when we measure them with the compasses, we find that they are exactly the same distance apart as the others, and the same distance from the edges and the bottom corner. The irresistible conclusion is that these four sheets came from the same packet."

The inspector started up from his chair, and faced Thorndyke. "Who is this Mr Barlow?" he asked.

"That," replied Thorndyke, "is for you to determine; but I can give you a useful hint. There is only one person who benefits by the death of Alfred Hartridge, but he benefits to the extent of twenty thousand pounds. His name is Leonard Wolfe, and I learn from Mr Marchmont that he is a man of indifferent character − a gambler and a spendthrift. By profession he is an engineer, and he is a capable mechanician. In appearance he is thin, short, fair, and clean-shaven, and he has lost the middle finger of his left hand. Mr Barlow is also short, thin, and fair, but wears a wig, a beard, and spectacles, and always wears a glove on his left hand. I have seen the handwriting of both these gentlemen, and should say that it would be difficult to distinguish one from the other."

"That's good enough for me," said the inspector. "Give me his address, and I'll have Miss Curtis released at once."

The same night Leonard Wolfe was arrested at Eltham, in the very act of burying in his garden a large and powerful compressed-air rifle. He was never brought to trial, however, for he had in his pocket a more portable weapon − a large-bore Derringer pistol − with which he managed to terminate an exceedingly ill-spent life.

"And, after all," was Thorndyke's comment, when he heard of the event, "he had his uses. He has relieved society of two very bad men, and he has given us a most instructive case. He has shown us how a clever and ingenious criminal may take endless pains to mislead and delude the police, and yet, by inattention to trivial details, may scatter clues broadcast. We can only say to the criminal class generally, in both respects, 'Go thou and do likewise.' "

EIGHT
A Message from the Deep Sea

The Whitechapel Road, though redeemed by scattered relics of a more picturesque past from the utter desolation of its neighbour the Commercial Road, is hardly a gay thoroughfare. Especially at its eastern end, where its sordid modernity seems to reflect the colourless lives of its inhabitants, does its grey and dreary length depress the spirits of the wayfarer. But the longest and dullest road can be made delightful by sprightly discourse seasoned with wit and wisdom, and so it was that, as I walked westward by the side of my friend John Thorndyke, the long, monotonous road seemed all too short.

We had been to the London Hospital to see a remarkable case of acromegaly, and, as we returned, we discussed this curious affection, and the allied condition of gigantism, in all their bearings, from the origin of the "Gibson chin" to the physique of Og, King of Bashan.

"It would have been interesting," Thorndyke remarked as we passed up Aldgate High Street, "to have put one's finger into His Majesty's pituitary fossa – after his decease, of course. By the way, here is Harrow Alley; you remember Defoe's description of the dead-cart waiting out here, and the ghastly procession coming down the alley." He took my arm, and led me up the narrow thoroughfare as far as the sharp turn by the "Star and Still" public-house, where we turned to look back.

"I never pass this place," he said musingly, "but I seem to hear the clang of the bell and the dismal cry of the carter – "

He broke off abruptly. Two figures had suddenly appeared framed in the archway, and now advanced at headlong speed. One, who led, was a stout, middle-aged Jewess, very breathless and dishevelled: the other was a well-dressed young man, hardly less agitated than his companion. As they approached, the young man suddenly recognized my colleague, and accosted him in agitated tones.

"I've just been sent for to a case of murder or suicide. Would you mind looking at it for me, sir? It's my first case, and I feel rather nervous."

Here the woman darted back, and plucked the young doctor by the arm.

"Hurry! hurry!" she exclaimed, "don't stop to talk." Her face was as white as lard, and shiny with sweat; her lips twitched, her hands shook, and she stared with the eyes of a frightened child.

"Of course I will come, Hart," said Thorndyke; and, turning back, we followed the woman as she elbowed her way frantically among the foot-passengers.

"Have you started in practice here?" Thorndyke asked as we hurried along.

"No, sir," replied Dr Hart; "I am an assistant. My principal is the police-surgeon, but he is out just now. It's very good of you to come with me, sir."

"Tut, tut," rejoined Thorndyke. "I am just coming to see that you do credit to my teaching. That looks like the house."

We had followed our guide into a side street, halfway down which we could see a knot of people clustered round a doorway. They watched us as we approached, and drew aside to let us enter. The woman whom we were following rushed into the passage with the same headlong haste with which she had traversed the streets, and so up the stairs. But as she neared the top of the flight she slowed down suddenly, and began to creep up on tiptoe with noiseless and hesitating steps. On the landing she turned to face us, and pointing a shaking forefinger at the door of the back room, whispered almost inaudibly, "She's in there," and then sank half-fainting on the bottom stair of the next flight.

I laid my hand on the knob of the door, and looked back at Thorndyke. He was coming slowly up the stairs, closely scrutinizing floor, walls, and handrail as he came. When he reached the landing, I turned the handle, and we entered the room together, closing the door after us. The blind was still down, and in the dim, uncertain light nothing out of the common was, at first, to be seen. The shabby little room looked trim and orderly enough, save for a heap of cast-off feminine clothing piled upon a chair. The bed appeared undisturbed except by the half-seen shape of its occupant, and the quiet face, dimly visible in its shadowy corner, might have been that of a sleeper but for its utter stillness and for a dark stain on the pillow by its side.

Dr Hart stole on tiptoe to the bedside, while Thorndyke drew up the blind; and as the garish daylight poured into the room, the young surgeon fell back with a gasp of horror.

"Good God!" he exclaimed; "poor creature! But this is a frightful thing, sir!"

The light streamed down upon the white face of a handsome girl of twenty-five, a face peaceful, placid, and beautiful with the austere and almost unearthly beauty of the youthful dead. The lips were slightly parted, the eyes half closed and drowsy, shaded with sweeping lashes; and a wealth of dark hair in massive plaits served as a foil to the translucent skin.

Our friend had drawn back the bedclothes a few inches, and now there was revealed, beneath the comely face, so serene and inscrutable, and yet so dreadful in its fixity and waxen pallor, a horrible, yawning wound that almost divided the shapely neck.

Thorndyke looked down with stern pity at the plump white face.

"It was savagely done," said he, "and yet mercifully, by reason of its very savagery. She must have died without waking."

"The brute!" exclaimed Hart, clenching his fists and turning crimson with wrath. "The infernal cowardly beast! He shall hang! By God, he shall hang!" In his fury the young fellow shook his fists in the air, even as the moisture welled up into his eyes.

Thorndyke touched him on the shoulder. "That is what we are here for, Hart," said he. "Get out your notebook;" and with this he bent down over the dead girl.

At the friendly reproof the young surgeon pulled himself together, and, with open notebook, commenced his investigation, while I, at Thorndyke's request, occupied myself in making a plan of the room, with a description of its contents and their arrangements. But this occupation did not prevent me from keeping an eye on Thorndyke's movements, and presently I suspended my labours to watch him as, with his pocket-knife, he scraped together some objects that he had found on the pillow.

"What do you make of this?" he asked, as I stepped over to his side. He pointed with the blade to a tiny heap of what looked like silver sand, and, as I looked more closely, I saw that similar particles were sprinkled on other parts of the pillow.

"Silver sand!" I exclaimed. "I don't understand at all how it can have got there. Do you?"

Thorndyke shook his head. "We will consider the explanation later," was his reply. He had produced from his pocket a small metal box which he always carried, and which contained such requisites as cover-slips, capillary tubes, moulding wax, and other "diagnostic materials". He now took from it a seed-envelope, into which he neatly shovelled the little pinch of sand with his knife. He had closed the envelope, and was writing a pencilled description on the outside, when we were startled by a cry from Hart.

"Good God, sir! Look at this! It was done by a woman!"

He had drawn back the bedclothes, and was staring aghast at the dead girl's left hand. It held a thin tress of long, red hair.

Thorndyke hastily pocketed his specimen, and, stepping round the little bedside table, bent over the hand with knitted brows. It was closed, though not tightly clenched, and when an attempt was made gently to separate the fingers, they were found to be as rigid as the fingers of a wooden hand. Thorndyke stooped yet more closely, and, taking out his lens, scrutinized the wisp of hair throughout its entire length.

"There is more here than meets the eye at the first glance," he remarked. "What say you, Hart?" He held out his lens to his quondam pupil, who was about to take it from him when the door opened, and three men entered. One was a police-inspector, the second appeared to be a plain-clothes officer, while the third was evidently the divisional surgeon.

"Friends of yours, Hart?" inquired the latter, regarding us with some disfavour.

Thorndyke gave a brief explanation of our presence, to which the newcomer rejoined: "Well, sir, your *locus standi* here is a matter for the inspector. My assistant was not authorized to call in outsiders. You needn't wait, Hart."

With this he proceeded to his inspection, while Thorndyke withdrew the pocket-thermometer that he had slipped under the body, and took the reading.

The inspector, however, was not disposed to exercise the prerogative at which the surgeon had hinted; for an expert has his uses.

"How long should you say she'd been dead, sir?" he asked affably.

"About ten hours," replied Thorndyke.

The inspector and the detective simultaneously looked at their watches. "That fixes it at two o'clock this morning," said the former. "What's that, sir?"

The surgeon was pointing to the wisp of hair in the dead girl's hand.

"My word!" exclaimed the inspector. "A woman, eh? She must be a tough customer. This looks like a soft job for you, sergeant."

"Yes," said the detective. "That accounts for that box with the hassock on it at the head of the bed. She had to stand on them to reach over. But she couldn't have been very tall."

"She must have been mighty strong, though," said the inspector; "why, she has nearly cut the poor wench's head off." He moved round to the head of the bed, and, stooping over, peered down at the gaping wound. Suddenly he began to draw his hand over the pillow, and then rub his fingers together. "Why," he exclaimed, "there's sand on the pillow – silver sand! Now, how can that have come there?"

The surgeon and the detective both came round to verify this discovery, and an earnest consultation took place as to its meaning.

"Did you notice it, sir?" the inspector asked Thorndyke.

"Yes," replied the latter; "it's an unaccountable thing, isn't it?"

"I don't know that it is, either," said the detective. He ran over to the washstand, and then uttered a grunt of satisfaction. "It's quite a simple matter, after all, you see," he said, glancing complacently at my colleague. "There's a ball of sand-soap on the washstand, and the basin is full of blood-stained water. You see, she must have washed the blood off her hands, and off the knife, too – a pretty cool customer she must be – and she used the sand-soap. Then, while she was drying her hands, she must have stood over the head of the bed, and let the sand fall on to the pillow. I think that's clear enough."

"Admirably clear," said Thorndyke; "and what do you suppose was the sequence of events?"

The gratified detective glanced round the room. "I take it," said he, "that the deceased read herself to sleep. There is a book on the table by the bed, and a candlestick with nothing in it but a bit of burnt wick at the bottom of the socket. I imagine that the woman came in quietly, lit the gas, put the box and the hassock at the bedhead, stood on them, and cut her victim's throat. Deceased must have waked up and clutched the murderess' hair – though there doesn't seem to have been much of a struggle; but no doubt she died almost at once. Then the murderess washed her hands, cleaned the knife, tidied up the bed a bit, and went away. That's about how things happened, I think, but how she got in without anyone hearing, and how she got out, and where she went to, are the things that we've got to find out."

"Perhaps," said the surgeon, drawing the bedclothes over the corpse, "we had better have the landlady in and make a few inquiries." He glanced significantly at Thorndyke, and the inspector coughed behind his hand. My colleague, however, chose to be obtuse to these hints: opening the door, he turned the key backwards and forwards several times, drew it out, examined it narrowly, and replaced it.

"The landlady is outside on the landing," he remarked, holding the door open.

Thereupon the inspector went out, and we all followed to hear the result of his inquiries.

"Now, Mrs Goldstein," said the officer, opening his notebook, "I want you to tell us all that you know about this affair, and about the girl herself. What was her name?"

The landlady, who had been joined by a white-faced, tremulous man, wiped her eyes, and replied in a shaky voice: "Her name, poor child, was Minna Adler. She was a German. She came from Bremen about two years ago. She had no friends in England – no relatives, I mean. She was a waitress at a restaurant in Fenchurch Street, and a good, quiet, hard-working girl."

"When did you discover what had happened?"

"About eleven o'clock. I thought she had gone to work as usual, but my husband noticed from the back yard that her blind was still down. So I went up and knocked, and when I got no answer, I opened the door and went in, and then I saw – " Here the poor soul, overcome by the dreadful recollection, burst into hysterical sobs.

"Her door was unlocked, then; did she usually lock it?"

"I think so," sobbed Mrs Goldstein. "The key was always inside."

"And the street door; was that secure when you came down this morning?"

"It was shut. We don't bolt it because some of the lodgers come home rather late."

"And now tell us, had she any enemies? Was there anyone who had a grudge against her?"

"No, no, poor child! Why should anyone have a grudge against her? No, she had no quarrel – no real quarrel – with anyone; not even with Miriam."

"Miriam?" inquired the inspector. "Who is she?"

"That was nothing," interposed the man hastily. "That was not a quarrel."

"Just a little unpleasantness, I suppose, Mr Goldstein?" suggested the inspector.

"Just a little foolishness about a young man," said Mr Goldstein. "That was all. Miriam was a little jealous. But it was nothing."

"No, no. Of course. We all know that young women are apt to – "

A soft footstep had been for some time audible, slowly descending the stair above, and at this moment a turn of the staircase brought the newcomer into view. And at that vision the inspector stopped short as if petrified, and a tense, startled silence fell upon us all. Down the remaining stairs there advanced towards us a young woman, powerful though short, wild-eyed, dishevelled, horror-stricken, and of a ghastly pallor: and her hair was a fiery red.

Stock still and speechless we all stood as this apparition came slowly towards us; but suddenly the detective slipped back into the room, closing the door after him, to reappear a few moments later holding a small paper packet, which, after a quick glance at the inspector, he placed in his breast pocket.

"This is my daughter Miriam that we spoke about, gentlemen," said Mr Goldstein. "Miriam, these are the doctors and the police."

The girl looked at us from one to the other. "You have seen her, then," she said in a strange, muffled voice, and added: "She isn't dead, is she? Not really dead?" The question was asked in a tone at once coaxing and despairing, such as a distracted mother might use over the corpse of her child. It filled me with vague discomfort, and, unconsciously, I looked round towards Thorndyke.

To my surprise he had vanished.

Noiselessly backing towards the head of the stairs, where I could command a view of the hall, or passage, I looked down, and saw him in the act of reaching up to a shelf behind the street door. He caught my eye, and beckoned, whereupon I crept away unnoticed by the party on the landing. When I reached the hall, he was wrapping up three small objects, each in a separate cigarette-paper; and I noticed that he handled them with more than ordinary tenderness.

"We didn't want to see that poor devil of a girl arrested," said he, as he deposited the three little packets gingerly in his pocket-box. "Let us be off." He opened the door noiselessly, and stood for a moment, turning the latch backwards and forwards, and closely examining its bolt.

I glanced up at the shelf behind the door. On it were two flat china candlesticks, in one of which I had happened to notice, as we came in, a short end of candle lying in the tray, and I now looked to see if that was what Thorndyke had annexed; but it was still there.

I followed my colleague out into the street, and for some time we walked on without speaking. "You guessed what the sergeant had in that paper, of course," said Thorndyke at length.

"Yes. It was the hair from the dead woman's hand; and I thought that he had much better have left it there."

"Undoubtedly. But that is the way in which well-meaning policemen destroy valuable evidence. Not that it matters much in this particular instance; but it might have been a fatal mistake."

"Do you intend to take any active part in this case?" I asked.

"That depends on circumstances. I have collected some evidence, but what it is worth I don't yet know. Neither do I know whether the police have observed the same set of facts; but I need not say that I shall do anything that seems necessary to assist the authorities. That is a matter of common citizenship."

The inroads made upon our time by the morning's adventures made it necessary that we should go each about his respective business without delay; so, after a perfunctory lunch at a tea-shop, we separated, and I did not see my colleague again until the day's work was finished, and I turned into our chambers just before dinner-time.

Here I found Thorndyke seated at the table, and evidently full of business. A microscope stood close by, with a condenser throwing a spot of light on to a pinch of powder that had been sprinkled on to the slide; his collecting-box lay open before him, and he was engaged, rather mysteriously, in squeezing a thick white cement from a tube on to three little pieces of moulding-wax.

"Useful stuff, this Fortafix," he remarked; "it makes excellent casts, and saves the trouble and mess of mixing plaster, which is a consideration for small work like this. By the way, if you want to know what was on that poor girl's pillow, just take a peep through the microscope. It is rather a pretty specimen."

I stepped across, and applied my eye to the instrument. The specimen was, indeed, pretty in more than a technical sense. Mingled with crystalline grains of quartz, glassy spicules, and water-worn fragments of coral, were a number of lovely little shells, some of the texture of fine porcelain, others like blown Venetian glass.

"These are Foraminifera!" I exclaimed.

"Yes."

"Then it is not silver sand, after all?"

"Certainly not."

"But what is it, then?"

Thorndyke smiled. "It is a message to us from the deep sea, Jervis; from the floor of the Eastern Mediterranean."

"And can you read the message?"

"I think I can," he replied, "but I shall know soon, I hope."

I looked down the microscope again, and wondered what message these tiny shells had conveyed to my friend. Deep-sea sand

214

on a dead woman's pillow! What could be more incongruous? What possible connection could there be between this sordid crime in the east of London and the deep bed of the "tideless sea"?

Meanwhile Thorndyke squeezed out more cement on to the three little pieces of moulding-wax (which I suspected to be the objects that I had seen him wrapping up with such care in the hall of the Goldsteins' house); then, laying one of them down on a glass slide, with its cemented side uppermost, he stood the other two upright on either side of it. Finally he squeezed out a fresh load of the thick cement, apparently to bind the three objects together, and carried the slide very carefully to a cupboard, where he deposited it, together with the envelope containing the sand and the slide from the stage of the microscope.

He was just locking the cupboard when a sharp rat-tat on our knocker sent him hurriedly to the door. A messenger-boy, standing on the threshold, held out a dirty envelope.

"Mr Goldstein kept me a awful long time, sir," said he; "I haven't been a-loitering."

Thorndyke took the envelope over to the gas-light, and, opening it, drew forth a sheet of paper, which he scanned quickly and almost eagerly; and, though his face remained as inscrutable as a mask of stone, I felt a conviction that the paper had told him something that he wished to know.

The boy having been sent on his way rejoicing, Thorndyke turned to the bookshelves, along which he ran his eye thoughtfully until it alighted on a shabbily-bound volume near one end. This he reached down, and as he laid it open on the table, I glanced at it, and was surprised to observe that it was a bi-lingual work, the opposite pages being apparently in Russian and Hebrew.

"The Old Testament in Russian and Yiddish," he remarked, noting my surprise. "I am going to get Polton to photograph a couple of specimen pages – is that the postman or a visitor?"

It turned out to be the postman, and as Thorndyke extracted from the letter-box a blue official envelope, he glanced significantly at me.

"This answers your question, I think, Jervis," said he. "Yes; coroner's subpœna and a very civil letter: 'sorry to trouble you, but I had no choice under the circumstances' – of course he hadn't – 'Dr Davidson has arranged to make the autopsy tomorrow at 4 p.m., and I should be glad if you could be present. The mortuary is in Barker Street, next to the school.' Well, we must go, I suppose, though Davidson will probably resent it." He took up the Testament, and went off with it to the laboratory.

We lunched at our chambers on the following day, and, after the meal, drew up our chairs to the fire and lit our pipes. Thorndyke was evidently preoccupied, for he laid his open notebook on his knee, and, gazing meditatively into the fire, made occasional entries with his pencil as though he were arranging the points of an argument. Assuming that the Aldgate murder was the subject of his cogitations, I ventured to ask: "Have you any material evidence to offer the coroner?"

He closed his notebook and put it away. "The evidence that I have," he said, "is material and important; but it is disjointed and rather inconclusive. If I can join it up into a coherent whole, as I hope to do before I reach the court, it will be very important indeed – but here is my invaluable familiar, with the instruments of research." He turned with a smile towards Polton, who had just entered the room, and master and man exchanged a friendly glance of mutual appreciation. The relations of Thorndyke and his assistant were a constant delight to me: on the one side, service, loyal and whole-hearted; on the other, frank and full recognition.

"I should think these will do, sir," said Polton, handing his principal a small cardboard box such as playing-cards are carried in. Thorndyke pulled off the lid, and I then saw that the box was fitted internally with grooves for plates, and contained two mounted photographs. The latter were very singular productions indeed; they were copies each of a page of the Testament, one

Russian and the other Yiddish; but the lettering appeared white on a black ground, of which it occupied only quite a small space in the middle, leaving a broad black margin. Each photograph was mounted on a stiff card, and each card had a duplicate photograph pasted on the back.

Thorndyke exhibited them to me with a provoking smile, holding them daintily by their edges, before he slid them back into the grooves of their box.

"We are making a little digression into philology, you see," he remarked, as he pocketed the box. "But we must be off now, or we shall keep Davidson waiting. Thank you, Polton."

The District Railway carried us swiftly eastward, and we emerged from Aldgate Station a full half-hour before we were due. Nevertheless, Thorndyke stepped out briskly, but instead of making directly for the mortuary, he strayed off unaccountably into Mansell Street, scanning the numbers of the houses as he went. A row of old houses, picturesque but grimy, on our right seemed specially to attract him, and he slowed down as we approached them.

"There is a quaint survival, Jervis," he remarked, pointing to a crudely painted, wooden effigy of an Indian standing on a bracket at the door of a small old-fashioned tobacconist's shop. We halted to look at the little image, and at that moment the side door opened, and a woman came out on to the doorstep, where she stood gazing up and down the street.

Thorndyke immediately crossed the pavement, and addressed her, apparently with some question, for I heard her answer presently: "A quarter-past six is his time, sir, and he is generally punctual to the minute."

"Thank you," said Thorndyke; "I'll bear that in mind;" and, lifting his hat, he walked on briskly, turning presently up a side-street which brought us out into Aldgate. It was now but five minutes to four, so we strode off quickly to keep our tryst at the mortuary; but although we arrived at the gate as the hour was striking, when we entered the building we found Dr Davidson hanging up his apron and preparing to depart.

"Sorry I couldn't wait for you," he said, with no great show of sincerity, "but a *post-mortem* is a mere farce in a case like this; you have seen all that there was to see. However, there is the body; Hart hasn't closed it up yet."

With this and a curt "good afternoon" he departed.

"I must apologize for Dr Davidson, sir," said Hart, looking up with a vexed face from the desk at which he was writing out his notes.

"You needn't," said Thorndyke; "you didn't supply him with manners; and don't let me disturb you. I only want to verify one or two points."

Accepting the hint, Hart and I remained at the desk, while Thorndyke, removing his hat, advanced to the long slate table, and bent over its burden of pitiful tragedy. For some time he remained motionless, running his eye gravely over the corpse, in search, no doubt, of bruises and indications of a struggle. Then he stooped and narrowly examined the wound, especially at its commencement and end. Suddenly he drew nearer, peering intently as if something had attracted his attention, and having taken out his lens, fetched a small sponge, with which he dried an exposed process of the spine. Holding his lens before the dried spot, he again scrutinized it closely, and then, with a scalpel and forceps, detached some object, which he carefully washed, and then once more examined through his lens as it lay in the palm of his hand. Finally, as I expected, he brought forth his "collecting-box", took from it a seed-envelope, into which he dropped the object — evidently something quite small — closed up the envelope, wrote on the outside of it, and replaced it in the box.

"I think I have seen all that I wanted to see," he said, as he pocketed the box and took up his hat. "We shall meet tomorrow morning at the inquest." He shook hands with Hart, and we went out into the relatively pure air.

On one pretext or another, Thorndyke lingered about the neighbourhood of Aldgate until a church bell struck six, when he bent his steps towards Harrow Alley. Through the narrow, winding passage he walked, slowly and with a thoughtful mien, along Little Somerset Street and out into Mansell Street, until just on the stroke of a quarter-past we found ourselves opposite the little tobacconist's shop.

Thorndyke glanced at his watch and halted, looking keenly up the street. A moment later he hastily took from his pocket the cardboard box, from which he extracted the two mounted photographs which had puzzled me so much. They now seemed to puzzle Thorndyke equally, to judge by his expression, for he held them close to his eyes, scrutinizing them with an anxious frown, and backing by degrees into the doorway at the side of the tobacconist's. At this moment I became aware of a man who, as he approached, seemed to eye my friend with some curiosity and more disfavour; a very short, burly young man, apparently a foreign Jew, whose face, naturally sinister and unprepossessing, was further disfigured by the marks of smallpox.

"Excuse me," he said brusquely, pushing past Thorndyke; "I live here."

"I am sorry," responded Thorndyke. He moved aside, and then suddenly asked: "By the way, I suppose you do not by any chance understand Yiddish?"

"Why do you ask?" the newcomer demanded gruffly.

"Because I have just had these two photographs of lettering given to me. One is in Greek, I think, and one in Yiddish, but I have forgotten which is which." He held out the two cards to the stranger, who took them from him, and looked at them with scowling curiosity.

"This one is Yiddish," said he, raising his right hand, "and this other is Russian, not Greek." He held out the two cards to Thorndyke, who took them from him, holding them carefully by the edges as before.

"I am greatly obliged to you for your kind assistance," said Thorndyke; but before he had time to finish his thanks, the man had entered, by means of his latchkey, and slammed the door. Thorndyke carefully slid the photographs back into their grooves, replaced the box in his pocket, and made an entry in his notebook.

"That," said he, "finishes my labours, with the exception of a small experiment which I can perform at home. By the way, I picked up a morsel of evidence that Davidson had overlooked. He will be annoyed, and I am not very fond of scoring off a colleague; but he is too uncivil for me to communicate with."

The coroner's subpœna had named ten o'clock as the hour at which Thorndyke was to attend to give evidence, but a consultation with a well-known solicitor so far interfered with his plans that we were a quarter of an hour late in starting from the Temple. My friend was evidently in excellent spirits, though silent and preoccupied, from which I inferred that he was satisfied with the results of his labours; but, as I sat by his side in the hansom, I forbore to question him, not from mere unselfishness, but rather from the desire to hear his evidence for the first time in conjunction with that of the other witnesses.

The room in which the inquest was held formed part of a school adjoining the mortuary. Its vacant bareness was on this occasion enlivened by a long, baize-covered table, at the head of which sat the coroner, while one side was occupied by the jury; and I was glad to observe that the latter consisted, for the most part, of genuine working men, instead of the stolid-faced, truculent "professional jurymen" who so often grace these tribunals.

A row of chairs accommodated the witnesses, a corner of the table was allotted to the accused woman's solicitor, a smart dapper gentleman in gold pince-nez, a portion of one side to the reporters, and several ranks of benches were occupied by a miscellaneous assembly representing the public.

There were one or two persons present whom I was somewhat surprised to see. There was, for instance, our pock-marked acquaintance of Mansell Street, who greeted us with a stare of hostile surprise; and there was Superintendent Miller of Scotland Yard, in whose manner I seemed to detect some kind of private understanding with Thorndyke. But I had little time to look about me, for when we arrived, the proceedings had already commenced. Mrs Goldstein, the first witness, was finishing her recital of the circumstances under which the crime was discovered, and, as she retired, weeping hysterically, she was followed by looks of commiseration from the sympathetic jurymen.

The next witness was a young woman named Kate Silver. As she stepped forward to be sworn she flung a glance of hatred and defiance at Miriam Goldstein, who, white-faced and wild of aspect, with her red hair streaming in dishevelled masses on to her shoulders, stood apart in custody of two policemen, staring about her as if in a dream.

"You were intimately acquainted with the deceased, I believe?" said the coroner.

"I was. We worked at the same place for a long time – the Empire Restaurant in Fenchurch Street – and we lived in the same house. She was my most intimate friend."

"Had she, as far as you know, any friends or relations in England?"

"No. She came to England from Bremen about three years ago. It was then that I made her acquaintance. All her relations were in Germany, but she had many friends here, because she was a very lively, amiable girl."

"Had she, as far as you know, any enemies – any persons, I mean, who bore any grudge against her and were likely to do her an injury?"

"Yes. Miriam Goldstein was her enemy. She hated her."

"You say Miriam Goldstein hated the deceased. How do you know that?"

"She made no secret of it. They had had a violent quarrel about a young man named Moses Cohen. He was formerly Miriam's sweetheart, and I think they were very fond of one another until Minna Adler came to lodge at the Goldsteins' house about three months ago. Then Moses took a fancy to Minna, and she encouraged him, although she had a sweetheart of her own, a young man named Paul Petrofsky, who also lodged in the Goldsteins' house. At last Moses broke off with Miriam, and engaged himself to Minna. Then Miriam was furious, and complained to Minna about what she called her perfidious conduct; but Minna only laughed, and told her she could have Petrofsky instead."

"And what did Minna say to that?" asked the coroner.

"She was still more angry, because Moses Cohen is a smart, good-looking young man, while Petrofsky is not much to look at. Besides, Miriam did not like Petrofsky; he had been rude to her, and she had made her father send him away from the house. So they were not friends, and it was just after that that the trouble came."

"The trouble?"

"I mean about Moses Cohen. Miriam is a very passionate girl, and she was furiously jealous of Minna, so when Petrofsky annoyed her by taunting her about Moses Cohen and Minna, she lost her temper, and said dreadful things about both of them."

"As, for instance — ?"

"She said that she would kill them both, and that she would like to cut Minna's throat."

"When was this?"

"It was the day before the murder."

"Who heard her say these things besides you?"

"Another lodger named Edith Bryant and Petrofsky. We were all standing in the hall at the time."

"But I thought you said Petrofsky had been turned away from the house."

"So he had, a week before; but he had left a box in his room, and on this day he had come to fetch it. That was what started the trouble. Miriam had taken his room for her bedroom, and turned her old one into a workroom. She said he should not go to her room to fetch his box."

"And did he?"

"I think so. Miriam and Edith and I went out, leaving him in the hall. When we came back the box was gone, and, as Mrs Goldstein was in the kitchen and there was nobody else in the house, he must have taken it."

"You spoke of Miriam's workroom. What work did she do?"

"She cut stencils for a firm of decorators."

Here the coroner took a peculiarly shaped knife from the table before him, and handed it to the witness.

"Have you ever seen that knife before?" he asked.

"Yes. It belongs to Miriam Goldstein. It is a stencil-knife that she used in her work."

This concluded the evidence of Kate Silver, and when the name of the next witness, Paul Petrofsky, was called, our Mansell Street friend came forward to be sworn. His evidence was quite brief, and merely corroborative of that of Kate Silver, as was that of the next witness, Edith Bryant. When these had been disposed of, the coroner announced: "Before taking the medical evidence, gentlemen, I propose to hear that of the police-officers, and first we will call Detective-sergeant Alfred Bates."

The sergeant stepped forward briskly, and proceeded to give his evidence with official readiness and precision.

"I was called by Constable Simmonds at eleven forty-nine, and reached the house at two minutes to twelve in company with Inspector Harris and Divisional Surgeon Davidson. When I arrived Dr Hart, Dr Thorndyke, and Dr Jervis were already in the room. I found the deceased woman, Minna Adler, lying in bed with her throat cut. She was dead and cold. There were no signs of a struggle, and the bed did not appear to have been disturbed. There was a table by the bedside on which was a book and an empty candlestick. The candle had apparently burnt out, for there was only a piece of charred wick at the bottom of the socket. A box had been placed on the floor at the head of the bed and a hassock stood on it. Apparently the murderer had stood on the hassock and leaned over the head of the bed to commit the murder. This was rendered necessary by the position of the table, which could not have been moved without making some noise and perhaps disturbing the deceased. I infer from the presence of the box and hassock that the murderer is a short person."

"Was there anything else that seemed to fix the identity of the murderer?"

"Yes. A tress of a woman's red hair was grasped in the left hand of the deceased."

As the detective uttered this statement, a simultaneous shriek of horror burst from the accused woman and her mother. Mrs Goldstein sank half-fainting on to a bench, while Miriam, pale as death, stood as one petrified, fixing the detective with a stare of terror, as he drew from his pocket two small paper packets, which he opened and handed to the coroner.

"The hair in the packet marked *A*," said he, "is that which was found in the hand of the deceased; that in the packet marked *B* is the hair of Miriam Goldstein."

Here the accused woman's solicitor rose. "Where did you obtain the hair in the packet marked *B*?" he demanded.

"I took it from a bag of combings that hung on the wall of Miriam Goldstein's bedroom," answered the detective.

"I object to this," said the solicitor. "There is no evidence that the hair from that bag was the hair of Miriam Goldstein at all."

Thorndyke chuckled softly. "The lawyer is as dense as the policeman," he remarked to me in an undertone. "Neither of them seems to see the significance of that bag in the least."

"Did you know about the bag, then?" I asked in surprise.

"No. I thought it was the hair-brush."

I gazed at my colleague in amazement, and was about to ask for some elucidation of this cryptic reply, when he held up his finger and turned again to listen.

"Very well, Mr Horwitz," the coroner was saying, "I will make a note of your objection, but I shall allow the sergeant to continue his evidence."

The solicitor sat down, and the detective resumed his statement.

"I have examined and compared the two samples of hair, and it is my opinion that they are from the head of the same person. The only other observation that I made in the room was that there was a small quantity of silver sand sprinkled on the pillow around the deceased woman's head."

"Silver sand!" exclaimed the coroner. "Surely that is a very singular material to find on a woman's pillow?"

"I think it is easily explained," replied the sergeant. "The wash-hand basin was full of bloodstained water, showing that the murderer had washed his – or her – hands, and probably the knife, too, after the crime. On the washstand was a ball of sand-soap, and I imagine that the murderer used this to cleanse his – or her – hands, and, while drying them, must have stood over the head of the bed and let the sand sprinkle down on to the pillow."

"A simple but highly ingenious explanation," commented the coroner approvingly, and the jurymen exchanged admiring nods and nudges.

"I searched the rooms occupied by the accused woman, Miriam Goldstein, and found there a knife of the kind used by stencil cutters, but larger than usual. There were stains of blood on it which the accused explained by saying that she cut her finger some days ago. She admitted that the knife was hers."

This concluded the sergeant's evidence, and he was about to sit down when the solicitor rose.

"I should like to ask this witness one or two questions," said he, and the coroner having nodded assent, he proceeded: "Has the finger of the accused been examined since her arrest?"

"I believe not," replied the sergeant. "Not to my knowledge, at any rate."

The solicitor noted the reply, and then asked: "With reference to the silver sand, did you find any at the bottom of the wash-hand basin?"

The sergeant's face reddened. "I did not examine the wash-hand basin," he answered.

"Did anybody examine it?"

"I think not."

"Thank you." Mr Horwitz sat down, and the triumphant squeak of his quill pen was heard above the muttered disapproval of the jury.

"We shall now take the evidence of the doctors, gentlemen," said the coroner, "and we will begin with that of the divisional surgeon. You saw the deceased, I believe, Doctor," he continued, when Dr Davidson had been sworn, "soon after the discovery of the murder, and you have since then made an examination of the body?"

"Yes. I found the body of the deceased lying in her bed, which had apparently not been disturbed. She had been dead about ten hours, and rigidity was complete in the limbs but not in the trunk. The cause of death was a deep wound extending right across the throat and dividing all the structures down to the spine. It had been inflicted with a single sweep of a knife while deceased was lying down, and was evidently homicidal. It was not possible for the deceased to have inflicted the wound herself. It was made with a single-edged knife, drawn from left to right; the assailant stood on a hassock placed on a box at the head of the bed and leaned over to strike the blow. The murderer is probably quite a short person, very muscular, and right-handed. There was no sign of a struggle, and, judging by the nature of the injuries, I should say that death was almost instantaneous. In the left hand of the deceased was a small tress of a woman's red hair. I have compared that hair with that of the accused, and am of opinion that it is her hair."

"You were shown a knife belonging to the accused?"

"Yes; a stencil-knife. There were stains of dried blood on it which I have examined and find to be mammalian blood. It is probably human blood, but I cannot say with certainty that it is."

"Could the wound have been inflicted with this knife?"

"Yes, though it is a small knife to produce so deep a wound. Still, it is quite possible."

The coroner glanced at Mr Horwitz. "Do you wish to ask this witness any questions?" he inquired.

"If you please, sir," was the reply. The solicitor rose, and, having glanced through his notes, commenced: "You have described certain blood-stains on this knife. But we have heard that there was bloodstained water in the wash-hand basin, and it is suggested, most reasonably, that the murderer washed his hands and the knife. But if the knife was washed, how do you account for the blood-stains on it?"

"Apparently the knife was not washed, only the hands."

"But is not that highly improbable?"

"No, I think not."

"You say that there was no struggle, and that death was practically instantaneous, but yet the deceased had torn out a lock of the murderess' hair. Are not those two statements inconsistent with one another?"

"No. The hair was probably grasped convulsively at the moment of death. At any rate, the hair was undoubtedly in the dead woman's hand."

"Is it possible to identify positively the hair of any individual?"

"No. Not with certainty. But this is very peculiar hair."

The solicitor sat down, and, Dr Hart having been called, and having briefly confirmed the evidence of his principal, the coroner announced: "The next witness, gentlemen, is Dr Thorndyke, who was present almost accidentally, but was actually the first on the scene of the murder. He has since made an examination of the body, and will, no doubt, be able to throw some further light on this horrible crime."

Thorndyke stood up, and, having been sworn, laid on the table a small box with a leather handle. Then, in answer to the coroner's questions, he described himself as the lecturer on Medical Jurisprudence at St Margaret's Hospital, and briefly explained his connection with the case. At this point the foreman of the jury interrupted to ask that his opinion might be taken on the hair and the knife, as these were matters of contention, and the objects in question were accordingly handed to him.

"Is the hair in the packet marked *A* in your opinion from the same person as that in the packet marked *B*?" the coroner asked.

"I have no doubt that they are from the same person," was the reply.

"Will you examine this knife and tell us if the wound on the deceased might have been inflicted with it?"

Thorndyke examined the blade attentively, and then handed the knife back to the coroner.

"The wound might have been inflicted with this knife," said he, "but I am quite sure it was not."

"Can you give us your reasons for that very definite opinion?"

"I think," said Thorndyke, "that it will save time if I give you the facts in a connected order." The coroner bowed assent, and he proceeded: "I will not waste your time by reiterating facts already stated. Sergeant Bates has fully described the state of the room, and I have nothing to add on that subject. Dr Davidson's description of the body covers all the facts: the woman had been dead about ten hours, the wound was unquestionably homicidal, and was inflicted in the manner that he has described. Death was apparently instantaneous, and I should say that the deceased never awakened from her sleep."

"But," objected the coroner, "the deceased held a lock of hair in her hand."

"That hair," replied Thorndyke, "was not the hair of the murderer. It was placed in the hand of the corpse for an obvious purpose; and the fact that the murderer had brought it with him shows that the crime was premeditated, and that it was committed by someone who had had access to the house and was acquainted with its inmates."

As Thorndyke made this statement, coroner, jurymen, and spectators alike gazed at him in open-mouthed amazement. There was an interval of intense silence, broken by a wild, hysteric laugh from Mrs Goldstein, and then the coroner asked: "How did you know that the hair in the hand of the corpse was not that of the murderer?"

"The inference was very obvious. At the first glance the peculiar and conspicuous colour of the hair struck me as suspicious. But there were three facts, each of which was in itself sufficient to prove that the hair was probably not that of the murderer.

"In the first place there was the condition of the hand. When a person, at the moment of death, grasps any object firmly, there is set up a condition known as cadaveric spasm. The muscular contraction passes immediately into *rigor mortis*, or death-stiffening, and the object remains grasped by the dead hand until the rigidity passes off. In this case the hand was perfectly rigid, but it did not grasp the hair at all. The little tress lay in the palm quite loosely and the hand was only partially closed. Obviously the hair had been placed in it after death. The other two facts had reference to the condition of the hair itself. Now, when a lock of hair is torn from the head, it is evident that all the roots will be found at the same end of the lock. But in the present instance this was not the case; the lock of hair which lay in the dead woman's hand had roots at both ends, and so could not have been torn from the head of the murderer. But the third fact that I observed was still more conclusive. The hairs of which that little tress was composed had not been pulled out at all. They had fallen out spontaneously. They were, in fact, shed hairs – probably combings. Let me explain the difference. When a hair is shed naturally, it drops out of the little tube in the skin called the root sheath, having been pushed out by the young hair growing up underneath; the root end of such a shed hair shows nothing but a small bulbous enlargement – the root bulb. But when a hair is forcibly pulled out, its root drags out the root sheath with it, and this can be plainly seen as a glistening mass on the end of the hair. If Miriam Goldstein will pull out a hair and pass it to me, I will show you the great difference between hair which is pulled out and hair which is shed."

The unfortunate Miriam needed no pressing. In a twinkling she had tweaked out a dozen hairs, which a constable handed across to Thorndyke, by whom they were at once fixed in a paper-clip. A second clip being produced from the box, half a dozen hairs taken from the tress which had been found in the dead woman's hand were fixed in it. Then Thorndyke handed the two clips, together with a lens, to the coroner.

"Remarkable!" exclaimed the latter, "and most conclusive." He passed the objects on to the foreman, and there was an interval of silence while the jury examined them with breathless interest and much facial contortion.

"The next question," resumed Thorndyke, "was, whence did the murderer obtain these hairs? I assumed that they had been taken from Miriam Goldstein's hair-brush; but the sergeant's evidence makes it pretty clear that they were obtained from the very bag of combings from which he took a sample for comparison."

"I think, Doctor," remarked the coroner, "you have disposed of the hair clue pretty completely. May I ask if you found anything that might throw any light on the identity of the murderer?"

"Yes," replied Thorndyke, "I observed certain things which determine the identity of the murderer quite conclusively." He turned a significant glance on Superintendent Miller, who immediately rose, stepped quietly to the door, and then returned, putting something into his pocket. "When I entered the hall," Thorndyke continued, "I noted the following facts: Behind the door was a shelf on which were two china candlesticks. Each was fitted with a candle, and in one was a short candle-end, about an inch long, lying in the tray. On the floor, close to the mat, was a spot of candle-wax and some faint marks of muddy feet. The oil-cloth on the stairs also bore faint footmarks, made by wet goloshes.

They were ascending the stairs, and grew fainter towards the top. There were two more spots of candle-wax on the stairs, and one on the handrail; a burnt end of a wax match halfway up the stairs, and another on the landing. There were no descending footmarks, but one of the spots of wax close to the balusters had been trodden on while warm and soft, and bore the mark of the front of the heel of a golosh descending the stairs. The lock of the street door had been recently oiled, as had also that of the bedroom door, and the latter had been unlocked from outside with a bent wire, which had made a mark on the key. Inside the room I made two further observations. One was that the dead woman's pillow was lightly sprinkled with sand, somewhat like silver sand, but greyer and less gritty. I shall return to this presently.

"The other was that the candlestick on the bedside table was empty. It was a peculiar candlestick, having a skeleton socket formed of eight flat strips of metal. The charred wick of a burnt-out candle was at the bottom of the socket, but a little fragment of wax on the top edge showed that another candle had been stuck in it and had been taken out, for otherwise that fragment would have been melted. I at once thought of the candle-end in the hall, and when I went down again I took that end from the tray and examined it. On it I found eight distinct marks corresponding to the eight bars of the candlestick in the bedroom. It had been carried in the right hand of some person, for the warm, soft wax had taken beautifully clear impressions of a right thumb and forefinger. I took three moulds of the candle-end in moulding wax, and from these moulds have made this cement cast, which shows both the fingerprints and the marks of the candlestick." He took from his box a small white object, which he handed to the coroner.

"And what do you gather from these facts?" asked the coroner.

"I gather that at about a quarter to two on the morning of the crime, a man (who had, on the previous day visited the house to obtain the tress of hair and oil the locks) entered the house by means of a latchkey. We can fix the time by the fact that it rained on that morning from half-past one to a quarter to two, this being the only rain that has fallen for a fortnight, and the murder was committed at about two o'clock. The man lit a wax match in the hall and another halfway up the stairs. He found the bedroom door locked, and turned the key from outside with a bent wire. He entered, lit the candle, placed the box and hassock, murdered his victim, washed his hands and knife, took the candle-end from the socket and went downstairs, where he blew out the candle and dropped it into the tray.

"The next clue is furnished by the sand on the pillow. I took a little of it, and examined it under the microscope, when it turned out to be deep-sea sand from the Eastern Mediterranean. It was full of the minute shells called 'Foraminifera', and as one of these happened to belong to a species which is found only in the Levant, I was able to fix the locality."

"But this is very remarkable," said the coroner. "How on earth could deep-sea sand have got on to this woman's pillow?"

"The explanation," replied Thorndyke, "is really quite simple. Sand of this kind is contained in considerable quantities in Turkey sponges. The warehouses in which the sponges are unpacked are often strewn with it ankle deep; the men who unpack the cases become dusted over with it, their clothes saturated and their pockets filled with it. If such a person, with his clothes and pockets full of sand, had committed this murder, it is pretty certain that in leaning over the head of the bed in a partly inverted position he would have let fall a certain quantity of the sand from his pockets and the interstices of his clothing. Now, as soon as I had examined this sand and ascertained its nature, I sent a message to Mr Goldstein asking him for a list of the persons who were acquainted with the deceased, with their addresses and occupations. He sent me the list by return, and among the persons mentioned was a man who was engaged as a packer in a wholesale sponge warehouse in the Minories. I further ascertained that the new season's crop of Turkey sponges had arrived a few days before the murder.

"The question that now arose was, whether this sponge-packer was the person whose fingerprints I had found on the candle-end. To settle this point, I prepared two mounted photographs, and having contrived to meet the man at his door on his return from work, I induced him to look at them and compare them. He took them from me, holding each one between a forefinger and thumb. When he returned them to me, I took them home and carefully dusted each on both sides with a certain surgical dusting-powder. The powder adhered to the places where his fingers and thumbs had pressed against the photographs, showing the fingerprints very distinctly. Those of the right hand were identical with the prints on the candle, as you will see if you compare them with the cast." He produced from the box the photograph of the Yiddish lettering, on the black margin of which there now stood out with startling distinctness a yellowish-white print of a thumb.

Thorndyke had just handed the card to the coroner when a very singular disturbance arose. While my friend had been giving the latter part of his evidence, I had observed the man Petrofsky rise from his seat and walk stealthily across to the door. He turned the handle softly and pulled, at first gently, and then with more force. But the door was locked. As he realized this, Petrofsky seized the handle with both hands and tore at it furiously, shaking it to and fro with the violence of a madman, and his shaking limbs, his starting eyes, glaring insanely at the astonished spectators, his ugly face, dead white, running with sweat and hideous with terror, made a picture that was truly shocking.

Suddenly he let go the handle, and with a horrible cry thrust his hand under the skirt of his coat and rushed at Thorndyke. But the superintendent was ready for this. There was a shout and a scuffle, and then Petrofsky was born down, kicking and biting like a maniac, while Miller hung on to his right hand and the formidable knife that it grasped.

"I will ask you to hand that knife to the coroner," said Thorndyke, when Petrofsky had been secured and handcuffed, and the superintendent had readjusted his collar. "Will you kindly examine it, sir," he continued, "and tell me if there is a notch in the edge, near to the point – a triangular notch about an eighth of an inch long?"

The coroner looked at the knife, and then said in a tone of surprise: "Yes, there is. You have seen this knife before, then?"

"No, I have not," replied Thorndyke. "But perhaps I had better continue my statement. There is no need for me to tell you that the fingerprints on the card and on the candle are those of Paul Petrofsky; I will proceed to the evidence furnished by the body.

"In accordance with your order, I went to the mortuary and examined the corpse of the deceased. The wound has been fully and accurately described by Dr Davidson, but I observed one fact which I presume he had overlooked. Embedded in the bone of the spine – in the left transverse process of the fourth vertebra – I discovered a small particle of steel, which I carefully extracted."

He drew his collecting-box from his pocket, and taking from it a seed-envelope, handed the latter to the coroner. "That fragment of steel is in this envelope," he said, "and it is possible that it may correspond to the notch in the knife-blade."

Amidst an intense silence the coroner opened the little envelope, and let the fragment of steel drop on to a sheet of paper. Laying the knife on the paper, he gently pushed the fragment towards the notch. Then he looked up at Thorndyke.

"It fits exactly," said he.

There was a heavy thud at the other end of the room and we all looked round.

Petrofsky had fallen on to the floor insensible.

"An instructive case, Jervis," remarked Thorndyke, as we walked homewards – "a case that reiterates the lesson that the authorities still refuse to learn."

"What is that?" I asked.

"It is this. When it is discovered that a murder has been committed, the scene of that murder should instantly become as the Palace of the Sleeping Beauty. Not a grain of dust should be moved, not a soul should be allowed to approach it, until the scientific observer has seen everything *in situ* and absolutely undisturbed. No tramplings of excited constables, no rummaging by detectives, no scrambling to and fro of bloodhounds. Consider what would have happened in this case if we had arrived a few hours later. The corpse would have been in the mortuary, the hair in the sergeant's pocket, the bed rummaged and the sand scattered abroad, the candle probably removed, and the stairs covered with fresh tracks.

"There would not have been the vestige of a clue."

"And," I added, "the deep sea would have uttered its message in vain."

R Austin Freeman

The D'Arblay Mystery
A Dr Thorndyke Mystery

When a man is found floating beneath the skin of a green-skimmed pond one morning, Dr Thorndyke becomes embroiled in an astonishing case. This wickedly entertaining detective fiction reveals that the victim was murdered through a lethal injection and someone out there is trying a cover-up.

Dr Thorndyke Intervenes
A Dr Thorndyke Mystery

What would you do if you opened a package to find a man's head? What would you do if the headless corpse had been swapped for a case of bullion? What would you do if you knew a brutal murderer was out there, somewhere, and waiting for you? Some people would run. Dr Thorndyke intervenes.

R Austin Freeman

Felo De Se
A Dr Thorndyke Mystery

John Gillam was a gambler. John Gillam faced financial ruin and was the victim of a sinister blackmail attempt. John Gillam is now dead. In this exceptional mystery, Dr Thorndyke is brought in to untangle the secrecy surrounding the death of John Gillam, a man not known for insanity and thoughts of suicide.

Flighty Phyllis

Chronicling the adventures and misadventures of Phyllis Dudley, Richard Austin Freeman brings to life a charming character always getting into scrapes. From impersonating a man to discovering mysterious trapdoors, *Flighty Phyllis* is an entertaining glimpse at the times and trials of a wayward woman.

R Austin Freeman

Helen Vardon's Confession
A Dr Thorndyke Mystery

Through the open door of a library, Helen Vardon hears an argument that changes her life forever. Helen's father and a man called Otway argue over missing funds in a trust one night. Otway proposes a marriage between him and Helen in exchange for his co-operation and silence. What transpires is a captivating tale of blackmail, fraud and death. Dr Thorndyke is left to piece together the clues in this enticing mystery.

Mr Pottermack's Oversight

Mr Pottermack is a law-abiding, settled homebody who has nothing to hide until the appearance of the shadowy Lewison, a gambler and blackmailer with an incredible story. It appears that Pottermack is in fact a runaway prisoner, convicted of fraud, and Lewison is about to spill the beans unless he receives a large bribe in return for his silence. But Pottermack protests his innocence, and resolves to shut Lewison up once and for all. Will he do it? And if he does, will he get away with it?